KP08

DR.

D0934883

MAR   2006

SPECIAL MESSAGE TO READERS

This book is published under the auspices of

THE ULVERSCROFT FOUNDATION

(registered charity No. 264873 UK)

Established in 1972 to provide funds for research, diagnosis and treatment of eye diseases. Examples of contributions made are: —

A Children's Assessment Unit at Moorfield's Hospital, London.

•

Twin operating theatres at the Western Ophthalmic Hospital, London.

•

A Chair of Ophthalmology at the Royal Australian College of Ophthalmologists.

•

The Ulverscroft Children's Eye Unit at the Great Ormond Street Hospital For Sick Children, London.

You can help further the work of the Foundation by making a donation or leaving a legacy. Every contribution, no matter how small, is received with gratitude. Please write for details to:

**THE ULVERSCROFT FOUNDATION,
The Green, Bradgate Road, Anstey,
Leicester LE7 7FU, England.
Telephone: (0116) 236 4325**

**In Australia write to:
THE ULVERSCROFT FOUNDATION,
c/o The Royal Australian and New Zealand
College of Ophthalmologists,
94-98 Chalmers Street, Surry Hills,
N.S.W. 2010, Australia**

K. T. McCaffrey was born in Ireland and worked for a number of Dublin's leading advertising agencies before setting up his own graphic practice. His interest in writing was sparked while illustrating children's books and he is now a full-time author. He lives in Co. Meath with his wife and son.

BISHOP'S PAWN

Shocked after reading her own obituary notice, investigative journalist Emma Boylan wants to discover who is behind the deception. She decides to re-examine reports she'd written as a rookie journalist. Seemingly relevant is the story of the illegitimate daughter of a Catholic Bishop who, in front of Emma and other witnesses, shot herself. Now, a decade later, some of these witnesses have met with mysterious ends. A killer is singling out victims. And, as Emma follows a trail of corruption and betrayal, her name is next on the list. Can she stop the killer before falling victim herself?

Come away, O human child!
To the waters and the wild
With a faery, hand in hand,
For the world's more full of weeping than
 you can understand.

The Stolen Child
William Butler Yeats
(1865-1939)

PROLOGUE

Helena is oblivious to the fact that she has emptied the contents of her bladder. Her body trembles as trickles of urine seep down both legs. One week shy of her twelfth birthday, the celebration she'd planned to mark the event has vanished from her consciousness. Moments earlier, when a gun had been pressed to her head, it seemed unlikely she'd ever see that birthday. She can still feel the circular imprint of the barrel on her temple. From somewhere — might be inside her own head for all she knows — she hears an alarm bell ringing, the continuous reverberations heightening the sense of doom all around her.

A skeletal-thin woman lies sprawled on the floor in front of her. Blood seeps from a gash in the woman's leg, soaking her nightdress and creeping steadily on to the carpet tiles. This woman had been the one holding the gun to her head. There are other people in the room, some speaking, some shouting, but to Helena their voices sound distorted, like a record played at too slow a speed. The faces peering at her appear to swim in and out of focus.

She wants to dismiss what's happening as a nightmare. After all, it's past midnight and several hours since she'd gone to bed. But this is no nightmare; this is real, the here and now, there's no escaping the fact. Less than two hours earlier, her biological mother, Susan Furlong, had come for her under the cover of darkness. She'd known who Susan was, but this represented her first time to come face to face with the woman. She'd been asleep when Susan entered her bedroom. Little persuasion had been needed to inveigle her to go into the night with her abductor. Susan Furlong had then driven several miles and taken her to a large grey building with a stone carved sign that read — *The Mother of Perpetual Succour Private Psychiatric Hospital.*

The room they are now in belongs to the woman who lies on the floor bleeding, a patient whose *nom de guerre* is Joan of Arc. It is a dimly lit, small room with a single bed, a chair, a bedside locker and a wash hand basin. Smells of antiseptic cream and stale cigarette ash linger in the room's stuffy atmosphere.

An obese man in clerical garb stands out from a group of five people bunched together at an open door on the opposite side of the

2

room to where Helena stands. She knows this man; he is Bishop John Treanor, her adoptive mother's uncle. She'd recently stayed in his house and hadn't liked him very much. His looks hadn't helped then, they don't help now. Layers of pink, blotchy fat hide his chin and ugly hairs stick out from his nose and ears. Right now, though, his presence gives her a faint sense of hope. The bishop and those beside him — two women and two men — want to rescue her, but they are prevented from doing so by the gun pointing in their direction. Susan Furlong, the woman now in possession of the weapon, clutches Helena's shoulder with her free hand. 'You all right?' she asks Helena. 'I had to tackle Joan of Arc, get the gun away from her, get you out of harm's way.'

'Please don't hurt me,' Helena whimpers.

'Nobody's going to hurt you, darling, as long as I'm here,' the woman says, giving her the benefit of a smile before turning her attention to the others. Helena's legs are shaking, barely able to sustain her but somehow she remains upright, too terrified to move. Above the sound of the clanging alarm, she can hear Susan Furlong engage in heated argument with the others but she's lost the ability to follow what's being said. It's only when the woman lets go of her shoulders that she realizes she's wet herself.

In spite of the terror consuming her, she wants to get to grips with the situation. She can't understand how she'd been so easily persuaded to leave the safety of her home. What had she seen in the woman to make her act in such an irrational way? Her parents, her teachers, even her pals had warned her a thousand times to beware of strangers. *This is different*, she tells herself, *Susan Furlong is not really a stranger; she's my real mother. We even look alike. We've got the same colouring, the same copper-coloured hair. That proves she's my real mother, doesn't it?* She's not convinced. She has first-hand knowledge of children being abused by adults, but she'd always believed that real parents were different. It dawns on her now that her assumptions might not be correct.

She forces her gaze on to the bishop. He is looking to Susan Furlong with imploring eyes, his face bathed in a vapour of sweat. Next to him, the two women and two men take it in turns to remonstrate with Susan Furlong. Susan rebuffs them with contempt. And then, suddenly, as though out from a fog of sounds, the alarm ceases to ring. Without this clamour to contend with she is able to follow some of what is being said.

She hears someone say, 'Bishop Treanor is

4

your father.' The words, spoken by one of the two women, are meant for Susan Furlong. 'I didn't want it to come out like this,' the woman is saying, 'but it's the truth. Bishop Treanor *is* your father. I'm a journalist; I've done my research. Your mother died giving birth to you. John Treanor made her pregnant. He was a lecturer back then, back before he entered the priesthood. He's your father . . . he's Helena's grandfather.'

Helena's legs finally give way and she flops on to the side of the bed. She hears her biological mother ask the bishop, 'Is this true?'

' 'Tis true,' he replies, 'you're my daughter . . . Helena's my grandchild.'

Susan Furlong lowers her right hand to her side, still gripping the gun. 'This is too fucking much,' she says with a mirthless chuckle, 'There is no Christ in Heaven; there's no justice in this world; it's all bile, misery, piss and pain.' There's a mad fervour in her eyes and she appears to have forgotten where she is.

Helena feels something snap inside her head. She leaps from the bed and barges into Susan, her fists pummelling furiously into the woman. 'You *are* a bad person,' she shouts. 'It's true what my friends say; you really are bad . . . bad and mad, just like everyone warned me. I hate you, I hate you . . . I want to go home to my mum and dad.'

Susan stares down at her, not fully understanding what is happening. Under her breath she murmurs, 'I'm out of here,' then opens her mouth, inserts the barrel of the gun and pulls the trigger. The force of the blast jerks her head backwards, knocking her on to the floor. Blood, grey brain matter and pink-flecked bone tissue splatter on to Helena's face. Through a red mist she sees the body of her biological mother sprawled beside her. She opens her mouth in a silent scream.

1

There was nothing to indicate that people would be reading her obituary in the following morning's papers. No premonition. No warning. No inkling at all of what lay ahead. Emma Boylan remained at her desk, reluctant to leave, even though the rest of the daytime staff at the *Post* had left for home hours earlier. It was after seven o'clock in the evening. Mid-October misery abounded. Darkness settled on the city like a shroud. The nightshift people had taken up their positions, slotting into their repetitive chores with lack-lustre mobility and bored detachment. Tonight, like every other night, they would produce the first edition of the morning paper. In the basement, the huge Roland web machine rumbled away like some snoring subterranean monster, churning out the weekly property supplement that would accompany the next day's main edition.

The building had slipped into what might be called *stupor mode*. Normally, Emma, who worked as an investigative journalist, would have left for home by now. Even the evening rush-hour traffic — which stretched

7

for over two hours in the city centre — had eased to an almost tolerable level. She stared out the newsroom window on the fourth-floor, observing the gloomy city. The Spire, Dublin's millennium monument, extended high above the surrounding buildings, its red beacon almost enveloped by the low-lying clouds. The 120-metre structure with its foundation in central O'Connell Street usurped the space where Vice Admiral Horatio Nelson once stood and was, according to its creator, a metaphor for Ireland's forward-looking vision. The city's older inhabitants weren't so sure. The tall, hollow, cylindrical structure put them in mind of a giant-sized hypodermic needle and symbolized the extent to which drug culture held sway over the city they once thought of as their *jewel and darlin' Dublin*.

But Emma's mind was not focused on the current drugs and alcohol problems bedevilling the city, her thoughts were preoccupied with reflections on the latest row she'd had with husband Vinny. Quite a long history preceded the subject leading to the argument. Eight years earlier, she'd miscarried on her first and only pregnancy. She'd failed to heed warnings that might have prevented the loss. Consequently, she blamed herself. Vinny had wanted to try again to start a family, but she'd been reluctant. Two years after the miscarriage he discovered she'd been taking birth-control pills. A major row ensued. Variations on the theme were re-enacted once or twice every year since. Last night's spat was the latest instalment.

The sound of her telephone put an end to her musings. It was an internal call. 'Tell us something,' Joe Nicholson said, in heavily accentuated inner-city vernacular, 'are ya all right, Emma?'

'Yes, Joe,' she answered, looking at her watch and wondering why she hadn't gone home, 'I was a thousand miles away . . . what can I do for you?'

'Well, I was gonna ask if you and Vinny were still alive?'

Emma had no doubt that the question was part of a wind-up. Nicholson held the position of print production manager and had gained a reputation as a practical joker. 'Last time I checked,' she replied, 'all our bodily functions still worked so I guess that means we're still alive. Could be wrong, of course. Why ask?'

'Because both your names are on the non-smoker's list, ready to roll off the bleedin' presses.'

Emma was not amused. Like everyone else working for the *Post*, she knew that the non-smoker's *list* was a euphemism for the paper's daily deaths column.

'Joe, if this is your idea of a joke, I don't — '

'No, Emma,' Joe cut in, 'I kid you not; both your funeral arrangements have been submitted for publication.'

'Joe, come on, this is not funny — '

'Hey, you hear me laughing? I don't think it's funny either. Tell you what, I'll punch it up on your terminal, let you see for yourself, OK?'

Emma watched the obituary column appear on her screen. She scrolled quickly through the names beginning with the As and stopped when she came to the Bs. The first name on the list was BAILEY.

BAILEY (Hubband Court, Percy Place, Dublin and late of Little Bray, Co. Wicklow.) Suddenly, Vincent (Vinny), much loved husband of Emma (Boylan). Deeply regretted by his father Ciarán, his relatives and his many friends in the fine art and antique business. R.I.P. Remains leaving Doolan's Funeral Home, Quinns Road Bray this Wednesday evening at 6.30, arriving at Church of the Holy Redeemer, Main St, Bray at 7.00. Requiem Mass Thursday at 11.30 followed by burial in Dean's Grange cemetery.

Emma felt the blood drain from her face. She still wasn't entirely sure whether or not this was some sort of daft prank dreamed up by Nicholson. She scrolled through the Bs. Vinny's entry was followed by BARRY, BOWEN and then her own name — BOYLAN. She swallowed her breath and read the notice.

BOYLAN (Hubband Court, Percy Place, Dublin and late of Slane, Co. Meath) Suddenly, Emma, deeply regretted by her husband Vinny Bailey, her father Arthur, her mother Hazel, her relatives and wide circle of friends from the press, radio and television media. R.I.P. Remains leaving Foley's Funeral Home, Mount St, Ballsbridge, Dublin 4, this Wednesday evening at 6.30, arriving St Oliver Plunkett Church, Slane at 8.00. Requiem Mass Thursday at 11.30 followed by burial in the adjoining cemetery.

A voice inside her head screamed — *This is a joke, a really lousy, shitty joke.* She reached to the swan-necked lamp on her desk, switched it on and off several times in rapid succession, an unconscious affirmation that her bodily faculties still functioned. 'This is bloody crazy,' she said aloud, 'I'm here, sitting at my desk, alive. I'm alive, what the hell's going on?' She called Joe Nicholson back, asked him to remove the notices. She then called Vinny, told him what had happened. Vinny acted as though the whole idea was comical. 'Would've been good to see how many friends turned up for the funeral,' he said, 'hear what they thought about us while we were alive.'

Emma presumed that Vinny's attempt at humour was the product of a nervous reaction, a residue from the row they'd had the previous night. 'What about your father?' she asked. 'How do you think he would feel if he read about your death in the paper. What about *my* parents?'

'Yeah, you're right Emma; it's not funny. It's the dumbest thing I've ever heard. You sure it's not one of your mates taking the piss?'

'Could be; I don't know, Vinny.' Emma thought about her new workmate, Mary-Jo Graham, but dismissed the notion. Mary-Jo had only been in the job a few weeks and was barely familiar with the various departments. Emma could not imagine her conceiving such a prank. 'I'll check it out,' she told Vinny. 'If I discover someone here is behind this messing, they'd better start making their own funeral arrangements.'

Emma finished the call to Vinny and redialled Joe Nicholson. 'Please tell me again that this isn't an in-house prank?'

'Give us a break, Emma,' Nicholson said. 'No one here would do such a lousy thing, swear to God, honest.'

'Thanks, Joe, I believe you. Tell me something, how did the notices come into the *Post*?'

'Checked that angle already; everything was lee-git. The undertakers put them through, all formalities adhered to.'

'In that case, I'll need to get in touch with them, find out who made the call, see if I can discover the identity of the sick prick behind this.'

'Good idea, Emma. Someone's playing silly buggers.'

Emma put the phone down. Yes, she thought, someone *is* playing silly buggers. A shiver ran through her body. She contacted the undertakers but only succeeded in getting recorded messages. She would have to wait until the next day to follow up that angle. Knowing there was little else she could do, she headed for home.

In the underground car-park attached to

her apartment, she sat for several minutes in her car. The ignition had been cut but her brain continued to turn over furiously. Thoughts of mortality had forced her to pause and think about her role in life, look into her soul, seek answers to some searching questions about the state of her marriage. The tenth anniversary was just a month away. A decade of wedded bliss? Questionable. Their union had been harmonious, sometimes sublime, but for the most part humdrum. They were comfortably well off, both earning good money — Vinny as a dealer in fine art and antiques and she as a top-flight journalist.

They lived in one of the city's better apartment blocks, overlooking the Grand Canal at Percy Place, on the affluent Ballsbridge side of town. They bought it at a time when their resources were stretched to the limits but their bravery and blind faith had paid off handsomely. The millstone they'd hung around their necks had come to represent their most sound investment. People looking at them would have said they had it all. And on a good day, Emma would have agreed.

As soon as she let herself into the apartment, Vinny informed her that her boss, Bob Crosby, had called. 'He wants you to get back to him straight away. Sounds urgent.'

'It's those blasted death notices,' Emma said. 'Joe Nicholson has probably been in touch with him.'

As news editors went, Crosby was in the top league but he tended to get over excited when things weren't going his way. Only then did he deem it necessary to call her at home. For more than a decade she'd worked at the *Post* and for most of that time she'd enjoyed it, picking up two Journalist of the Year awards along the way. She'd been offered countless opportunities to switch employment, but she'd remained on. Bob Crosby, the person who had given her the job in the first place, was partly responsible for her unwillingness to leave. As her mentor, she felt a huge sense of loyalty to him. He could be demanding and downright impossible at times, but he was always fair. Over the years they'd forged a healthy working relationship and had become true friends.

Emma felt apprehensive as she dialled his number, trying to second-guess what he'd say. 'Hello Bob,' she said, as soon as she heard him pick up the phone. 'Vinny says you were on; is there a problem?'

'I don't know; you tell me. I've just heard the weirdest damn thing about some death notices involving you and Vinny. I've had a call from — '

'It's all sorted Bob,' Emma cut in, 'I got Joe Nicholson to — '

'No, no, Emma. I'm not talking about *our* paper. I'm talking about the *Irish Times*, the *Indo* and the *Examiner*. I've just had a call from Tommy Collins at the *Times*. He rang to find out what arrangements were being made for the two funerals. I asked what the hell he was talking about and then he read a death notice from his paper. It's already printed — '

'Oh, Christ no,' Emma gasped. She told him what had happened in the *Post* and how she had managed to have the notices pulled. 'It never occurred to me that the other dailies would be contacted. What can I do, Bob?'

'I don't know, Emma. Never heard of this happening before. I got Tommy Collins to check with his opposite numbers in the *Indo* and *Examiner*. The story's the same: they've got you and Vinny in their obituary columns. I'd better call them, have them to pull it from their later editions.'

'But it's already on the streets. Isn't that what you said?'

'Well, yes, but so far only the country and overseas editions have been dispatched. I can have it pulled from the main run.'

'Yes Bob, please, do what you can. This is bloody surreal. What will my friends say

16

. . . my parents, and Vinny's dad . . . his pals?'

'We'll run a small headline on the front page . . . have the others do the same; let people know it's a hoax. Meanwhile, I suggest you get on the blower, call the cops, let them know what's happened.'

'Fine, Bob. Thanks for your help.'

'No problem, Emma. Just be thankful the notices are not for real.'

Emma would have laughed at this remark under normal circumstances, but right now she was beyond humour. She felt numb. Vinny took her by the arm, sat her down and brought coffee. He then rang his father and warned him about the fake death notices, passing it off as someone's idea of a practical joke. Emma contacted her parents, gave them a similar story. After that, they sat discussing the strange predicament they found themselves in, trying to figure who could have conceived such a notion. Who did they know that would go to such lengths to falsify their deaths? No names came immediately to mind. At one point, after a prolonged soul-sapping silence, Vinny looked at his wife and said, 'Hey, let's go out and grab a bite, what do you say? It's like a wake in here.'

Emma attempted a smile, failed to come close. 'Yeah, right, let's have a really good meal. Might be the last one we have in peace for some time. Things are going to get hectic tomorrow when news of our demise hits the street.'

Vinny took hold of her hands, pulled her from the seat and kissed her lightly on the lips. 'Come on then,' he said, 'we're not dead yet.'

'No, not until tomorrow morning,' Emma replied, 'that's when we're supposed to wake up dead.'

2

It never stopped, never went away. It was, Helena Andrews believed, her curse, her destiny, to relive the night she witnessed the suicide over and over again. How could she ever forget it? It marked the only time she'd met Susan Furlong, her biological mother. It marked the first time she'd been inside a psychiatric hospital. Seeing the mother she'd never known put a gun in her mouth and pull the trigger had left an indelible impression on her mind. And now, a full ten years later, the experience was about to be re-enacted yet again.

It hadn't always been like that.

Following the traumatic occurrence, she'd managed to bury the memories, at least on a temporary basis. It had taken a full-blown breakdown and prolonged psychotherapy to reactivate the dark deeds from the past. Since then the images were never further than the blink of an eye away, perfect recall, perfect sound, perfect vision. Like some video loop on continuous playback, the details and sequence of events remained consistent, the outcome always the same.

Right now, a re-enactment consumed Helena.

★ ★ ★

— It's ten years earlier. It's past midnight. The night is dark. Wearing the trainers, scruffy jeans and baggy jumper she'd so hastily slipped into before sneaking out of her house with the woman, Helena allows herself to be taken by the hand and led inside the big building. Shadows loom from every angle, dark amorphous shapes, appearing to shrink and enlarge as they pass a maze of double doors and passageways before eventually halting in front of a heavy timber door. 'Right,' Susan whispers, pushing the door open, 'we'll be safe here.'

The room they enter is bathed in a diffused yellowish glow no stronger than a candle flame. Shadows and ill-defined shapes create ghostly patterns. Helena finds herself gripping Susan's hand with increased force.

'No need to be afraid,' Susan whispers. 'This room belongs to an old friend of mine . . . we call her Joan of Arc . . . can't remember her real name. Bit of a nutter I'm afraid, but she's harmless. Got to be quiet though . . . best not to wake her.'

Helena's eyes adjust to the dim light. From

20

the hillock shape of the blankets on a bed, it's obvious that someone is sleeping there. When the shape stirs, Helena jumps in fright and presses against Susan.

'Nothing to be scared of,' Susan soothes. 'Joan of Arc hasn't been out of the bed in ages. We don't bother her, she won't bother us.'

Helena is far from convinced. She watches as the blankets are thrown aside by a stick-thin woman who rises slowly, ghost-like, from the bed.

'What are you doing in my room?' a croaking voice asks.

Susan gropes for words. 'Joan, Jeez, Joan, bloody hell,' she gasps, 'you put the heart crossways in me. But, hey, what's this? You're speaking . . . you're talking again. Why it's . . . it's great. Always said you'd pull through.'

Joan of Arc swings her legs out of the bed and stands. Susan places a protective arm around Helena's shoulder. 'I don't understand this,' she whispers. 'All the time I've been here, I've never seen Joan of Arc out of the bed.'

To Helena, the woman looks like a Hallowe'en ghoul. A white, full-length gown clings to the woman's bony frame and accentuates her height. Waist-length, straw-coloured hair, falls untidily over her shoulders. The face has deep hollow cheeks, made more ghastly by the dim light. Her deep recessed eyes dart erratically from Susan to Helena and back again. 'You abandoned me like the others,' she whines.

'Look,' Susan says, 'I'll tell you all about what — '

'Shut up,' Joan of Arc snaps, her voice taking on a chilling note. 'As I recall, you did a lot of mouthing in your time here; yap, yap, bloody yap all the time, going on and on *ad nauseam* about the big shot who'd raped you. You were like a record stuck in the same groove, going over and over about his cohorts, the ones you claimed had you locked away in this madhouse. Then you gave birth — result of the rape sez you — and failed to stop them taking the child away from you. Proper order, sez I; who in their right mind would want to rear a child in this godforsaken hole? I've had to listen to your plans for escape; listen to how you were going to take revenge on your enemies. Oh, you were the cute whore and no mistake, pretending to be my buddy-buddy in order to extract information from me, information to help you on the outside. Yeah, you're a devious bitch, I see that now. Had me fooled all right, made me think you really were a friend, had me on your side, then you went and legged it without a shagging word.'

'Look, Joan, it wasn't like that. If you let me explain — '

'But what the hell . . . water under the bridge, eh? What's done is done, right?' Joan of Arc moves closer to Susan. 'Let me get a good look at you.' She places her hands on Susan's shoulders and smiles. She seems about to hug her but head-butts her forcefully instead. Susan staggers backwards, her legs buckling beneath her. She lies there, stunned, flat out on the floor, her eyes closed, her body still. Joan of Arc clamps her bare foot on Susan's neck, stomps hard.

Helena starts to cry. She's never felt so scared in her life. Alarm bells are ringing and raised voices boom and echo in the building. Through tear-filled eyes she watches the woman named Joan of Arc sink to her knees and rifle Susan's pockets. The ghost-like woman extracts a handgun and a pair of knives. She stands up unhurriedly, oblivious to the alarm bells and throws the knives to the floor. She is totally absorbed by the gun in her hands.

Helena can hear running footsteps approaching. Joan of Arc too, finally acknowledges the commotion. 'Come 'ere, child,' she snaps. But Helena is incapable of moving; she stands as though welded to the floor. The woman grabs her by the hair and pulls her back towards the bed as the door to the room bursts open. A group of people fill its frame. A small, middle-aged woman with a pretty face and boyish haircut stands at the head of the group. Behind her, three men and another woman gape enquiringly into the room. 'What's going on here?' the woman at the front asks, her eyes fixed on Joan of Arc.

'Well, will yo' look who's here,' Joan of Arc says in a reedy voice. 'We are privileged indeed. A visit from the medical director no less. My, my, my, if it isn't Sister Dympna! Don't see you too often down here in the wards. Never thought you'd be the one heading up the posse to capture Susan.'

'Give me the weapon, please,' the woman identified as Sr Dympna says, stepping forward.

'Back up,' Joan of Arc yells, pressing the gun to Helena's head. 'Move an inch further, I'll blow the kid's head off, understand?'

'Take it easy. We won't do anything,' Sr Dympna says, 'but for God's sake be careful.' Getting no reply, she looks at the body on the floor. 'Oh, my God, that's Susan . . . Susan Furlong. What . . . what have you done to her?'

'Gave her a bloody good thumping, that's what; nothing the two-faced bitch didn't deserve. Your pet patient if I'm not mistaken.

Huh, looks like she fooled you too.'

Helena feels the gun press against the side of her head and tries not to think what will happen if the trigger is pulled. Nobody moves. Nobody speaks. Alarm bells continue to clamour. Suddenly there is movement among the three men behind the medical director. Helena knows one of them. Partially hidden behind a tall muscular man she recognizes her adoptive mother's uncle, Bishop John Treanor. He is dressed in full clerical garb and looks scared. Helena is about to call out to him when the tall muscular man steps forward. 'I'm Detective Sergeant Larry Lawlor,' he says, looking directly at Joan of Arc, 'why don't you put the gun down, let the kid go, then we can — '

'Shove that big skull of yours up your arse Mr Detective and whistle *Danny Boy* while you're at it,' Joan barks.

A second man from the group speaks. He is big and handsome but nowhere near the size of the detective 'Hey Joan,' he says, sounding friendly, 'it's me, Vinny, remember?'

'Who? Vinny? Not *that* Vinny, not the fare-weather freedom fighter? Vinny, Vinny what's your-name?'

'Bailey, Vinny Bailey. This is my friend Emma,' he says, indicating the woman beside him. 'She's the journalist, the one who's written articles about the movement. She knows you and I were friends once . . . I came to visit you a few times, remember? You can trust me. Put the weapon down and I'll try to sort this out . . . I promise.'

'Yeah, I remember you all right. Still got the looks I see. Used to be lean as a whippet. Filled out a bit since. Well, you were frig all use to me back when it mattered and you're even less bloody use to me now.'

While this exchange is taking place Helena notices movement from the body on the floor. Susan has regained consciousness and is observing what's happening through partially opened eyelids. A knife lies in front of her, its blade no more than six inches away. Helena senses that something is about to happen. She is right. Susan lifts her body from the floor in an acrobatic manoeuvre and cork-screws her feet into Joan's midriff, managing at the same time to grab the knife. Before Joan of Arc realizes what is happening the blade rips through her nightdress and cuts deep into her thigh. Air belches from the stricken woman's lungs as she presses her finger home on the trigger.

Helena feels, and hears, the mechanical click against the side of her skull. There is no explosive bang, no deafening boom. The shooter has failed to slide the barrel mechanism forward and back to release the firing hammer. In disbelief, Helena realizes she's still breathing. Her brain can't take much more; the action around her appears to have slipped into some kind of time warp, each move fragmented and played out in slow motion. Susan dislodges the gun from Joan of Arc's hand and knocks her to the floor. Blood gushes from the wound on Joan of Arc's thigh where the knife has struck home to the bone.

Detective Lawlor breaks from the group of stunned onlookers and lunges for the weapon. The full weight of his body crashes to the floor as his hand reaches for the gun. His fingers make contact just as Susan's foot, in a simultaneous move, crunches down on his wrist. He bellows in pain. By the time he realizes what has happened, he is staring into the gun's barrel. The weapon is held firmly in both of Susan Furlong's hands.

'Back off,' Susan yells, 'back off. I've got the gun now.'

★   ★   ★

It was at this point that Helena froze the playback loop. 'Enough!' she said aloud. She knew only too well what happened next and had no wish to revisit the segment where her biological mother's suicide was re-enacted yet

27

again. Instead, she dwelled on the faces of those who'd been in the room when the dreadful event took place. In particular, she conjured up a still of Detective Larry Lawlor's face from the darkest corner of her mind.

3

Surviving one's own funeral, Emma discovered, could be quite an ordeal. The notices proclaiming her death had been pulled from the main editions of the papers but enough people had got hold of the news to cause quite a stir. The national dailies ran front-page pieces on the false obituaries alongside a picture of an alive and smiling Emma Boylan. Accompanying text borrowed from Mark Twain's quip about the rumours of his death being greatly exaggerated. Notices had been posted in the two funeral homes and churches involved lest any would-be mourners turned up to pay their last respects.

On the behest of Bob Crosby, Emma stayed away from work on the day leading up to and including the 'burial'. 'You'll have well-wishers calling to the apartment, better be there to greet them,' he said with a smile. 'I've asked Mary-Jo Graham to man your desk. Half the calls will probably be queries about your untimely demise.'

Crosby had got it right: the situation in the apartment was hectic. Her landline and mobile phone rang continuously. Friends and acquaintances turned up at her door in droves. Some brought flowers.

Before the 'mourners' arrived, Emma slipped out to the hairdressers. She was blessed with luxuriant toffee-coloured hair and natural highlights but she needed a quick cut, wash and blow-dry. Wasn't every day you got the chance to attend your own wake. She was determined to make the best of it. The reflection in the hairdresser's mirror showed a young woman — if mid-thirties could be considered young — who took care of her appearance, had a perfect symmetrical face, employed make-up cleverly and, on a good day, offered the world a bright smile. Not bad for someone supposed to be dead. Her reaction to the death notices had gone from confusion and disbelief to numbness, then irritation, anger and finally, a determination not to let the whole bizarre episode get to her. If someone had gone to so much trouble to tell the world she was dead, then by God, she was going to make damn sure they knew she was alive.

She decided to dress for the occasion, but resisted the urge to go for the goth look. According to her mother, she possessed an innate sense of style and an unerring eye for picking suitable clothes. Her mother's assessment was certainly right in one respect:

Emma was blessed with the kind of figure that made most clothes look good on her. She had a flair for picking outfits that complemented her personality and never failed to cut a dash when the occasion called for it. Dressing up for her own 'death' came easy. The timing would never be more opportune to wear what Christian Dior once called the most essential item in a woman's wardrobe: the little black dress.

Vinny dressed as Vinny always dressed. Deaf to all fashion dictates, he wore a denim button-down shirt, well-worn twill trousers and a cord jacket. Hardly sartorial elegance, but comfortable. His hair, aided by a flick from his fingers, fell across his forehead in an unkempt manner that managed to look stylishly flamboyant. Like Emma, he had remained at home to help with the throng who called to sympathize. In keeping with the tradition of Irish wakes, drinks were consumed by the well-wishers and tributes to both of them were on everyone's lips. The old ballad of *Tim Finnegan's Wake* got an airing with all the 'bereaved' joining in the last verse:

Then Mickey Maloney ducked his head
When a naggin of whiskey flew at him
It missed him, falling on the bed
The liquor splattered over Tim.

Bedad, he revives and see how he rises
And Timothy rising from the bed
Says 'Fling your whiskey round like blazes
Thunderin' Jaysus, do you think I'm dead?'

One friend of Vinny's, a little the worse for drink, wiped a tear from his eye, declaring, 'Vinny and Emma would have loved this.'

Friends that Emma had known since schooldays came to pay their respects. There were others too, people she'd forgotten about, all anxious to let her know how glad they were that she was still in the land of the living. But mostly, the 'mourners' were from the media, fellow hacks that she rubbed shoulders with on a daily basis. The most unexpected caller to pay respects came in the person of Detective Inspector Jim Connolly. The debonair detective, who enjoyed an amiable working relationship with Emma joked with her, saying how things had come to a sorry pass when she'd had to resort to faking her own death to grab front-page headlines. On a more serious note, Connolly said there was a matter he'd like to discuss with her as soon as she rejoined the living. Intrigued by the detective's request, Emma agreed to contact him 'when the dust settled'. She spoke with the other well-wishers in a similar vein, the gallows humour wearing thin as the day progressed. They were glad, when eventually the 'wake' drew to a close.

Emma and Vinny collapsed on to the sofa after closing the door on the last visitor.

'Well, I'm glad that's over,' Vinny said.

'Me too,' Emma agreed, 'being dead isn't all it's cracked up to be.'

'Still, we got a decent send off. Did you notice I had the most mourners?'

'Liar, I had twice as many and besides, my lot were far classier.'

Vinny was trying to think of a witty rejoinder when the doorbell sounded. 'Ah, for Pete's sake, not another one,' he said, getting up from the settee, 'I wish they'd let us rest in peace; we're supposed to be bloody-well dead.' He made his way to the door pretending to walk like a zombie. Emma grabbed a cushion and threw it at him. 'Stop it, Vinny, mocking is catching.'

Vinny wiped the smile from his face and opened the door. He recognized the woman standing there but couldn't dredge up the name. 'Come in,' he said, racking his brain. 'Good of you to come. Emma's inside; she'll be glad to see you.'

'Always the gentleman, Vinny,' the caller said, shaking his hand, 'I don't expect you'll remember me; I'm Grace . . . Grace McCormack. You haven't changed a bit since we last met.'

'Well, that's nice to know, Grace,' Vinny said, still not making the connection. Only when Emma greeted the woman and called her Sister Dympna did the penny drop. Now, he knew who she was. The recognition brought with it memories from a period of his life he'd rather forget. Sister Dympna had been the medical director of a private psychiatric hospital when he'd first met her. How long ago had it been, eight years, nine, more? He settled for ten. Racing back through the years, the circumstances that had brought them together clicked into place.

He had just met Emma Boylan at the time. She'd been investigating the death of a powerful businessman and, for reasons that escaped him now, she'd sought his help with the investigation. This was at a time when he had turned his back on his love affair with the Irish republican movement. In his mid-twenties then, he'd befriended a number of impressionable young people like himself who saw the six counties of Ulster as some kind of brave new world — a land to be liberated, unshackled from British imperialism. He had dropped out of art college to fight for the 'cause'. However, his romantic notion of patriotism had been short lived. The leaders he looked up to turned out to be nothing more than crime godfathers and drug pushers, their war merely a means to an end; an end that had nothing to do with achieving peace in Ireland.

Now he remembered why Emma Boylan had made contact with him initially. One of the republican activists he had known from that period had come to Emma's notice in the course of her investigation into the businessman's murder. The activist's name was Bernadette Maxwell but the tabloid press gave her the name Joan of Arc because she'd declared, 'They can burn me at the stake before I'll surrender my republican ideals', at a protest rally outside the British Embassy in Dublin. After this declaration, she became a leading light with the subversives operating in England. The reign of terror that she and her cell wrought made worldwide headlines. They bombed, killed and maimed men, women, children and animals. In one particular operation, she almost died in a premature explosion. Two of the terrorists working with her were blown to pieces; bits of their bodies splattered over her mangled limbs.

Miraculously, Joan of Arc survived. British surgeons reassembled most of her limbs, but they made no attempt to unscramble her mind. That problem had been left to The Mother of Perpetual Succour Private Psychiatric Hospital. Grace McCormick had been in charge at the time. Back then she was a member of a religious order and answered to the name of Sister Dympna. Emma Boylan had persuaded Vinny to accompany her on a visit to the hospital to meet with Joan of Arc. But before either of them could make contact with the patient they had to go through Sister Dympna.

And now, a decade later, Grace McCormick, having shed the Sister Dympna persona, had turned up on his doorstep. She looked no older than when he'd last seen her but he suspected her age to be hovering somewhere in or around the forty-five mark. Her hair was cut short in a way that helped accentuate the finely sculpted head, not unlike that of the latter day Sinead O'Connor. Her clothes, a tasteful ensemble of black and crimson, fitted her petite figure to perfection and her make-up had been applied with skill and care. Around her neck, a silver crucifix hung from an old-fashioned rosary-beads chain, the effect strangely at odds with her overall appearance. Grace had dispensed with the nun's habit but her core religious beliefs, it appeared, had survived.

'Get you a drink . . . something to eat?' Vinny offered, after the preliminary small talk had been dispensed with.

'Thanks, Vinny, a cup of tea wouldn't go

amiss, I've just come from the airport and I'm a little thirsty.'

'The airport?' Emma asked, 'where've you come from?'

'Liverpool. I live there now; have my practice there. It's only a short hop and a skip across the Irish Sea.'

'You've travelled from Liverpool just to visit myself and Vinny?'

'Well yes, yes I have. You see, I make a point of getting the Irish papers every day and I always read the obituaries. You can imagine the shock I got . . . seeing your names. I couldn't understand how both of you could have died at the same time. I didn't want to believe it. Your names brought back memories of the dreadful trauma we shared when Susan Furlong took her life. My immediate reaction was to come to Ireland and pay my respects. It was only when I got on the plane today that I read the piece saying it had been a hoax. I let out a whoop of delight and punched the paper. The other passengers thought I'd gone bonkers.'

'This whole thing *is* bonkers,' Emma said, 'but I can't believe you'd go to all the bother of flying over here . . . irrespective of whether we were dead or alive.'

Grace took the cup of tea offered by Vinny. 'I have to admit,' she said, 'that my reasons for making the journey are twofold. I do have something else I need to check out. I'd no reason to disbelieve your death notices when I first read them and I genuinely wanted to pay my respects ... but there's another matter; this is going to sound just as daft as your reported deaths.' Grace McCormick stopped talking and opened the slim handbag she'd been carrying. She extracted a white envelope and handed it to Emma. 'Have a look at that,' she said, 'it came in the post just over a week ago.'

Emma opened the envelope. 'It's a sympathy card,' she said, taking out a card from the envelope.

'See what it says,' Grace said.

Emma did as requested. After reading its content she stared open-eyed at her visitor. 'This is crazy! The sender thinks you're dead. What's this all about?'

'Wish I knew! As you can see there's no name, no signature.'

'Any idea who sent it?'

'Until today I'd no idea whatsoever. And then, when I discovered that you and Vinny weren't really dead, I got an eerie feeling.'

'You're not suggesting there's a connection?'

'Well, yes, yes I am; could be totally off the wall, seeing conspiracies where none exists, but I believe there's a link between what's happened to us and another disturbing event that took place recently.'

'What event?' Emma asked.

'Two months ago, Caroline and Jim Andrews were shot dead in the villa they owned in Mijas, Spain.'

Emma nodded. She knew about the incident. Because of her previous involvement with the victims, she'd followed the saturation media coverage it received. Ten years earlier, along with Vinny, she had visited the Andrews's opulent home in Castleknock. She'd been anxious to see how Helena was coping in the aftermath of her exposure to the violent death of Susan Furlong. Jim and Caroline Andrews, however, had not appreciated her concern and after one particularly strained meeting, during which Jim was downright rude, the visits ended. 'Yes, I read about it,' Emma said, 'saw footage on the television. Dreadful business. According to the reports, the Andrews disturbed burglars in the process of robbing their villa and ended up dead. Far as I know there's been no arrests.'

'That's right,' Grace said, 'and the strange thing is, nothing was stolen.'

'Could be the robbers panicked and legged it.'

'No, Emma, they didn't run. You see, that's the whole point; they hung around long enough to butcher Jim and Caroline Andrews.'

'So, what's your theory?'

'I believe Jim and Caroline Andrews were executed.'

'But why, I mean who . . . who'd want to kill the Andrews?'

'The same person who sent me a sympathy card; the same person who put your death notices in the papers.'

4

The eleven-year-old who'd watched her mother blow her brains out had changed. Ten years on from that dreadful event, Helena Andrews had become a woman of head-turning beauty. She'd been subjected to a series of traumatic twists and turns during the decade, the most recent being the deaths of her adoptive parents. The mysterious break-in at the Andrews's Spanish villa remained the subject of ongoing inquiries in that jurisdiction. Tragedy and upset were inextricably linked to Helena, but she'd managed to put aside the recent bereavement. Right now, confronting ex-Detective Sergeant Larry Lawlor, one of the people who had witnessed her biological mother's death, had become the most pressing aspect of her life.

For six weeks, she'd been on his trail in London, gathering scraps of information, stalking him relentlessly, familiarizing herself with his moves. She frequented his pubs, identified those he hung with, infiltrated his circle of acquaintances. She quickly estab-lished that his drinking buddies were not real 'buddies'. From unguarded snippets they'd let slip it was obvious that no one had anything good to say about Lawlor. A picture emerged of a man with a hold over all his contacts, a crook who was into all manner of illegal operations; everything from loan-sharking to debt collecting. His operations encompassed CD counterfeiting, fake-brand merchandizing, protection enforcement, and drug trafficking.

Helena needed to know more. She jettisoned her softly-softly overtures, ditched subtlety, and elevated the art of prick-teasing to shameless heights. It was a strategy that bore fruit. A few of Lawlor's cohorts succumbed to her seductive advances. After being sucked clean of information, these would-be paramours were left high and dry. The dossier she'd built up on Lawlor was substantial, and none too pretty.

Dumped from the *Garda Síochána*, the Irish Police Force, for being on the take, Lawlor quit Ireland and headed for London. He picked up work as a bouncer in some of the rougher pubs and clubs in and around Brixton and Camden Town. Over six-feet tall, with a body-builder's physique and mean attitude, he quickly earned a reputation as a 'heavy'. Anyone stupid enough to cause him grief was taken aside and beaten to a pulp.

For a man who'd once been an officer of the law, he took to the seamy side of life with all the relish of a starving rat in a well-stocked abattoir. His insider's knowledge of how police operations worked gave him an edge over fellow low-life scum. Within a few years he'd established himself as a serious villain in London's murky underworld.

He'd quickly graduated to working the more respectable establishments, securing a footing in Hampstead. One of the city's most desirable residential areas, Hampstead had a reputation for attracting artists and writers. More recently a number of wealthy Irish had taken up residency there. These blow-ins had been forced to flee their home base on account of the effectiveness of Ireland's all-powerful Criminal Assets Bureau. With their ill-gotten gains, the ex-pats snapped up the perfectly maintained Georgian mansions and town houses that came on the market. Lawlor knew these criminals from his time as a cop and used this knowledge to full advantage.

Helena made sure that Lawlor remained unaware of her keen interest in him. But that was all about to change. Sitting with her 'date' at a table for two in the 4PLAY night club, off Hampstead's Heath Street, Helena could see him standing inside the main exit door. His eyes were alert, roving like a security camera lens, ever watchful, taking in all that was happening on the dance floor, scrutinizing the surrounding tables, noting every patron, storing pictures of each face in his memory banks. His face was that of a man used to getting his way, the face of a bully. His bullish head, broad shoulders and pugilistic physique were enough to ward off those who might be tempted to trifle with him. Once or twice, Helena felt, rather than saw, his eyes flit across her face but she remained confident that he was unaware of her identity.

How could he be expected to know her?

She'd been a mere child when last he had encountered her. Her face then had been that of a frightened eleven-year old. Her transformation in the interim had been comprehensive. Gone forever, the awkwardness, the sweet innocence of youth and the boyish figure. In its place stood a worldly, glamorous, self-assured 21-year-old woman. Her hair style owed much to the likes of celebrities such as Charlize Theron; her eyes benefited from the use of vibrant green contact lenses and her figure had developed a voluptuousness of its own. Not a trace of the gawky kid remained for Lawlor to identify.

But she remembered him. God, yes! How

could she ever forget that face and those merciless eyes.

4PLAY featured garage and hardcore house music and like a handful of similar London venues, it encouraged innovative dress codes for men. The young, the trendy, the preposterous, and a scattering of weirdly dressed persons of indeterminable gender regarded the club nights at the 4PLAY as a must-be-seen-at gig. It was not the sort of place Helena would frequent by choice but it suited her purpose tonight. Besides, it allowed her to exhibit her chameleon-like talent for blending with the scene; going with the flow, she called it. Even her accent was adaptable; no hint of Irish brogue. Home-counties crisp utterances tripped off her tongue with all the assurance and nuance of a native Brit. For tonight's gig she'd chosen a fluttering, cobweb-light black dress. She looked, and felt, sexy and classy at the same time.

She'd attended the venue twice already in the company of Geoff Blackburn, a computer programmer who owned his own business in London's financial district. Geoff was tall, well built and had the chiselled perfection of a male model's face. For a white, middle-class, straight man in his mid-twenties, he dressed like a camp glam-rocker. The fact

45

that he was good in the sack came as a welcome bonus. Helena was well aware that together they made a handsome couple, but unlike Geoff, she had no desire to prolong their relationship for a minute longer than her needs dictated.

At a table for four, directly across the dance floor from Helena, two young men and their lady friends sat quaffing champagne, engrossed in highly animated conversation, their chatter and laughter drowned by the all-pervasive pounding music. Unobtrusively, Helena observed the two men; one was tall, had bottle-blond, tight curly hair and wore a sleek, hip-hugging white suit, a clingy silk shirt and stack-heeled boots; the other was short, dark and muscular and had a noticeable scar down his right cheek. He wore a studded leather harness across one shoulder, had tight black combat pants and sported bright red leather boots. Helena knew the two men by their nicknames, Scarface and Pubes. Easy to figure how Scarface had come by his nickname, a little harder to ascertain how Pubes had come by his, but Helena suspected it might have something to do with the pubic-like growth adorning his head. The two men were in the 4PLAY because Helena had hired them to do a job for her.

46

She was careful to ensure that Geoff remained unaware of her interest in the men. When the one with the scar cast an almost imperceptible glance in her direction, she reciprocated with a flick of her eyelids. Minimalist contact established, Scarface nudged Pubes and gestured to their female companions that they would be gone for a few minutes.

Pubes sauntered up to where Larry Lawlor stood and whispered something in his ear. Scarface headed for a door to one side of the raised platform used by the club's dee-jays. Lights on the dance floor changed to a wash of indigo blue, pulsating music pumped at full volume from the powerful Bose speakers. Helena watched as Lawlor followed Pubes to where Scarface had disappeared seconds earlier. The ex-detective glanced around furtively before disappearing through the doorway. Helena engaged Geoff in conversation while keeping a discreet eye on the door, smiling when appropriate and feigning interest in the anecdote Geoff was labouring. Pubes reappeared at the door, nodded in her direction.

'Got to powder my nose,' Helena said to Geoff, cutting him off in mid-sentence. 'Be back in five.' Without waiting for a reply, she left the table and headed in the general direction of the Ladies' Room. Using the dancers and the swirling lights as camouflage, she doubled back and slipped through the door where the men had gone. It was a small windowless room, used by the dee-jays to change into their stage gear and store their day clothes. Larry Lawlor's body lay sprawled on the floor. Scarface stood above him, brandishing an iron bar in his hand, his legs straddling the prone figure. Helena said nothing, content to watch the two men do what she'd hired them to do. Scarface set the iron bar down, dragged Lawlor's unconscious body across the floor and propped him against the wall.

'He's not dead?' Helena asked, concern in her voice.

'No, not yet.' Scarface said. 'Big dumb Oirish Mick . . . strong as a fuckin' bull, man. Had to whop his thick skull real hard 'fore he crashed to the canvas. Best hurry with the dope 'fore he comes round.' Quickly, he removed Lawlor's dinner jacket, pulled back the sleeve of his dress shirt, secured a leather strap below the bicep and pumped a vein, all the time watching for signs that might indicate Lawlor was regaining consciousness. Pubes pulled on surgical gloves, opened a small pouch and extracted a syringe along with a small clear plastic pill bottle.

'This concoction,' he said to Helena, pointing to piss-yellow liquid in the bottle, 'is lethal enough to ground a fuckin' elephant.' He sucked up the liquid from the bottle with the syringe and handed it to Helena. 'Best hurry, little lady, he's 'bout to come round.'

Helena, who had by now fitted on surgical gloves, saw one of Lawlor's eyelids struggle to open. Hurriedly, she stuck the needle into his swollen vein, careful to avoid contact with the fine mist of blood that sprayed from the puncture. Both Lawlor's eyelids flicked open, the eyes, wild and pulsing, revealing an expression of incomprehension and terror. With a glow of satisfaction, Helena pushed the plunger home, sending a lethal solution racing through his bloodstream. 'That,' she said, staring into his eyes, 'is for my mother, Susan Furlong.'

Lawlor jerked, moaned and convulsed for a few seconds before falling still. Scarface gently moved Helena to one side, took hold of Lawlor's left arm and removed a plastic package that had been secured with tape beneath the armpit. 'Heroin,' he said, opening the package and tasting its content. He scattered the remainder of the white powder on the floor, then took hold of Lawlor's hand and wrapped it round the syringe. 'That should confuse the heat for a while. Now let's be having the bread and get the fuck outa here.'

Helena removed her surgical gloves, then took off her left shoe and extracted an envelope. 'It's all there,' she said. 'I should like to avail of your services again in the near future.'

Scarface took the envelope, opened it, flicked through the notes with his fingers, nodded and smiled. 'Any time ya want, babe. Been a blast doin' business with you.'

5

Emma stared at Grace McCormick, an expression of incredulity on her face. 'You're saying a hired assassin killed Jim and Caroline Andrews?'

'Yes,' Grace replied. 'And . . . I think whoever hired the assassin is also responsible for killing Larry Lawlor.'

'What? But . . . ? You're serious, yeah?' Emma asked, shaking her head. She'd read about the London gangland killing some weeks earlier. That Lawlor should come to a sticky end hadn't surprised her. She'd gained first-hand experience in the past of the ex-detective's law-enforcement methods. 'You think his death is connected to . . . ? No, this is way too — '

'Too fantastic,' Grace cut in, anticipating Emma's reaction 'Yes it is . . . truly fantastic. Nevertheless, I believe the deaths of the Andrews and Larry Lawlor were organized by the same person . . . the same person who sent my sympathy card; the same person who wrote your obituary.'

'And you know this person, right?' Emma asked, making no attempt to mask her scepticism.

Grace fingered the small crucifix that hung from her neck. 'Matter of fact I do,' she said with a slight bow of the head.

More scepticism from Emma. 'Then tell us; we're all ears.'

'Fine, I will tell you, but first let me fill in the background; let me tell you a story. We'll call it Helena Andrews's story. I'm not at liberty to divulge certain factors, things told to me in confidence, but much of what I've learned is already in the public domain. What I'm about to relate is, to some extent, the product of Helena's overwrought imagination. Most of it represents the truth . . . or at least the truth from her perspective.'

★ ★ ★

— After Susan Furlong took her own life, young Helena continued to live with Caroline and Jim Andrews. She appeared to have survived the incident unscathed at first, but signs of disturbance became evident within eighteen months. Personality changes; brooding silences during the day; fitful nightmares at night. During this period Caroline Andrews was caught up in her own world of charity dos and social engagements. The few odd behavioural traits she did notice in Helena were attributed to the normal growing pains associated with any 13-year-old. However, this period of change proved to be a precursor to far more serious and long lasting developments.

Twice in the same week Helena's mother was summoned to meet Mrs Whitehead, headmistress in St Theresa's Secondary School. This was unexpected. Helena had been happy in school; her report cards showed above average grades. Mrs Whitehead, a strict disciplinarian, sat Caroline down in her study and told her about the problems the school was experiencing with Helena. Some students had reported items stolen from their lockers, small amounts of money, CDs, magazines, personal belongings, trinkets of no value to anyone but themselves. They blamed Helena. Caroline Andrews insisted that Helena couldn't have been responsible and demanded tangible proof. Mrs Whitehead was more than willing to oblige. On the strength of the girls' complaints she'd had a close-circuit camera installed in the locker-room. On seeing the tape Caroline had no choice but to accept the evidence.

That evening after school, Caroline confronted Helena and demanded an explanation. Helena screamed abuse — *They're all liars in St Theresa's*, she yelled, before taunting Caroline with — *what do you care, you're not my real mother, you don't give a shit.* Caroline's attempt at reassurance brought further invective on her head — *You're just interested in your snooty friends. What the hell am I, Mother? A fashion accessory to go with your other possessions?*

Two days later matters came to a head. A midday telephone call from Mrs Whitehead demanded that Caroline come to the school straight away. This time the headmistress looked flushed and overwrought. She informed Caroline that Helena had been found in the chemistry lab, her face covered in blood, her underclothes scattered on the floor. She'd been simulating the sex act with a test tube. 'At first,' Mrs Whitehead explained, 'it was thought the test tube might have broken internally.' Helena hadn't responded to her own name and seemed unaware of the people in the room. Mrs Whitehead had shaken her to elicit a response, but Helena just stared at her with wild, defiant eyes and began shouting. The words pouring from her made little sense at first, but after a while they became more coherent; she claimed that her father did this to her on a regular basis.

She used the 'f' word to describe sexual intercourse and claimed that what she was doing was cleaner than what her father did. After several minutes she calmed down and began to shake. Mrs Whitehead sent for a doctor. The doctor established that she hadn't cut herself. Turns out she'd been menstruating. He arranged to have her taken to hospital. Just when Caroline thought it couldn't get any worse she received further bad news. School policy, she was informed, demanded that when a pupil made accusations of a sexual nature, the authorities had to be notified.

In the days that followed, Caroline saw her world turn upside down.

⋆ ⋆ ⋆

Grace McCormick had been talking for half an hour without interruption. Emma and Vinny's expressions reflected the horror they felt. Emma took advantage of a pause in the narrative to interrupt. 'We had no idea,' she said, looking to Vinny for support. 'Helena seemed to be doing so well, it never occurred to us that . . . that anything like . . . like what you're describing could possibly happen.'

Vinny nodded his agreement.

Grace McCormick looked at both of them. 'You'd no idea?'

Vinny sensed a note of censure. 'On our visit to the Andrews's house which was, let me think, about three months after Susan

Furlong's death, Helena seemed like any normal twelve-year old. We *did* detect a strained relationship between Caroline and Jim Andrews.'

'Yes,' Emma agreed, 'Jim Andrews was always a bit on the gruff side, but on that occasion he was particularly offhand with his wife and rude to us. It was fairly obvious he didn't welcome our continued interest in Helena.'

'So, you decided not to visit Helena again?' Grace said.

'No,' Emma said defensively. 'We didn't decide *not* to see her. It's just that, well, I suppose we felt Helena had got over what happened. We intended to keep in touch but, what with one thing and another . . . '

'Look, I'm not trying to lay a guilt trip on you,' Grace explained, all the while fingering the crucifix, 'it's just that to understand this current business with death notices and sympathy cards, you need to know about Helena. If my theory's right, then we might just get to the bottom of the mystery. Do you want to hear what happened to Helena after the episode in St Theresa's chemistry lab?'

'Yes please,' Emma replied.

Vinny nodded.

★   ★   ★

— Helena suffered a full-blown mental breakdown and was admitted to Bartholomew's, a private clinic in Foxrock. Top neurologists there hypothesized that Helena's emotional disturbance stemmed from some repressed trauma. But pinpointing the roots of her trauma proved more elusive. In essence, it narrowed down to two options: one, the witnessing of the horrific death of her mother, an event that Helena had managed to repress for eighteen months, or two, the alleged sexual abuse by her father — if it happened.

Jim and Caroline gave consent to have their daughter hospitalized for a longer period of observation. Helena went for psychoanalysis to the exclusive Oakwoods Psychiatric Clinic in Bray. Appraisal of her situation remained unclear; results were slow. The patient was adrift and disjointed, marooned in some impenetrable inner world. She was pale and thin and went from periods of seething rage to periods of stillness when she remained remote, aloof, veering towards catatonia. Every possibility was considered and examined in an effort to identify the trigger or the incubator of her neurosis.

While Helena remained in Oakwoods, the police were busy with their investigations into whether or not there was substance to her assertion that Jim Andrews had sexually abused her. It turned out to be a fruitless exercise. Helena refused to make any further charges against Andrews. Without allegations of interference, probes into this area were confined to basic procedures.

After six months of treatment and round the clock observation in Oakwoods, Helena was discharged. The experts admitted that they had not been entirely successful in establishing what had set off Helena's neurosis. Provided Helena took the medication prescribed by them, they claimed she should be able to continue with a normal and productive life.

First indications of trouble came when she was refused readmittance to St Theresa's Secondary School. This represented a serious setback and meant she could not be with the school-friends she'd known there. After strenuous effort on Caroline's part a college was found. That it was a boarding-school did not help matters. Helena was allowed home for weekends, but the periods of separation had the effect of further fracturing the fragile relationship that existed between daughter and parents.

Caroline and Jim Andrews were not the sort of parents to engage with Helena's inner life during this rough period. As head of an independent television production company, Jim Andrews's hectic work schedule meant that his daughter's needs did not receive the attention they required. Caroline Andrews's priorities left a lot to be desired; she immersed herself in a number of the more glamorous fund-raising activities, absorbed in her own self-interests.

Helena's grades in boarding-school remained impressive. Academically, she was a bright spark, earning enough points in her Leaving Certificate examination to allow her a choice of subjects in whichever university she cared to attend. She opted for Languages in Dublin's Trinity College. Her parent's palatial pile in Castleknock was close enough to the university to allow her to commute on a daily basis but she insisted on moving out. She found a spacious basement flat in Rathmines where she shared accommodation with three other students, two females, one male. For a while it looked as though her troubles were behind her. To use her own term — she'd got her shit together. She joined the university drama group and became one of the leading lights on the campus stage.

Halfway through her second year at Trinity, Helena dropped out. One day she was there, an industrious student with no apparent difficulties, next day she had disappeared without trace. Her flatmates contacted Jim and Caroline Andrews to report her missing. But a week after Helena's vanishing act, Caroline Andrews received a telephone call from London.

Grace McCormick paused with her story for a moment. 'I was the one who made the call. I let Caroline know that Helena was safe.'

'She went to you?' Emma asked. 'Why?'

'I was working in a clinic in London at the time. Somehow or other Helena had traced my whereabouts. The frightened child I remembered was gone; an exceptionally pretty young lady stood in her place. Like you, I asked her why she'd come to me. Her answer couldn't be more direct. She needed to know the nature of her biological mother's mental illness. On the basis that I'd been Susan Furlong's therapist and the one who'd experienced her mother's breakdown, she figured I could supply her with the information she required.'

'And did you?' Emma asked.

'At first, no. I made some excuse about not having case files with me, told her I never ever discuss details of a patient's condition, even after that patient had passed on. That didn't satisfy her. She insisted I tell her everything. I asked her what purpose would be served by raking over Susan Furlong's medical records? She said she needed the information because she was concerned that she might be afflicted by a similar mental state of mind.'

'She thought — ' Emma started to say.

' — that she was going mad,' Grace said, finishing the sentence.

6

The morning sky was dull and miserable. Start of a typical October day in Dublin. Detective Inspector Connolly stared disconsolately at the rain washing down his office window. Below him, cars rumbled along Pearse Street, their tyres hissing on the road's surface, creating a sound like sizzling bacon in a pan but without the inherent pleasant smell. The earthly elements were, for once, in total accord with his dark mood.

His subordinates, DS Dorsett and DS McFadden, wouldn't make an appearance until lunchtime. Bridie McFadden, a rosy-cheeked woman in her thirties who hailed from Tipperary, was tied up on court duty — two drug-pushers she'd prosecuted were standing trial. Her sidekick, Mike Dorsett, a lanky Donegal man of few words, had been called to help sort out a city-centre traffic snarl-up that had resulted from a collision between a government minister's speeding Mercedes and a Guinness lorry on O'Connell's Bridge.

Three slim files fanned out on Connolly's desktop remained ignored. He was reluctant to undertake a more thorough examination. Sitting in his ergonomically contoured chair, the 48-year-old detective drummed his fingers on the desk's shiny surface, loath to do anything. The chair — not the standard issue decreed by the Justice Department — was one of the few items he'd managed to salvage from his bankrupt marriage before his house went under the auctioneer's hammer. There was a time, back when he lived in the house, that the chair hugged his large frame like a snug glove, but today it failed to offer any measure of comfort or contentment.

Like so many mornings of late he didn't feel like activating his brain or concerning himself with work. In appearance he looked the same as always: handsome, well groomed, wearing a tailor-fitted suit, sparkling white shirt, sedate tie and shoes that glistened, the perfect façade to cloak what lay beneath. His inertia was a product of the torturous separation procedures he and his ex-wife had recently experienced.

The house he now rented didn't feel much like home. A transient abode on life's journey might best describe it. Most of his belongings remained in cardboard boxes and refuse sacks; his books and music collection lay stacked in the hallway. Allocating them to more appropriate locations proved a bridge too far. Clothes and footwear remained in plastic bags. Cupboards and kitchen presses gathered dust in the absence of culinary activity. In short, his domestic life was a mess, suspended in a state of limbo. What's more, it was on show for the neighbours to see because, as yet, he hadn't got around to hanging curtains at the windows.

His thoughts were interrupted by the sound of his telephone, a peculiar purring sound he likened to the wails of a castrated tomcat. Wearily, he picked it up, heard Chief Superintendent Smith's secretary, a charming young woman named Ellen Furey, remind him that he had a noonday meeting with her boss. Connolly assured her he hadn't forgotten and hung up. The meeting had been arranged to evaluate the information contained in the three unexamined files. Hearing Ellen's cheerful voice partially eased his despondency. Thoughts of domestic strife were parked temporarily as he reached for one of the files.

The Spanish police had forwarded a brief account of the deaths of Jim and Caroline Andrews from their Malaga headquarters. Two top fact sheets, translated into English, were attached to several pages of a tightly spaced report in Spanish. The smattering of the language he knew had been picked up during holidays he'd spent in Ibiza and Mallorca back in his early twenties. The ability to mouth the words *Puedo ver la carta de vinos, por favor?* when looking for the wine list hardly qualified him to decipher the formal police text contained in the dossier. The top fact sheets contained a synopsized, point by point, account of the relevant facts. It would suffice for the moment to bring him up to speed with the deaths in Spain.

The facts were straightforward enough. The Andrews had been staying in Mijas, an Andalusian mountain village a few kilometres north of Fuengirola on the Costa del Sol. Some years earlier, they'd purchased one of the small white-washed villas that dotted the slopes above Mijas golf club. Their most recent visit to the holiday home had ended in tragedy. Jim Andrews had arranged to play golf with some business acquaintances. Caroline, more than a match for her husband on the eighteen holes, decided to let the men have their fun without her. She needed a few items for her wardrobe and had taken the train to Malaga. Receipts from purchases showed that she had gone shopping in the El Cortes Ingles store.

Later that evening Jim and Caroline met for a meal in the Valpariso Restaurant, Mijas' most popular eating establishment, located less than two kilometres below the Andrews's villa. They dined well, drank a little too deep on the rioja grape, and then ordered a taxi. The driver remembered dropping them off outside their wall-enclosed villa.

What happened next remains open to conjecture. Apparently, their arrival interrupted a burglary in progress. Next morning a local woman, who came by twice a week to clean the place, found their dead bodies. She called the police. They examined the scene, established that the Andrews had both been shot through the head at close range. Initial investigations plumped for the simplest solution: the Andrews were victims of a break-in that had gone wrong. But, further enquiries into circumstances surrounding the crime gave cause for concern.

A groundsman in the golf course who knew Jim Andrews, remembered seeing a man and a woman pay particular interest to the Irishman. He hadn't thought much of it at the time, but when he'd heard what had happened subsequently, he thought that perhaps Jim Andrews was being stalked. A barman in the Valpariso added weight to this theory; he remembered seeing a man and woman acting suspiciously while Jim Andrews enjoyed a drink with his golfing friends.

The fact that nothing was stolen from the

villa led the Malaga *Comisaría de Policia* to conclude that it had all the hallmarks of a vengeance killing. They'd sought co-operation from the Irish *Garda Síochána* with their enquiries. Their reasons, Connolly suspected, had as much to do with the effects the killing was having on tourism as it had with the crime itself. If the Spanish authorities could demonstrate that the murder had its origins outside their jurisdiction it would deflect the blame from them.

The second file on Connolly's desk was connected to the first, albeit by a somewhat tenuous link. It concerned the death of ex-detective Larry Lawlor, a bent cop who'd been found murdered in a London night club. A division of London's Criminal Investigation Department, based in Hampstead, had sent a report to their counterparts in Dublin requesting background information on the ex-detective. Alongside their request they provided a detailed account complete with pictures of the crime scene. Lawlor had been hit on the head with a blunt instrument before being injected with a lethal mixture of rogue heroin and washing-up liquid. According to the report, Lawlor had been heavily involved in London's drug scene and had been known to mix it with some of the city's most hardened villains.

Like the report from Spain, the CID boys believed an Irish connection existed. Snitches reported seeing a young woman doing the rounds of Lawlor's haunts prior to his death. Descriptions varied; some had her blonde, other reports had her as brunette, redhead, black, straight, curls, long, short, but the police believed it was the same woman wearing disguises. They hinted that the order to 'take Lawlor out' might have come from Ireland, suggesting that the culprit might be someone with a grudge.

The third file on Connolly's desk contained information on the life and times of Susan Furlong. It included several articles that had been penned ten years earlier by Emma Boylan. Connolly had gone to Emma's fake wake hoping to have a word with her on the subject but there had been too many 'mourners' present to conduct a meaningful conversation. He would contact her later, discover what insights she might have with regard to Larry Lawlor and the Andrews's murders.

He felt reasonably sure that Susan Furlong's death had a bearing on the events outlined in the first two files and he couldn't dislodge the notion that Emma Boylan could be a significant factor in tying all three reports together. There was something bizarre about the notices proclaiming the demise of Emma and her husband. Was it some sort of practical joke? Or, did the episode have a more sinister aspect? He knew from case records that Emma had been involved in the Susan Furlong case and had known the Andrews and their daughter Helena. She'd also known Larry Lawlor and had witnessed the dreadful finale in the Mother of Perpetual Succour Private Psychiatric Hospital. Records showed that four other people had been present at Susan Furlong's suicide:

Bernadette Maxwell: *Patient in the psychiatric hospital. Aka Joan of Arc*
Sister Dympna: (Grace McCormick) *Medical Director of MOPSPH*
John Treanor: *(retired bishop) Father of Susan Furlong and uncle of Caroline Andrews*
Helena Andrews: *Jim and Caroline Andrews's adopted daughter*

Connolly would have to trace these names but first he'd like to talk to Emma Boylan. If she could provide him with short-cuts, it would be most helpful. Right now he needed all the help he could get. At the scheduled noonday meeting with Chief Superintendent Smith he was expected to outline how he proposed to deal with the overseas enquiries.

He moved from his desk to the window, a frown working its way across his face. The rain was still bucketing down. On the far side of the street a skeleton walked the footpath, leaning forward into the diagonal sheets of rain and strong wind, moving in the direction of Trinity College. Pedestrians, struggling to hold umbrellas at forty-five degrees, glanced at the skeleton and shook their heads. Connolly suspected that the spectacle, a young man wearing black leotard outfit with white skeletal bones embossed on its surface, had probably been to a fancy-dress affair the previous night. There was, of course, the possibility that he was one of the growing band of drug addicts and binge-drinkers that seemed to inhabit the city of late.

He felt his own mood plummet. Domestic troubles regrouped, ready to commence battle, determined to sap his energies and take him to a place he didn't wish to inhabit. Momentarily he was lost. In a bout of agitated reverie, his wife Iseult materialized in all her glory. She was stunning. That had always been the trouble: her beauty; it had blinded him, dazzled him, fucked up his brain big time. Her flawless face, every feature looking as though it had been modelled in exquisite porcelain, the head perched delicately above a long graceful neck, her blonde hair neatly swept back and held in place with a dark-green velvet bow.

The expression on Iseult's face morphed to that of a snarling she-devil, the same she-devil who'd snapped defiantly at him when he'd caught her *in flagrante* with her lover. A clamour of voices threatened to blow his skull apart. He wanted to kill her, smash that face, stop her breathing. And for the briefest fraction of a second he'd been capable of doing it. Unbridled chaos funnelled into that millisecond. He would destroy her, wipe that mocking sneer off her face. Then he would kill himself. But packed into that same millisecond, some rational part of his brain kicked in. To murder her would make him no better that the low-life he spent his working life trying to apprehend.

To quell the sound and vision spinning out of control in his head, he closed his eyes, leaned his body forward and pressed the palms of his hands against the glass. He would descend into full-blown madness if he did not find an antidote to the torturous re-enactments. For just the briefest of seconds his thoughts broke free from the bleakness. With little enthusiasm, he forced his mind back to the humdrum chores requiring his attention, back to the monoto-nous daily grind of getting on with life. He would meet with Chief Superintendent Smith, try to hold it together for the rest of the day, and then as soon as he could get away, he would do something he hadn't done for a long, long time; he would get smashed.

7

Grace McCormick favoured Vinny with a beneficent nod after he'd served her breakfast: fresh orange juice, Fruit 'n' Fibre, toast, marmalade and a cup of Earl Grey tea. What was it he saw in her expression? An echo from her time as a nun? Hard to tell but it puzzled him. The previous night, after much persuasion, Grace had agreed to stay overnight. She'd made prior arrangements to stay in The Fitzwilliam Lodge but Emma, at her most persuasive, got her to cancel the reservation.

Accommodation sorted, the conversation flowed, concentrating for the most part on the subject of Helena Andrews and Helena's biological mother, Susan Furlong. Midnight had come and gone before a yawning Grace McCormick, pleading travel exhaustion, begged leave to go to bed.

And now, next morning, after a leisurely breakfast Vinny excused himself and left the two women to each other. He had an auction to attend in the Adam's showroom on the corner of Kildare Street and Stephen's Green. A number of Patrick Scott's finest canvasses had come on the market and he fancied his chances of acquiring one or two of them. If successful he would turn a decent profit on the deal. As an antique and fine art dealer, he made a comfortable living specializing in the purchase and sale of paintings. Back in his student days at the College of Art and Design, he had learned to appreciate aesthetic values in works of art but his real instruction, he readily admitted, had come from the apprenticeship he'd gained in his father's studio. Working under the expert tutelage of Ciarán Bailey had helped him develop a love of paintings and all manner of *objet d'art*.

Grace McCormick was scheduled to board her plane in Dublin Airport at 11.30 a.m. This gave Emma Boylan the best part of an hour to chat uninterrupted with the psychiatrist before her departure. The previous night, Emma had lain awake for ages digesting the disturbing tale she'd been told about Helena Andrews. Sleep had eluded her as she tossed and turned, hearing Vinny softly snore, her mind whirling in several directions at once, regurgitating the revelations. The fact that she'd been a part player in the ten-year-old drama made it all the more intriguing. Yet, there were aspects of the story that bothered her, details she'd like to probe further.

While Grace helped her put away the

breakfast things Emma broached the subject once more. 'How long did you say Helena continued to visit your practice in London?'

Grace seemed happy enough to revisit the subject, 'About a year, I'd say.'

'How did she react to what you told her?'

'Hard to say. Helena developed a mechanism for hiding emotions but I discerned that beneath her calm exterior, a rage lurked, a burning desire to hit back at those she blamed for her mother's misfortune.'

'Who exactly did she blame?'

'All of us,' Grace said, reaching for the small silver crucifix around her neck and cupping it in her hand, a mannerism she'd exhibited continually during conversation. 'Helena felt we all failed Susan Furlong. Her greatest resentment was reserved for the people who should have righted the wrongs, the people who saw the injustice and failed to intervene.'

'Who did she think should have put these wrongs to right?'

'I think you know the answer to that one, Emma. She blamed church and state; she blamed your lot — the media, and my profession — the so-called healers.'

'So, in Helena's eyes, we're all damned.'

'That's one way of putting it, yes.'

'And you think she's involved in this

business with the death notices and sympathy cards?'

'I'd say it's a strong possibility.'

'What? A mission to punish those of us who, in her opinion, let Susan Furlong down?'

'Yes. Like I said last night, I believe her search for vengeance has begun.'

'I'm having difficulty taking this on board,' Emma said. 'The notion that Helena Andrews could have something to do with the death of Larry Lawlor is hard to grasp. But, that's what you're suggesting, yeah?'

'Well yes, yes I am.'

Emma took a deep breath and shook her head. 'According to reports in the British media, Lawlor's killing was drug-related. If he operated as a drug trafficker then it wouldn't be unusual. I mean, you read about it every day: territorial wars, intimidation and the like. So, it begs the question, how would Helena, a woman just shy of twenty-two, get to someone like that?'

'Helena is wise beyond her years; she is — '

'And where would she get the resources, the money, to go after him?'

'You're forgetting something, Emma. Helena's worth a few million, maybe more. As the sole beneficiary in her adoptive parents' last will and testament she inherited all the funds she required.'

'A bit fortuitous then . . . that they died, I mean.'

'Fortuitous? No, not *fortuitous*. Might be more accurate to say that the Andrews's deaths were *deliberately* engineered.'

Emma held up her hands and splayed her fingers. 'Let me get this right: are you saying that Helena was responsible for their deaths? Are you seriously suggesting that she went to Spain, broke into their villa and murdered them?'

'OK, all right, I admit it's pretty fantastic. I don't know how she did it. But bear this in mind: Helena knew every inch of that villa. She'd been there several times on holidays. She could have given the layout of the place to some criminals; supplied duplicate keys and the code for the alarm system. She could have got them to break-in, paid them to kill her parents.'

'Anything's possible, I suppose,' Emma conceded, 'but even if we accept your hypothesis, how would she know where to contact the low-life? And another thing . . . her parents were alive then so where would she get the funds?'

'I don't know, Emma. It's possible I'm wrong about the whole thing . . . but I don't think so. You see, I got to know her pretty well during her visits to my clinic. It's not my place to make moral judgements, but it *is* my job to delve beyond the words, actions and personality traits of my patients. I became alarmed about her state of mind and persuaded her to allow me to conduct some professional psychoanalysis. I wondered if the root cause of Helena's eruptive behaviour might not stem back to events that happened *before* she was exposed to the brutal killing of her mother.

'With Helena's full co-operation, I set about helping her. I attempted to break down her defences, probe the most obscure regions of her psyche. She developed a total trust in me. That helped tremendously. I managed to strip away the façades and pretences she'd built up. One by one, I demolished the false structures and negative forces that had, until then, been controlling her disordered personality. I began to reconstruct her like a jigsaw puzzle, except that in her case the pieces I forged and clicked into position had to be cleansed of their ill-gotten baggage from her past.'

'Sounds as though you cured her,' Emma said.

A tight little smile from Grace. '*Cured* is not a word I use,' she said. 'Yes, I was some help, but unfortunately I didn't get to finish the treatment; without the final pieces of the puzzle in place, the *whole* remains incomplete, the exercise in abeyance.'

'You didn't finish the therapy?'

'No, I was almost there, my goal in sight, when Helena stopped coming. Some time after this, I moved from St Albans to Liverpool.'

'You didn't make contact when you heard about the Andrews's deaths?'

'I didn't hear about it until a week after the event. Unfortunately, Helena never gave me a contact address. She may have been renting a place nearby, somewhere like Harpenden or Luton but I was never sure. I should have tried harder . . . but I didn't, that's the tragedy. And then, in this past week, three events happened to bring the whole thing into sharp focus.'

'You're talking about the sympathy card you got and our deaths notices?'

'That, and the death of Larry Lawlor, yes. Put them together with the mysterious deaths of her parents and it's hard to escape the conclusion: Helena's involved.'

'It's a staggering theory,' Emma admitted, 'but you're right about one thing: the coincidence is compelling. What do you suggest we do?'

'Well, there's little point in going to the

police. There's no evidence to give them, at least nothing tangible to link Helena to the events. I have to get back to Liverpool, but I think it might be worth your while to contact the others who were involved with Susan Furlong, find out if they've received threats. In the meanwhile, I suggest you and Vinny keep a sharp lookout for anything suspicious. I hate to sound melodramatic but if I'm right — and I pray to God I'm not — your lives could be in danger.'

'Don't worry, Grace, forewarned is fore-armed.'

'Trouble is, I am worried. There's so much you still don't know. What Helena's told me is truly frightening.'

'Would it help if I saw a transcript of your sessions?'

'I'm sure it might,' Grace said with a hint of a smile, 'but as you know, I'm bound by the oath of confidentiality.'

'One could argue,' Emma pressed, 'that in this particular instance it might be prudent, in the interest of safety, to let me see selected passages.'

'Sorry, Emma, I could never betray a confidence under any condition.'

Emma sighed. 'Yeah, OK, you're right, I understand.'

'However, I will revisit my notes. If I find

there is any useful purpose — or benefit — in talking to you in regard to certain areas . . . without breaking confidences, then I will fill you in. Can't promise any more than that.'

'That's fine by me, thanks, Grace, I understand your position and I can appreciate your concern. I know you'll do what you think is right.'

'Exactly. I don't want to read about your funeral arrangements again.'

Emma smiled. 'Hey, neither do I.'

8

Joan Quinn was enjoying her day trip to Dublin. Along with sixteen other 9- and 10-year-olds from the Jesus and Mary Primary School she'd set out on the twelve-mile journey from the village of Leixlip earlier that morning in a luxury coach. Under the ever-watchful eye of teacher, Ms Thompson, she had visited the National Gallery of Ireland where the curator had taken her and her classmates on a guided tour, explaining the stories and meanings behind the works of art on exhibit. After this enforced exposure to culture, they were marched from Clare Street to Grafton Street and treated to an early lunch in McDonalds where Big Macs and McFlurrys were devoured with an enthusiasm that had been notably lacking on the visit to the art gallery.

Following this gluttonous and noisy extravaganza, Ms Thompson marshalled her charges with military precision along St Stephen's Green North and past the top of Dawson Street. Before turning into Kildare Street the girls' progress was disrupted by the appearance of three rough-looking young men, all of them inebriated, all clutching flagons of cider. Ms

Thompson's concern for the safety of the children shot to full alert, determined to avoid confrontation at all costs. A pile of filthy blankets alongside some empty bottles and syringes lay scattered on the steps of a nearby Georgian doorway. She felt compassion for the growing number of homeless people living rough in the city but the children's welfare was her main concern. The sight of their school uniforms had, it appeared to her, ignited some primitive urge in the men. One of the trio, a bearded man with a woollen hat pulled low on his forehead, pushed unsteadily into their midst, waving his bottle about and sloshing drink in all directions.

Ms Thompson, a slight, soft-spoken woman in her thirties, had no hesitation in confronting the drunk. The man looked at her, a lop-sided smirk on his face, and passed the flagon of cider to one of his companions. Winking lecherously at her, he lowered one hand and thrust it into his trouser pocket. 'Got something here for you,' he slurred, his fingers groping deep inside the pocket. In a move totally out of character for Ms Thompson, she rammed her knee into his crotch. The leer on the man's face turned to an angry scowl. 'You stupid cow,' he yelled, withdrawing his hand from the pocket, 'Gonna-haf-to beat the shit outa you for doin' that.' He raised his hand to strike her but stopped when one of the schoolgirls pushed her way between him and the teacher. It was Joan Quinn.

'You leave my teacher alone,' the 9-year-old demanded with surprising authority, 'or I'll have my mum throw you in jail.'

The homeless trio fell about with laughter. Pedestrians, passing by the confrontation ignored what was happening. Collectively, they appeared to have gone blind, deaf and dumb as they stepped across spilt drink and urine that trickled across the footpath towards a row of taxi cabs parked by the kerb-side. The taxi drivers were no better; they watched the situation develop with apparent indifference.

'What d'fuck have we here?' said the man, who'd verbally abused Ms Thomson. 'Hey, lads, we gonna haf-ta teach this precocious little piss-ant a t'ing or two.' He grabbed Joan by the hair and began to jerk her from side to side. Ms Thompson, with fire in her eyes and both fists flaying, laid into him. The man's two companions lurched to stop her, but from out of nowhere, two uniformed officers materialized. Perhaps the taxi drivers, seeing the children at risk, had been shaken out of their inertia and had called for help. For whatever reason, the uniforms had arrived in the nick of time. Within seconds, the three offenders had been cuffed and the girls allowed to proceed. This experience was by far the most exciting thing to happen so far on the girls' big day in the city.

Midway down Kildare Street they came to a halt outside the gates of Leinster House, the seat of Ireland's Government and Senate. Before talking to the *garda* officer on gate duty Ms Thompson beckoned Joan Quinn to her side. Joan's composure like that of her teacher had not been unduly ruffled by the altercation with the cider heads. If anything, Joan's spirits were heightened, helped no doubt by the admiring glances coming from her school pals. It was her mother, Niamh O'Flynn, an elected parliamentarian, who had arranged for her daughter's school to visit the government building. (O'Flynn didn't use her married name, Quinn, in political circles.) Ms Thompson introduced Joan to the *garda* officer, a slim young man with bad skin, and showed him a copy of the school's invitation. He read the letter, gave Joan what approximated for a smile, then spoke into his radio phone.

A few minutes later, teacher and pupils stood in the front hall of Leinster House, a massive space taking up two storeys, paved in black and white squares and crowned with a coffered ceiling. Sunlight shafted in from three central windows, flooding the area with brilliant light. Niamh O'Flynn stood in front of a chimney breast of Portland stone to welcome the group.

Joan couldn't wait to tell her mother about her meeting with the drunks. Her classmates joined in a babble of enthusiastic approval for how Joan had stood up to the trio. Ms Thompson eventually restored order and formally thanked the politician for inviting them to what she called 'the heart, soul, and seat of our country's democracy'.

Currently opposition spokesperson on Justice, Niamh O'Flynn had been Minister for Justice during her party's brief stint in government ten years earlier. At the time she'd been seen as a potential party leader. Some even saw her as Ireland's equivalent to Margaret Thatcher, equipped with the qualities necessary to grab hold of the country's reins. It never happened. The subsequent general election saw Niamh O'Flynn lose her seat. She bided her time in the Senate for three years before regaining her seat in the following general election. Her party, still in opposition, appointed her as shadow spokesperson for Justice.

Impeccably dressed in an elegant black trouser suit, grey blouse and matching grey shoes, the aura of power and magnetism she exuded so naturally on the TV tube was notably absent. Neither beautiful nor plain, at 44, she teetered on the edge of both. The slender face, the almond-shaped eyes, the character and shrewdness evident in her features all combined to project a no-nonsense image. And yet, as she placed her hand on her daughter's shoulder and pressed her closer to her side, the mask slipped momentarily. Joan sensed something odd in her mother's behaviour.

Niamh O'Flynn introduced the teacher and students to a middle-aged man in uniform, telling them that he would act as their guide for their tour of the building. As the group set off, she remained by the fireplace, a troubled expression on her face. She could hear the guide launch into his practised spiel, telling the children that Richard Castle had originally built the house for James FitzGerald, the twentieth Earl of Kildare. As the commentary faded she made her way upstairs to her own office.

She opened a drawer in her desk and withdrew a small white envelope that had been delivered that morning. Although she'd studied its contents several times already the shock she'd received on the initial examination failed to lessen with subsequent readings.

She unfolded the letter and forced herself to read.

F.A.O. Niamh O'Flynn, TD.
A decade has passed since you held office. During your time as Minister for Justice you allowed the perpetrators of injustice go unpunished and deprived me of the one person I held most dearly. You have no concept of the loss I speak of, therefore to acquaint you with my grief I intend to offer you an opportunity to experience a similar loss. Look to your nearest and dearest.

She put the letter back in the envelope. The reference to her *nearest and dearest* had obvious implications for her husband and daughter. Seeing Joan just now brought home the seriousness of the situation. On the positive side, she knew how plucky her daughter could be. She'd taught Joan to stand up for what was right and truthful. The account she'd just heard of Joan's spirited behaviour in front of the drunks should have reassured her, but served instead to illustrate how easily it would be for someone to get to Joan.

And what of her husband? Bill Quinn worked overseas at the Commission in

Brussels, a high-flying Director General in the Regional Policy division. Their union had been reasonably harmonious, give or take the odd spat over twelve years. Bill's work demanded that he commute between Dublin and Brussels. What if someone decided to harm him while on a flight or in an airport or perhaps in his apartment in Brussels?

Niamh thought about the letter's author. Was it the work of a crank, someone bearing a grudge from her time in office? Offhand she could think of dozens of conflicts that had arisen during her watch in the Justice Department. She had championed many un-popular issues. Disgruntled lobbyists, opposed to her policies, had attempted to trip her up at every turn. Some battles she lost, some she won. And yes, she had made enemies.

She considered putting a call through to Bill to warn him to be careful, but thought better of it. She hated to bother him, knowing that he was particularly busy at the moment. Besides, there wasn't a whole lot he could do about it over in Belgium. Instead she would contact the Chief Superintendent Harry Smith, and seek his opinion. He would know what to do.

9

It was difficult to look at the man in the bed. Ten years had elapsed since Emma had last been this close up to Bishop John Treanor. An unkind thought struck her: *I fervently hope the intervening years have been kinder to me.* A more wasted specimen of manhood would be hard to imagine. The once portly cleric had shrunk to a mere shell of his former self. Yellowed flesh hung from the face's bone structure in crimped layers. Age-spots textured the coarsely dried skin of his hands and skeletal fingers. Propped up on three pillows, amid mountainous folds of white sheets, the ravaged face looking back at her induced a feeling of nausea. Were it not for his eyes she would have thought him dead. Treanor's eyes, what she could see of them, were very much alive. They soaked her in with a remorseless, cold-blooded, calculating stare.

Emma sat on an easy chair that had been strategically angled so as to face him. On the ground floor of a two-storey modern building, the room was warm and spacious, had plush carpet flooring and a large bay window facing a well-cultivated garden. A belt of mature beech, oak and elms screened off the neighbouring buildings. The nurse who had shown her to the room told her that 'His Grace', the title she used when referring to Treanor, had lost the use of his speech. The once formidable man of the cloth had clocked up three years in St Joseph's, a rest home for retired clerics, set in the grounds of the bishop's palace. With all the comforts of a five-star hotel, St Joseph's was strictly reserved for those clerics who had reached the highest echelons in the service of the church.

In John Treanor's case, however, the comforts and benefits were of little avail; he had suffered a series of strokes, the first attack happening within months of his arrival. Emma got the distinct impression from the brief conversation she'd had with the nurse that nobody in the retirement home missed the vitriolic verbosity that spewed from him in the period leading up to his enfeeblement.

The other residents, Emma learned, consisted of six retired churchmen; the youngest of them in his mid-sixties. This comparatively young man had been an Adjunct Bishop before the onset of Parkinson's disease brought his career to a shuddering stop. Two of the more elderly inhabitants had risen to the rank of Monsignor before being consigned to their present comfortable surroundings. The remaining three residents had worked as professors of theology in various seminaries throughout the country. This meant that John Treanor was, theoretically at least, top dog in the pecking order.

Emma introduced herself to the retired churchman and made reference to the fact that they had met before. His mouth remained resolutely closed, the lips reduced to a tight jagged line with the corners turned down in a permanent scowl. She could not help but remember how those same lips, ten years earlier, then plump and cherubic, had been prised apart to admit the barrel of Susan Furlong's gun. She was more chilled by how the lips looked today.

Nurse Daly, who had escorted Emma to Treanor's room, assured her that 'His Grace' was crafty as a mongrel fox, didn't miss a trick and understood everything that was going on around him. She told how, in the past, he'd shown his displeasure when certain dishes were served by deliberately tossing the offending food to the floor.

Emma spoke to Treanor as though she were conducting a regular conversation. She told him about the recent visit she'd had from Sister Dympna, deliberately using the psychiatrist's now defunct religious appellation, knowing that the name Grace McCormick would mean nothing. Back in the days when the bishop knew Grace McCormick she was still with her religious order.

Nothing that Emma said induced the slightest flicker of reaction, making her wonder what exactly she'd hoped to gain from the visit. Surely a moment of lucidity wasn't too much to hope for, was it? She was about to finish her one-sided discourse when the mention of Helena Andrews's name seemed to register with Treanor. 'Ah, you remember Helena, then?' Emma said to see if she'd get the response again. This time there was no mistake. A wince appeared on the muscles around Treanor's mouth. Emma edged her chair nearer to the bed, brought her face closer to his and spoke more earnestly. She repeated what Grace McCormick had told her about suspecting Helena of being responsible for a number of unexplained deaths.

A tremor appeared on Treanor's seamed cheeks. The mottled cords in his neck, though wasted and dangling like a turkey's gullet, showed the kind of movement that might suggest a struggle for breath. The dark blue trace of a vein throbbed visibly on the man's pasty white temple. The eyes, though deep and partially hidden, challenged her. His bloodless lips quivered, appearing to grope for expression. For a moment Emma believed she was about to get a response, but with the same suddenness that his distress had appeared, all routes to his critical faculties closed down. Treanor had regained control of his emotions and shut her out. Everything she said was, once again, met with the noncommittal stare and a face as inanimate as a mask made from plasterers' putty.

She thought about how this man had been pivotal in making Susan Furlong's life a hell on earth. But his part in the tragedy could be traced back further than that; it had begun with Susan Furlong's mother, a woman named Sarah Purcell.

At seventeen years of age Sarah Purcell came to Dublin to attend university. Up until then, she'd led a sheltered life in a small town in the midlands. Campus life and the liberal lifestyle of new-found friends proved seductive. Like a flower exposed to sunlight, she blossomed. Within weeks she fell headlong for her lecturer, John Treanor. This was at a time before Treanor had decided to take Holy Orders. Because he was a lecturer and she a student, the affair remained clandestine. However, when she became pregnant by him, there was no way of hiding the fact. In keeping with the university's prevailing ethos at the time she was obliged to leave.

As a reward for not naming him, Treanor looked after her financial needs. He continued to work for a time at the university and when her time came to have the baby he arranged for her to go to St John's Private Maternity Hospital in Marlborough Street. It was not the practice to take unwed pregnant girls into St John's but there were exceptions to the rule: if someone from one of the Catholic societies agreed to sponsor the expectant mother and agreed to have the child brought up in the Catholic faith, it was acceptable. In such cases the mother never saw her child again after the birth.

John Treanor arranged for Sarah Purcell to go to St John's under the patronage of his friend, James Furlong, a leading member of the Knights of St Patrick. However, Sarah died giving birth and the baby, a healthy girl, was handed over to James Furlong and his wife Jane. They named her Susan Furlong. She enjoyed a normal upbringing with the Furlongs until she reached her twelfth birthday, at which point Jane Furlong died. From that period on the relationship she had once enjoyed with her adoptive father deteriorated. James Furlong, inconsolable after his wife's death, began to drink heavily and generally lose interest in the world. By the time Susan's eighteenth birthday came around, his interest in her was non-existent.

At a celebration bash in her workplace to mark her eighteenth birthday Susan drank too much and had to allow her employer to drive her home. Her boss took advantage of her condition and raped her. For Susan, it represented the first downward step on the road to hell. Her employer, with the help of influential friends from the highest echelons of church and state, conspired to cover up the whole affair. James Furlong, in no state to help anyone, allowed himself to be bought off with money rather than pursue justice.

In the eighteen years that followed on from Susan's birth, John Treanor had joined the priesthood and risen meteorically through the ranks to the position of Monsignor. Throughout this period he had kept a watching, if distant, eye on Susan's progress. But apart from sending a monthly cheque to the Furlongs he never made himself known to her. Fearing for his own position in the church, he did nothing to help Susan in her hour of need. He refused to intervene on her behalf when she was confined to a mental institution.

When Susan Furlong gave birth to the baby she'd conceived in the rape, Treanor arranged for the baby to be adopted by his niece Caroline. Caroline was married to Jim Andrews, an up and coming advertising executive at the time in question. The Andrews called the baby Helena.

Emma, who had gleaned all this information ten years earlier while investigating the Susan Furlong case, looked once more at the figure in the bed. It was hard to credit that this man, so wasted, so feeble, could have wrought such misery and destruction on three generations of the same family. He'd ruined Sarah Purcell, been responsible for Susan Furlong's downfall, and it now looked as though his past deeds were having detrimental effects on Helena Andrews.

Before leaving the retirement home, Emma had another word with Nurse Daly. The nurse, wearing everyday clothes, explained that the absence of uniforms made the residence feel less institutionalized. 'We try our best,' she said, her tone bright and cheerful, 'to make the old boys feel at home. With some it's easy . . . with others, well . . .'

'And what of Bishop Treanor?' Emma asked. 'Strikes me he could be a bit of a handful.'

Nurse Daly shrugged her shoulders and gave a sad fleeting smile. In her forties, she was a neat petite person with a pleasant face and agile movements. 'Ah yes, His Grace, a troubled soul if ever I saw one, but God love him, he's been good as gold this last while. He's fine as long as no one disturbs him.'

'Has he had many visitors?'

'No, not really. Those who came in the beginning got little or no response and ceased coming. Can't say I blame them. Nobody bothers any more except his grandniece. Such a pretty woman.'

'His grandniece?' Emma queried, 'Do you mean Caroline Andrews?'

'No, no. Mrs Andrews, the Lord have mercy on her, seldom visited her uncle. Hard to believe she's no longer with us.'

'So who — ?'

'Sorry, it's Caroline's *daughter* I'm talking about, *Helena* Andrews.'

Emma tried to hide her surprise. 'When did she last visit?'

'This day three weeks ago exactly. I'm unlikely to forget it.'

'Why is that?'

'Seeing Helena was a bit too much for His Grace. I suppose she reminded him of the better days but for whatever reason her visit upset him terribly.'

'What happened?'

'I entered the room, saw Helena whisper something in his ear. Whatever she said brought on a severe bout of agitation. His face turned blue, his body began to tremble uncontrollably, his legs and arms thrashing about like you wouldn't believe. The whole spasm lasted no longer than thirty seconds or so but I can tell you it didn't half put the heart crossways in me. I really thought His Grace was about to meet his Maker. As soon as Helena left he returned to his former self and acted as though nothing had happened.'

'And that was the last time Helena came here?'

'Yes. Such a lovely young woman.'

'And you say you've no idea what Helena said to upset him?'

Nurse Daly stiffened. 'Well now, I certainly don't go round eavesdropping on what visitors say.'

'No, no, I meant no offence. I — '

'But even if I did,' the nurse said, regaining her friendly disposition, 'what Helena said was *whispered* in His Grace's ear.'

After some further innocuous chit-chat, Emma took her leave and headed back to a meeting she'd arranged with Detective Inspector Connolly. What she'd learned from the nurse made her wish she'd been a fly on the wall on the day of Helena Andrews's visit. What exactly had Helena said to her grandfather to induce such violent reaction? Did it confirm Grace McCormick's darkest fears in regard to Helena? Mention of Helena's name had sparked off some sort of reaction in Treanor; surely that lent more credence to Grace McCormick's assertions.

If only Treanor could talk. If only . . . if only . . .

10

Of the 700 pubs — give or take a half-dozen — in the greater Dublin area, The Turk's Head represented one of the most flamboyant and popular. Situated in Parliament Street, on the edge of the trendy Temple Bar district, a stone's throw from the River Liffey, it was the place where many of the city's 'pretty people' gravitate to at night. During daylight hours its clientele tended to be more varied with customers coming from all walks of life. Barristers, solicitors, PR gurus and the occasional judge from Dublin Castle, braved the biting breezes blowing up from the river to sample the pub's wares. Away from the rarefied atmosphere of the Castle, and the ever present reporters and television cameras, they enjoyed rubbing shoulders with tradesmen, sales executives, shoppers and tourists alike, the normal mix to be found in any city-centre watering hole.

Waiting at the counter for Emma Boylan, Connolly caught his reflection in the mirror slots between the upturned optics for dispensing spirits and raised a questioning eyebrow. Either the mirror had a built-in distortion or he was looking a hell of a lot more dishevelled than he thought possible. He'd gone on a bender the previous night, got stoned and ended up sleeping in his car. Such behaviour was for him an aberration, a one-off flight into madness. What the hell had driven him to act so out of character? Pondering this quandary, he saw the reflection of Emma making her way across the floor to him. She looked perfect, proving were proof needed that the mirror held no distortions. The wind had blown her hair all over the place, a factor that in her case only served to accentuate her attractiveness. Connolly was drawn to her mouth, wide and sensuous, and wondered what it would be like to kiss those lips. *Stop it*, he told himself. He didn't want notions like that messing up his mind. 'What're you having,' he asked, turning to greet her, 'coffee . . . something stronger?'

Emma looked at her watch. 'Three o'clock, hmmm, bit early in the day to hit the sauce.'

'Well then, you'll pardon me if I fortify my coffee with a measure of Hennessy; it's been a god-awful day. Want something similar?'

'I don't know, I — '

''Course you will! Grab some seats,' he said, indicating an alcove, 'How about an Irish coffee or a French one like I'm having. Something to warm the cockles, eh? There's a breeze out there that'd freeze a pawnbroker's balls. What'd you say?'

'Yeah, all right then, to hell with the begrudgers,' Emma said, moving away from the bar. 'I'll have a shot of brandy in mine.'

In all the time Emma had known Connolly she'd never known him to touch alcohol. Not only that but she suspected he'd already put away a few shots before making it to The Turk's Head. This was a new departure. The scowl on his face did not sit well on his handsome features. What was wrong with the man? Usually, the detective was turned out in pin-sharp fashion, neat as a high street shop mannequin, his hair groomed to perfection, the silver strands at the temple swept back stylishly above the ears, the shoes shone bright enough to dazzle a sergeant major on reveille inspection. Not today! The shirt and tie were just about passable but the suit, a charcoal three-piece, looked as though he'd slept in it; his hair was a mess and the lace on one of his shoes remained untied. Emma was aware that the detective's wife had left him but until now she had no idea how much the upheaval had affected him.

Connolly brought the laced coffees to the alcove, placed them on the small table, and slouched into a seat beside her. 'D'you know what I'm going to tell you, Emma? You're a sight for sore eyes.'

'Well, bearing in mind that my obituary appeared in the papers last week, I'm not doing so bad,' she said, taking a sip from her glass.

'Ah yes, greatest return from the dead since Finnegan's wake — '

' — Or since Lazarus took up his bed and walked. I do see the funny side now but discovering I was dead was a bit unsettling.'

'Now that you mention it, I've done some investigating on your behalf to see if I could identify the culprit.'

'Any joy?'

'No. Enquiries ran into sand. Whoever's responsible hid all trace of involvement. Any idea yourself who's behind it?'

'I've a few theories, yes, each one more daft than the next.'

'Tell me, Emma, would any of those theories be connected with events that happened ten years ago?'

'Ah haaa!' Emma said, a knowing look on her face, 'so this is the reason you called to my 'wake', right?'

'Guilty as charged! Yes, I wanted a quiet word but there were far too many well-wishers mourning your passing.'

'Well, you've got my undivided attention now.'

'This death notice business, Emma, is it linked to Susan Furlong?'

'Could be! But how on earth did you make that connection; you weren't involved in that case.'

'True, I wasn't. Which might be just as well considering that the two officers investigating the case are now dead. Susan Furlong, as I recall, shot DI Tom Costello dead at the time, and more recently Larry Lawlor's been murdered. On top of that the Andrews came to grief in Spain. Strange, wouldn't you say?'

'Yes,' Emma agreed, 'Seems to me like all of us who stood in the room where Susan Furlong took her life are an endangered species.'

'Open season more like, but not just for the people who were in the room.'

'What do you mean?'

Connolly took a deep swig from his drink. 'I'm not sure I know myself. Had a meeting yesterday with the Chief Super back at HQ. He's got the British and Spanish police authorities asking for help with their enquiries into the deaths of Lawlor and the Andrews. I've been given the task of going abroad to meet with them. I'm not complaining on that score; anything that gets me away from the wet and misery of this sodden country has got to be a bonus. But there's been a worrying development that might have a bearing on what we're

105

talking about. The Chief Super had a call from ex-government minister, Niamh O'Flynn.'

'We don't hear too much from her these days.'

'Let's be thankful for small mercies,' Connolly said, attempting to smooth back some wayward strands of hair with his hand. 'The opposition benches have softened that one's cough. But don't forget she was responsible for mishandling Susan Furlong's case. And now, all these years later, she gets a threatening letter.'

'What kind of threatening letter?'

'The worst kind. Whoever sent it issued O'Flynn with a veiled warning that she would soon know the meaning of loss and grieving.'

'And you think it's connected to Susan Furlong?'

'Strong possibility, wouldn't you say! The timing inclines me towards the Susan Furlong business. What do you think?'

'I think I'll have another coffee Royale.' Emma went to the counter rather than look for floor service. She needed to get away from the detective to think about what she should tell him. Her trust in Connolly was total. They had co-operated on cases before and had established a respect for each other. After she'd lost her baby he'd been the one to help her shake off the despondency. He'd visited her at the time and used his power of persuasion to shock her into facing realities. For that she would always be grateful. A bond of friendship had been forged, a bond she hoped never to abuse.

But with Connolly's recent marriage difficulties, she had a problem defining where the borderline lay when it came to friendship versus something more intimate. She could not fail to notice the way he looked at her. What was it she saw in those eyes? More importantly, how was she supposed to reconcile the undoubted effect Connolly had on her equilibrium. She couldn't deny the quickening pulse and fluttering heartbeat she experienced every time he brushed against her or accidentally touched her.

Emma gave an almost imperceptible shake of the head, annoyed with herself for entertaining such idle speculation. She was a married woman for God's sake, not some impressionable teenage girl dreaming of impossible romantic liaisons with an equally impossible and unobtainable member of the opposite sex. It was important to maintain the status quo: friendship; just plain old-fashioned, safe, reliable platonic friendship, nothing more.

The look of expectation on Connolly's face when she returned with the two steaming glasses of fortified coffee was like that of a child on Christmas morning. Pretending not to notice, Emma sat down and told him about the visit she'd had from Grace McCormick. She told him about the death-sympathy card the psychiatrist had received, and the suspicions she'd articulated in regard to Helena Andrews. Connolly listened without interruption as she talked about her visit to John Treanor and the conversation she'd had with Nurse Daly.

'This is all crazy,' Connolly said when she'd finished. 'The way this is stacking up it looks as though Helena Andrews, a 21-year-old girl, is going around bumping off people. Are we seriously suggesting that this woman has turned into some kind of serial killer? And why, because she blames . . . what, a bunch of people for not preventing her mother's suicide? Is that what we're saying?'

'When you put it like that, it does sound pretty incredible. I don't know what the hell is going on but we've got far too many coincidences here not to believe there isn't something sinister afoot.'

'I don't know, Emma; I'm getting too friggin' old for this stuff; I mean, you see serial killers on television cop shows and . . . and soaps, but never as far as I know have we had a serial killer in this country. I try to kid myself that we're getting a bit fanciful here, jumping to the wrong conclusions and getting spooked because of a few unfortunate coincidences.'

'But how do you explain the threat to Niamh O'Flynn? What about the death notices? And who sent the sympathy card to Grace McCormick?'

'Yeah, I know, we keep coming back to that and I have to admit there's a pattern. I'll know better after I've talked to my opposite numbers in London and Malaga.'

'When do you go abroad?'

'Day after tomorrow. A few hours in London, then off to Spain.'

'Hey, sounds good. The weather in Spain isn't bad even for this time of year. You want to take me with you? I could do with a break.'

'If I thought you were serious Emma, I'd take you in a flash. You're not serious though, are you?'

''Fraid not, wishful thinking on my part. Too much to do here, that's the problem. You could always take one of your colleagues.'

Connolly sighed. 'Ah, Emma, Emma my dear, the kind of company I'm looking for is not to be found in a cop shop. What I need is the milk of human kindness, a fellow human being to converse with . . . preferably female.'

Emma felt herself blush. She wanted to reach out to him but refrained. How would such a gesture be interpreted?

Connolly, seeing the look of confusion on her face came to her rescue. 'I'm sorry Emma,' he said, making a little grimace with his mouth, 'I shouldn't be laying my misfortune on you. It's just that with the house gone and Iseult playing the field, I'm feeling a bit sorry for myself. Being on my own isn't good for the soul . . . and yet, the paradox is: I'm glad the sham that was my marriage is over.' A sad smile crossed his face. 'You want to hear a joke?'

'A joke?' Emma said, surprised by the sudden turn of conversation.

'Yes, a joke. Iseult's getting great mileage out of this one down at the pony club. Goes something like this: name the worthless piece of baggage attached to the base of a penis.'

'I don't think I want to know the answer,' Emma lied.

'The answer, Iseult informs her friends through shrieks of laughter is — *a husband.*' Connolly's eyes misted over. He forced a smile on to his face. 'You're not laughing, Emma? Sure as hell cracks them up down at the club.'

Emma reached across the table and took his hand in hers.

11

Helena Andrews hunched her shoulders and shivered. November in Belgium.

Barely two weeks in Brussels and every day so far had been cold. Pushing against a biting breeze she made her way past the designer shops on Avenue Louise before turning a corner into Toison d'Or. She was on her way to meet Bill Quinn for lunch. Unlike the fur-clad Italians who habitually strutted their stuff in this part of town Helena had purposely dressed down: sensible boots and wool trouser suit in black, winter coat, also black, and large wrap-around scarf in creamy white. This lunchtime date meant that her ploy to forge a relationship with the man had succeeded. She shivered again but it was the thrill of conquest, not the chill factor, that induced the bodily shudder. Her game plan was about to shift to another level.

Niamh O'Flynn's husband Bill Quinn worked at the Commission headquarters and Helena had compiled quite a dossier on him before deciding on the Belgian adventure. Luckily for Helena she had a contact in Brussels, a young woman she'd known from her college days. Tracey Cusack worked as a Grade C official in Regional Policy Directorate and had a small apartment off the Avenue des Nerviens — two bedrooms, a kitchen and bathroom on the fifth floor of a poorly maintained building. Though cramped for space, the apartment had two plus factors: it was close to Tracey's place of work and the rent was reasonable. Tracey allowed Helena the use of her second bedroom, a tiny but well-lit room that, according to the estate agent who'd sold it, offered a view of Parc Cinquantenaire. It was almost true; it was indeed possible to get a glimpse of the park but to do so meant having to stand on a chair and lean to the edge of the window.

Helena could have taken on a more expensive apartment on the prestigious Avenue de la Renaissance or Avenue du Cortenberg but she'd chosen instead to share with Tracey Cusack, a person who could bring her up to speed with the *modus operandi* of the various EU establishments. Together, they had visited the vast modern Parliament Quarter, a gleaming state-of-the-art structure that housed the 600 plus Members of Parliament. There was, however, one small area of information where Helena's knowledge was superior to that of her guide. When Tracey took Helena to the Cours St

Michel 2 building and pointed out the Regional Policy HQ she didn't know it also represented the workplace of Bill Quinn.

As a Director General, Bill Quinn had a large office, situated on the same floor as a number of units under his control. These units were staffed by nationalities from most of the existing member states. Outside of office hours Bill Quinn frequented the Irish bars. In the first week of shadowing him Helena noted that he was on first-name terms with bar staff in the Old Oak, the James Joyce, Kitty O'Shea's, the Wild Geese and the Hairy Canary. He walked with a loping gait and smiled easily. His favourite tipple was Chimay beer but he occasionally ordered Jameson whiskey.

Helena had spent ten days in Brussels before making her move on Quinn. It was a Sunday, a day when many of the citizens visited the Grand Place. On the stroke of midday, she spotted him sitting in La Chaloupe d'Or, a copy of *The Irish Times* in his hands, a glass of Chimay in front of him. He had that pinkish skin unique to the Irish, the kind of skin that turns tomato red when exposed to the sun. Lifeless sandy hair, thinning towards the forehead, sat on his head as though arranged by a taxidermist. His age was difficult to pinpoint but she put him somewhere between 45 and 55. Almost six feet in height, he carried a little weight, a factor he managed to conceal by a judicious choice of well-cut clothes. He had the kind of face that was instantly forgettable, his features being uniformly unremarkable except for a neatly trimmed moustache that was a few shades darker than his hair.

Helena sat in a seat beside him and made her first tentative move. 'Anything of interest in the paper?' she asked.

Quinn lowered the newspaper. 'It's yesterday's I'm afraid,' he said, sneaking a sideways glance at her. 'Saturday's *Times*. Usual stuff, nothing startling. You're Irish, yeah? With the Commission, I suppose?'

'Irish, yes, but I'm here on a holiday break. Trying to get to know the city. I like what I've seen so far.'

'Hah!' Quinn said, stroking his moustache between finger and thumb. 'Then you've managed to avoid the dog-shit on the pavements; the motorists who see every pedestrian as the enemy, and the shop assistants who give the impression they're doing you a favour by serving you.'

Helena's smile was all encompassing. 'Oh, come now, I like the place. They make great chocolate and the food's not bad,' she said, guessing that Quinn habitually trotted out these same sentiments, 'I especially like the people, so many nationalities . . . all those languages . . . I think it's rather charming.'

'You do? Hah!' Quinn said, a know-all grin on his face. 'Well then, perhaps you'll allow me to buy you a drink?'

'I'd love that, thanks. What do you recommend?'

'Well now, the beer here is one of the good things about Brussels, but I think you should have something more special. Let's see; the name of this pub translates to The Golden Lifeboat and they have a special cocktail called The Golden. There's eating and drinking in it. You want to try it?'

'Well, you know what they say: when in Rome . . . '

The relationship had begun; a few pleasantries, then a few more, a couple of drinks and an exchange of names. Their personalities had gelled and the conversation had come easily. A lot had happened in the intervening two days. And now, she was about to meet him for lunch.

★ ★ ★

Emma had finished her breakfast and was about to head for work when the telephone rang. Should she answer it? Should she leave

115

it ringing in the hope that it encouraged Vinny to get out of bed? Of course not. Curiosity always won out. Could be important, she told herself. It was her mother. Hazel Boylan rarely telephoned in the morning and when she did Emma always feared the worst.

'Nothing wrong, Mum?' she asked.

'No, nothing wrong,' Hazel said, a little hesitantly, 'it's a daft thing really. A letter came this morning addressed to your dad and I, concerning you.'

'Concerning me? In what way?'

'Well, it's really a sales letter offering to design and erect a gravestone. I expect it's got something to do with that dreadful obituary business.'

Emma was speechless for a moment. 'You sure it's not just some junk mail . . . you know, sales stuff that goes to — '

'Could be, but the letter specifically names you and they even have a photo showing a gravestone with your name carved on a marble plaque. I don't mind telling you it gives me the heebie-jeebies. Still, I expect you're right, they probably send a similar thing to the next of kin of everyone whose name appears in the deaths' column. Morbid way to do business if you ask me.'

'Yes, Mum, I think it's just a sales pitch,'

Emma said, trying not to betray her unease. 'Hold on to it, I might be down your way over the next day or so, I'll look at it.' Emma hung up, turned around and let out a frightened little yelp. 'Vinny,' she managed to say, catching her breath, 'you frightened the life out of me creeping up on me like that.'

'Sorry, Emma,' he said, standing beside her, naked except for his boxer shorts. 'The phone woke me. Had to get out of bed, needed a pee. Didn't mean to frighten you. You look as though you've seen a ghost. Bad news?'

'I don't know, Vinny. Weird, more like.' Emma repeated what she'd heard from her mother. Vinny listened while he set about brewing coffee. 'Whoever placed those notices in the papers is intent on playing silly buggers.'

'Yes, but this time they've gone direct to my parents. I just hope they haven't been on to Ciarán.'

'What? Hey, you don't think they'll get on to Dad, do you?'

'I don't know what they'll do. Damn thing is infuriating.'

'What if *he* got a letter this morning . . . ?'

'You could ring him, I suppose.'

'I think I will. Don't want some prankster putting the wind up him.'

Vinny dialled his father's number. 'No answer,' he said to Emma, a look of apprehension on his face. 'He's always out of bed by now . . . all his life. You don't think — '

'No, Vinny, I don't think; I don't think anything. Could be any number of reasons why he's not answering.'

'You're right, Emma. I'll try later. If I don't hear from him, I'll pop out to the studio.'

'Good idea. And when you see him, invite him to dinner next Sunday. I worry that he's not feeding himself properly, living all alone in that big house, stuck in that studio all hours of the day and night.'

'You know what Dad's like, never happy till he has a brush in his hand and a canvas on the easel, only thing that really matters to him. I'll try and entice him out on Sunday, take him for a few pints first.'

'He'd enjoy that.'

'Yeah, he would. I'll call on him later, see if he's OK.'

'Call me as soon as you get there,' Emma said, placing a quick kiss on Vinny's lips. 'Got to run, I'm already late for a meeting with Crosby. I might drive down to see Mum later, check out that letter she got.'

'OK. Talk to you later.' As soon as she was out the door Vinny hit the redial button. Still no answer from his father. He tried to reassure himself that there was a rational explanation. But doubts assailed him. He would have no peace of mind until he called at the studio.

12

Helena's lunch with Bill Quinn had not worked out as planned. Quinn had invited two friends along, colleagues from the Council of Ministers' complex. Limp handshakes and brittle smiles were exchanged. They were pleasant enough company, a well-dressed handsome Irish man in his thirties named Willie Gilbert, and a slightly younger woman, equally well attired, named Rebecca Scott, also from Ireland. As far as Helena could tell, the two were not romantically linked.

Helena cloaked her displeasure as Willie Gilbert, a consummate raconteur, regaled them with an inexhaustible supply of anecdotes. At no time during the hour-long lunch did she have an opportunity to have a tête-à-tête with Bill Quinn.

A full hour after Quinn and his two friends made their way back to their respective offices he called her. 'Hope you didn't mind Willie and Rebecca joining us for the lunch,' he offered, apologetically.

'No, not at all,' she lied smoothly, 'they were fun.'

'Willie, huh? Must've swallowed the Blarney Stone.'

'Know what you mean, all those stories; smashing.'

'He's a walking-talking repository of useless information and tall tales. Trouble is, I didn't get a chance to ask in front of them, but would you fancy going out this evening . . . just the two of us, a nice meal, glass of wine, visit the Lower Town before you leave us. What do you say?'

'Yeah sure, why not!'

Helena listened as he gave directions for getting to a tavern called La Maison Royale. The location, he warned, was mostly residential, a bit off the beaten track, but well worth the trouble. 'The place is full of character and charm, part of the city that tourists don't usually get to see.'

'You've sold me. What time should I get there?'

'I'll be waiting for you there at, say, seven-thirty. How's that sound?'

'Fine, that's fine; look forward to it.'

Helena hit the 'end' button on her mobile and consulted the street map in her visitor's guide. She pinpointed the location easily enough. On earlier tours of the city with Tracey Cusack, she'd been greatly impressed by the Lower Town and its architecture. The location in question was well away from the business and legislative zones, nowhere near Quinn's apartment. Implications were clear; he wanted to be alone with her in a place where friends and work colleagues were unlikely to see him.

At 7.30 p.m. precisely, her taxicab pulled to a stop in a quiet side street. 'We're here, madam,' the driver said, his words overlaid with a Flemish accent. Helena got out, paid the fare and stood for a moment observing the building, a three-storey, cut stone establishment dimly illuminated by street lamps. The name — La Maison Royale — painted in faded characters on a timber awning looked decidedly unprepossessing. A coppery haze of warm light issued from a multicoloured stained-glass window beneath the awning.

Quinn was waiting for her inside, his wave of welcome expansive. She joined him at a table beside a pot-bellied stove. The place was not overly busy and the atmosphere was warm and pleasant. A dozen people or more, all Flemish speakers, supped drinks and talked quietly among themselves.

Quinn ordered two Chimay beers in what sounded like well-rounded Flemish to Helena. A scowling barman placed two fat tulip-shaped glasses in front of them without bothering to utter a word, the question of languages not a problem as far as he was concerned.

'We have three official languages in Belgium,' Quinn explained, 'and English is not one of them. I have a fair smattering of French and can get by with my Flemish.'

After two rounds of Chimay, Quinn suggested they have something to eat. Customers in the tavern were consuming shrimps and cheese croquettes with their beers, the aroma enough to entice Helena to do the same. When she agreed, Quinn reached out and took hold of her hand. 'Not here though,' he said, 'I thought we might go back to my place. I learned to do a bit of cooking since I came out here; don't often get a chance to try it out. What do you say?'

Helena nodded happily. 'Sounds good to me.'

'That's great!' Quinn said, draining his glass, 'my place is just around the corner, walking distance.'

Helena hid her surprise. She knew he was lying. Quinn's apartment was located down the road from the Justice Lipsius building. She'd tracked him there on two occasions, seen him come and go from the apartment building, a luxury 1920s complex that housed several floors of private flats. She'd seen his nameplate and his letterbox in the foyer, seen him extract post from it before taking the lift to his floor. Yet, here he was telling her that he lived just around the corner in a different part of town.

★ ★ ★

It was mid-morning by the time Vinny made it to Little Bray. He managed to find a parking spot outside Bailey's Fine Art & Antique Studio. He let himself in by the side door, made his way to the kitchen and called out to his father. There was no response. The smell of burnt toast hung in the air. The teapot was still warm. Since the death of Vinny's mother more than a dozen years earlier Ciarán had looked after himself. Unfortunately, he sometimes got so engrossed in his commissions that he forgot to eat. On other occasions he'd been known to go on the booze for days at a time. Yet it was Ciarán, not Vinny, who brought the bulk of income into the business. As long as the art galleries required his skills for retouching and art restoration needs, and his health held out, that would remain the case.

The pungent odours of linseed oil and solvent that permeated the whole house was especially strong as Vinny made his way to the art studio. It was a smell he had associated with his father's workplace for as long as he could remember. The scene seldom varied: piles of canvases angled against the walls, frames of every size and shape, brushes, paints, palettes, easels, rags, pots of varnish, bottles of Sansodor solvent and the inevitable splattered smocks, combining to create a riot of colour.

Much to Vinny's relief, he saw Ciarán's frail figure standing in front of an easel, palette balanced on his left arm and wrist, a brush poised in his other hand. Two spotlights, mounted on old-fashioned steel tripods, illuminated a still-life composition set on a table to one side of the easel. During the winter months it was Ciarán's habit to close the blinds and rely on the consistent spill of white arc light. The old artist, donned in a multi-daubed smock, seemed oblivious to his son's entrance.

'Hi Dad,' Vinny said, making his way through the obstacle course of objects strewn about the studio floor. 'How yo' doing?'

'Oh, Vinny, 'tis you,' he said, without averting his eyes from the canvas. 'What brings you here this morning?'

'Hadn't planned to come,' Vinny said pleasantly, 'but when you didn't bother your backside to answer the phone I decided to see if you were all right.'

Ciarán made no reply, his concentration totally absorbed with the painting. Vinny knew better than to force the pace when his father was at the easel. In the silence that followed, the realization that his father had become an old man hit him forcibly. What little hair remained on his head gleamed like silver threads in the artificial light. The face, though drained of colour and vigour, still bespoke a merciless pragmatism and intelligence. His cheekbones protruded, his mouth drooped a little at the corners but his eyes shone bright as ever from beneath their drooping lids.

'Heard the ringing all right,' Ciarán said, 'didn't want to leave this . . . wanted to capture the life and sap in these flowers before they began to wilt.'

Vinny looked at the arrangement. White lilies surrounded by a base of wild flowers. 'Not like you to bother with flowers, Dad; what brought this on?'

'You're right, I don't paint flowers as a rule but, well, there were certain circumstances . . .'

'Circumstances? Sounds intriguing. Sent by a lover, were they?'

'Lover me arse! If you must know, they were for you.'

'For me?'

'Well, yes, in a round about sort of way.'

'Dad, what are you talking about?'

Ciarán put his palette and brushes down, turned to face Vinny. 'I could do with a cup of tea, son. Come into the kitchen, I'll tell you about the flowers.'

Vinny led the way to the kitchen, plugged in the kettle and found some tea bags in a jam jar. 'Now tell me,' he said, when he'd sat down at the table with Ciarán, 'what's this about the flowers being for me?'

'Fellow from Interflora delivered them yesterday evening. I couldn't think for the life of me who'd sent them and was about to bin them when I saw the card. Apparently, someone bought the story about your death; didn't know it was a hoax. The message said — 'Deepest sympathy on the death of your son Vinny'.'

'Was there a name?'

'No, I couldn't find a signature . . . I've no idea who sent them. Anyway, I couldn't very well throw them out after that, could I? And the more I looked at them, the more the idea came to me, maybe I should paint them.'

Vinny said nothing. He had no doubt that the same person who'd been in touch with Emma's mother had sent the flowers. Someone out there was orchestrating a campaign of fear.

* * *

'My very own gastronomic speciality,' Quinn proclaimed brashly, 'Carbonnades flamandes.' His culinary expertise was indeed formidable, surprising Helena. He served up fillets of beef, braised in *kriek* — cherry fruit beer — with all the flourish of a trained chef. For dessert he brought upside-down apple cake to the table. 'It's a reminder,' he said, winking, 'that sometimes things can be more fun when what's usually on the bottom is allowed on top.'

The sexual innuendo came as no surprise to Helena. She could see lust lurking in his eyes. Since entering the apartment his manner had remained gracious, straightforward, yet all the time his eyes spoke volumes, their glint, a window to the machinations of his mind. That suited Helena's plans admirably. She hadn't exactly been subtle herself in signalling her intentions: two undone blouse buttons displaying her seductive cleavage and using the tip of her tongue to teasingly caress her teeth.

Earlier, while Quinn toiled in the kitchen she'd explored the apartment. It struck her as odd that no family photographs were on display. Discreetly, she'd peeped into cupboards and opened drawers. In one drawer she found a series of framed photographs, turned face downward. She recognized the smiling image of Willie Gilbert. The woman in the photo with Gilbert, his wife she suspected, was not the woman who'd been with him earlier for lunch. Other photographs showed two children, a boy of five or six, and a girl some years younger. His children, she had no doubt. So, Quinn was using Willie Gilbert's apartment for his extra-curricular activities.

With the meal out of the way, Quinn quickly cleared the table, stacked the dishwasher, and moved into the lounge with Helena. He put Pachelbel's Canon in D Major for Strings on the CD machine and fixed drinks. He dimmed the lights, sat next to Helena and placed a furtive kiss on her cheek. Helena stifled a yawn. This was going to be painful and slow. Quinn, she decided, would take forever to get his act together. He belonged to the category she termed *fumblers*, a breed of inept lover capable of turning the unhooking of a bra into a marathon event. 'Why don't we cut to the chase,' she said, moving her hand on to his thigh and allowing her fingers to gently squeeze. 'You brought me here to get it on, right?'

'Well, er, I . . . of course, ah — '

'Exactly! So let's make ourselves comfortable and move to the bedroom?'

'Yes, yes, yes, let's,' Quinn said excitedly, taking her by the hand. In the bedroom, a small, expensively furnished room with a large double bed, he tried to kiss her as his hands fumbled to help her out of her clothes. She stopped him, suggesting that he return to the kitchen for some glasses and a bottle of wine. Quinn, visibly aroused by now, readily agreed. As soon as he'd left the bedroom, Helena checked her handbag. The syringe and mobile phone were still there. Satisfied, that all was in order, she removed the mobile from one of the compartments and placed it under the pillows on the bed.

With a smirk of satisfaction, she looked at her reflection in a full-length wardrobe mirror, winked at her own image and mouthed the words — *show time*. She discarded her clothes with all the aplomb of a young woman fully conscious of the allure her voluptuous body held for others.

13

'Mom, hey, Mom, telephone!' Joan Quinn yelled.

'Be there in a sec,' her mother shouted from upstairs. Niamh O'Flynn had been getting ready to go to a party fund-raiser. Before descending the stairs she took a final across-the-shoulder glance in the mirror; a well-preserved woman of 44, stared back. She was pleased with her choice of wardrobe; an elegant sage-green wool suit, a designer hat that had cost a fortune and an equally expensive patent leather bag. She'd pinned her good-luck charm, a gold shamrock studded with green olivine, to the right side of her jacket. A second yell from Joan hurried her to the phone. 'Must be a crossed line,' the 9-year-old said, 'just weird noises and stuff.'

Niamh pressed the phone to her ear. 'Hello' she said impatiently, 'Quinn residence; who *is* this?' She could hear a muffled suction sound. Hard to identify the source but she felt certain it had a human dimension. An image sprang to mind: fornication. She was glad Joan had gone to her room; thoughts of her daughter being subjected to an obscene call frightened her.

Using her most authoritative inflection she demanded acknowledgement. Getting no response, she was about to hang up but stopped; she could hear a man and a woman speaking. Even though the sound was muffled she thought she recognized the male.

'You're gorgeous!' the man was saying, his voice slurred. Sounded like her husband. It couldn't be Bill, could it? He was in Brussels. The man spoke again. She was not mistaken. It *was* Bill. Her body tensed. She could hear breathing, indistinct whispering and hissing, then guttural moans from her husband, depraved utterances of a kind she'd never heard him use with her. Her hand shot to her mouth as she took an intake of breath.

'Where'd you learn to do *that*, Billy boy?' a honeyed voice asked. 'You're quite a lover. How much of this do you save for the little woman back home?'

'Who said anything about a little woman?' Niamh heard her husband ask.

The woman giggled. 'Oh, come now, a *big boy* like you must have a regular, like maybe a little wife tucked away somewhere.'

There was silence, then the rustle of sheets.

'I do as a matter of fact.' Bill was saying. 'Wouldn't lie to you . . . have a wife. But our marriage has long since run its course.'

Niamh felt her legs weaken. She sat on the stool, wanting to slam the phone down but pressed it tight enough to her ear to hurt.

The woman was speaking again. 'You have kids?'

Bill cleared his throat, spoke hesitantly. 'Have a daughter.'

'Must have been a spark for that to happen?' the woman said.

'Jesus, can we talk about something else?'

'All I'm saying is: you must have loved her once.'

'Thought I did.'

'Hmmm, past tense? You no longer love her? Does she love you?'

'She loves herself, period. Her nearest and dearest is her own sweet self. Now, can we change the subject? I'm losing my hard-on.'

'Sorry. Just wanted to establish that you once — '

'And I said I don't wish to talk about it, OK?'

A short silence was followed by the sound of Bill yawning. 'Jesus, I'm really sleepy. Must be the drink. Can we get back to — '

'I don't think we're going anywhere with our limp friend here — '

'Don't know what's wrong. I'm falling asleep, can't keep my eyes . . . '

Niamh could hear the sound of a face

being slapped followed by a sigh of exasperation from the woman. 'Sleep, sleep you dork,' the woman said, the voice no longer seductive. 'Thought you'd never pass out.'

There was a click, then silence. Niamh O'Flynn took the phone away from her ear and allowed it to fall back in its cradle. The noise it made seemed distant and other worldly. She was marooned in a mind-numbing stupor, unsure whether the experience she'd just had was part of an awful nightmare or, worse still, reality. The ceiling above her floated in a crazy out of kilter surreal world.

Gradually, mercifully, a kind of normality returned. She could feel herself tremble as she wiped tears from her eyes. Niamh O'Flynn didn't do crying; crying was a sign of weakness, not something a tough politician indulged in. She inhaled deep breaths, removed her hat and tried to clear her mind. Her trembles abated. *I'm stronger than this*, she told herself, *I can deal with this, I will deal with this*.

With robotic-like animation, her fingertip dialled the number that would connect her to Bill's mobile phone. After a short delay, a disembodied voice informed her that the number was not currently active; would she like to leave a message? No, she didn't wish to leave a message; what she had to say could not be accommodated on an answering machine.

She got up from the stool, reached for the small notebook that contained the telephone numbers of friends, relations, and emergency services. Under normal circumstances she could remember Bill's landline number without recourse to the mini directory, but these were not normal circumstances. She thumbed through the pages and found his listing. It surprised her how steady her fingers remained as she punched the digits.

A male voice answered. 'Hello, yes?' The speaker was not her husband.

'Niamh O'Flynn here,' she said, 'I want to speak with Bill.'

'Oh, hello, Niamh . . . ah emmm, Mrs Quinn, this is Willie Gilbert. You might remember me; we met at a few receptions, I'm a friend of Bill's.'

Niamh dredged up a picture of Gilbert. Yes, she remembered him: tallish, mid-thirties, good-looking, roving eyes, salesman's smile and over-familiar banter. 'Yes, Willie, I remember you . . . and your wife. Look I don't wish to be rude but could you put Bill on the line.'

'Well, I can't right now. He's not here. He's ah . . . had to work late in the office. Busy time here right now . . . sorting out the new member states. You wouldn't believe the amount — '

'Please, Willie,' she cut in, 'give me a number where I can contact him.'

'Now let me see; he could be in any part of the Commission complex. I tell you what: why don't I ring around, see if I can track him down.'

Niamh could hear the faint sound of another person. It sounded like a woman's voice, an intoxicated woman's voice, and it sounded like she was calling out to Willie.

'Someone there with you, Willie?'

She heard sssssh-ing and giggling in the background.

'Ah, it's just the TV set — ' Gilbert started to say.

'What exactly are you doing in Bill's flat? I mean, if *he's* not there, why would you — ?'

'Ah, well now, Niamh, that's . . . well, that's easy to explain. You see, Bill asked me to help with this report he's putting together, a bloody huge report, full of statistics and all that malarkey. Has to be ready for a Council of Ministers' meeting next week. He's under pressure so I offered to help. But look, Niamh, I'll ring around, track him down, have him call you back as soon as — '

Niamh hung up. Better to say nothing than give oxygen to the ugly thoughts in her head.

She stared at the mute phone. Willie Gilbert was lying through his teeth; she'd had enough dealings with liars to spot one a mile off, even over a phone line. It was what lay behind the lies that bothered her. She picked up her hat, moved to the lounge and slumped into a chair. The television was on in the corner of the room, its volume turned down, but even if it had been blaring it's doubtful she'd have heard it. Unaware that her hands were twisting her millinery creation out of shape, she attempted to envisage a likely scenario for what was going down in Brussels. Willie Gilbert was in Bill's apartment with a fancy woman; Bill was in Willie's apartment with his bit-on-the-side. Christ, it was a story old as time. In her husband's case she suspected that someone had accidentally activated a mobile phone. Somehow or other the mobile had called her number. She had another thought: what if someone had purposely opened the line; what if someone wanted her to overhear what Bill was up to in Brussels?

14

Halfway into her thirty-mile journey back to the city Emma's mobile bleeped. *Must be mother.* Hazel Boylan always remembered something she'd forgotten to say as soon as Emma drove away. The gravestone business had upset her and Emma suspected she was about to hear more on the subject. But she was wrong. The caller was Connolly.

'Emma, can you talk?'

'I'm fine; what's up?'

'Been a development . . . affects what we were talking about.'

Emma did a mental speed check on all that had passed between them on the previous day. They'd talked about Susan Furlong; they'd also aired some personal matters. Connolly had opened up his heart, exposed the hurt his marriage break-up had caused. She'd reached out and taken his hand. The moment was, as the old John Travolta/Olivia Newton-John song put it — *electrifying.* She'd felt sure that a surge of similar intensity had coursed through Connolly's veins.

Connolly's voice cut through her thoughts. 'Can you meet me in St Joseph's Rest Home?'

'Bishop Treanor, right?'

'Afraid so. The man's dead. Suspicious circumstances.'

'What? I don't get it. He was on his last legs anyway. Why would — '

'Can't talk about it on an open line. Can you get here?'

'Yes, sure. Be there in half an hour.'

Connolly clicked off.

Emma's curiosity was at boiling point. Could it really be that someone had done-in the retired cleric? What would be the point; he was only a whisper away from the grave as it was? One way or another she was about to find out.

★　★　★

A uniformed *garda* officer stopped her. 'Can't let you in, miss, restricted area.'

'No, it's OK,' Emma assured him, 'Detective Inspector Connolly asked me to get here.'

'Oh, I see. Let me check that out, miss, will ya?' The officer, a young pink-faced man in his mid-twenties, spoke into his walkie-talkie, nodded vigorously several times, then stood aside and indicated that Emma should pass through.

Connolly, in conversation with Nurse Daly,

nodded to Emma, his eyes telling her that he would be with her presently. Emma nodded back compliantly, then switched her gaze to the white-clad forensic team gathered around Treanor's bed. She could see the dead bishop's face propped up on pillows, a purplish hue through the slack skin and a trace of white froth on his lips. Emma made an involuntary sign of the cross, a throwback to her Catholic upbringing. It seemed to her that Treanor's parting from this world had not been easy. She was about to move closer when Connolly approached.

'We've got to get out of here,' he said, 'forensic are through with this stage but the autopsy needs to be set up. There's a small office down the corridor; we can talk there.'

Emma, following him, asked, 'What happened?'

'Looks like Treanor was poisoned.'

'Poisoned? But how would anyone — '

'Nurse Daly saw someone leave his room. She knew from reception that no visitors had been admitted so she called out to the person, whereupon the intruder ran. The nurse wanted to give chase but decided her priority lay with checking Treanor.

'Did she see who it was?'

'No, the runner's back was towards her. When she got to the bishop he was frothing at the mouth, his arms and legs flaying frantically. In the few minutes it took to summon medical assistance, the struggling ceased.'

'So, some unidentified person got to Treanor, poisoned him, and then legged it.'

'Looks that way. That's why I called you. We've got a hairy situation on our hands: everyone who witnessed the Furlong suicide, with the exception of yourself, Vinny and the medical director, is dead.'

'There were two other people present at the time. Bernadette Maxwell was there in the thick of it — '

'Ah, yes, our brain-damaged friend, Joan of Arc.'

'Yes, she witnessed the whole episode.'

'Yes, but luckily she's locked up. We can safely discount that unfortunate creature from our enquiries.'

'That *unfortunate creature* as you call her was once a proficient killing-machine. Remember, I was there when she held a gun against Helena's head and pulled the trigger. Would have killed the child except that the safety mechanism hadn't been released.'

'Odd thing, that, don't you think? I mean, Joan of Arc was with the paramilitaries back then, right? So how come she didn't know how to fire a gun?'

'Wondered about that myself, at the time, but it transpired that the weapon used was a Semmerling, an unusual piece of hardware. At any rate, Joan was unfamiliar with its intricacies; had to do with her not having the breech properly closed and the hammer being disengaged when she pulled the trigger, something like that. That make sense?'

'No, not really, but I think I get the picture. Sounds as though Joan of Arc could be in need of protection herself. I certainly don't see her as a threat.'

'I agree; it's unlikely she's a danger to anyone except herself . . . given her present state of mind. But there's another person who witnessed the death of Susan Furlong: you're forgetting Helena Andrews.'

'I'm *not* forgetting her. I now consider her the prime suspect. It's time I asked that young lady some serious questions. My immediate concern, however, is for your safety. No point fooling ourselves any longer.'

Emma nodded gravely. 'A few strange developments *have* taken place since we last spoke.'

'Like what?'

Emma told him about the gravestone leaflet and the flowers. Connolly shook his head, 'Someone's waging a psychological war, trying to scare you.'

'Yeah, right, and they're succeeding. I just wish they'd come out and say exactly what we're supposed to have done.'

'The next few days should tell us a lot. I talk with the police in London and Malaga tomorrow. Should help establish what links exist between these mysterious deaths. Meanwhile, I suggest you take care of yourself.'

'My concern is for Vinny's dad and my own parents.'

'We'll just have to remain alert.' Connolly said, standing up. 'Right now I've got to get back to Treanor's room. I have to ask you not to report what you've witnessed here for the moment. We should be able to identify the cause of death within a few hours. When that happens and his next of kin have been informed I'll contact you, OK?' Connolly took hold of her hands. 'Take care of yourself Emma; I don't want anything to happen to you while I'm gone.'

'Thanks, I'll bear that in mind,' Emma said, trying not to blush.

'There is one thing you could do while I'm away.'

'What's that?'

'I was supposed to talk to Niamh O'Flynn, but it looks like I won't get a chance to see her before my travels. I should send

McFadden or Dorsett but it might be better to keep this unofficial . . . could be more beneficial if you were to invent some pretext for talking to her.'

'I might just do that.'

'A warning though: be subtle, she's tough as nails and has the ear of some very important heads . . . including my boss. No point getting her all upset.'

'I'll be the soul of discretion.'

Connolly leaned into Emma, kissed her forehead, let go of her hands, turned on his heels and left.

Emma clasped her two hands together, pressed them to her mouth and kissed them.

15

The Boeing engines soared into the clouds above Zaventem, the sound spiralling back to Belgium's national airport like a protracted roll of thunder. Secure in her seat, safety belt fastened, sitting next to a window, Helena closed her eyes and exhaled a deep body-felt sigh. She'd accomplished what she'd set out to do and was now on her way to Dublin Airport. With no desire to cast a farewell glance at the city below she pulled the window blind down and began to contemplate the next phase of her plan. Yet, she couldn't help but take a little time out to savour the success of her mission in Brussels.

After Bill Quinn had passed out she'd cut the open line between the mobile phone and Niamh O'Flynn's house. During her encounter with Quinn it had been difficult to maintain the mobile in strategic positions. Fortunately, Quinn's thoughts had been fixated on pleasure to the exclusion of all other concerns. The powder she'd slipped into his wine had taken longer to work than anticipated. It meant having to endure his inept sexual skills for longer than she would have liked. However, it provided additional time for Quinn to be overheard by his wife. She'd enjoyed that bit. The man was such a creep, saying those awful things; it couldn't have been better had she written a script for him.

When she'd asked if his wife loved him his reply had been — *She loves herself, period.* Quinn couldn't have known it then but those words had given him a stay of execution. She'd been prepared to inject Quinn with a lethal concoction — the same mixture she'd pumped into Larry Lawlor — but changed her mind.

A hastily concocted plan B came into play.

Back in London when she'd bought the lethal hypodermic from Scarface and Pubes, she'd also acquired a vial of AIDS infected blood. At the time she hadn't had a specific use for it but looking at Quinn's naked body the urge to infect him with the virus became an unstoppable compulsion. It represented a more appropriate solution than the instantaneous death she'd initially planned and would have the benefit of prolonging his suffering. The stigma attached to his demise would, she hoped, inflict a degree of reflected shame on Niamh O'Flynn. He would discover the syringe as soon as he awoke. Lest he be in any doubts about its contents she'd inscribed the letters AIDS on the casing.

As the stewardess offered her a coffee, a niggling thought bothered her. Would Quinn report what happened to the police, give them her description? Not likely, she told herself. And what of Quinn's wife? Would she divulge what she'd overheard on the phone? Unlikely. O'Flynn wasn't likely to wash her dirty linen in public; not when that same public was the one she relied on for votes. No, the truth was, O'Flynn would exact whatever punishment she deemed necessary directly on her husband.

And how would the husband react? What would he do when he discovered he was carrying the AIDS virus? Would he admit as much to his wife? Doubtful. The notion that he could infect Niamh held its attraction for Helena but she didn't think that Quinn and his wife were likely to get it on after what took place in Brussels. Pity. She suspected that Quinn would claim he'd contracted the virus while he was a patient in some clinic or hospital. He was the kind that would probably sue the state for compensation.

The passenger sitting next to Helena, a middle-aged, overweight executive type, attempted to strike up a conversation. One withering look from Helena let him know she wasn't interested. She wanted to think about Susan Furlong.

She remembered how she had rejected her

mother in the last moments of her life. The awful guilt provided a constant driving force for the course of action she'd embarked upon. She'd been just one week shy of her twelfth birthday when the incident occurred, a very frightened child; the others, all adults, could have stopped what happened but they'd failed to intervene at the crucial moment. Worse, they were the very people who'd driven her mother to such a pitiful end.

She'd learned much from Grace McCormick. Harrowing stuff, all of it. In her mind she liked to re-enact the events related by the psychiatrist. It helped bring her closer to her mother. One particular episode never failed to make her flesh crawl: the day of her own conception.

Susan Furlong was raped that day. When she named the rapist, he had her certified insane. This extraordinary feat could not have been achieved without the compliance of willing participants, all of them ensnared by the lure of huge cash inducements. The rapist, a powerful businessman with influential friends in high places, bought off the foster father, the police, the doctor, the Church and anyone else in a position to stand in his way. He got away with it because the Mental Treatment Act 1945 — dealing with the subject of mental hospitals and the treatment of psychiatric illness — has no provisions for allowing a compulsorily detained person appeal against detention.

Helena had read an article on the subject of the abuses in the mental health system given to her by Grace McCormick. The article, written by Emma Boylan, was a damning indictment of the legislators who allowed this state of affairs to continue without trying to remedy the situation. Far from thinking Emma Boylan praiseworthy for highlighting the subject, Helena held her in contempt. In her opinion Emma Boylan should have moved heaven and earth to have the matter resolved. Writing an article wasn't enough. Like all the others she had failed Susan Furlong in her hour of need.

While locked up in the psychiatric hospital, Susan Furlong discovered she was pregnant. The thought of carrying the rapist's child repelled her initially but as the months dragged by she changed her mind. What else did she have to live for? Four days after the baby arrived, it was forcibly removed from her, the result of an arrangement organized by John Treanor.

In the seven years that followed, independent psychiatrists diagnosed Susan as normal. These assessments stated that she was angry, rebellious, destructive, mentally and emotionally on the edge but, importantly, they insisted she was sane. Yet with one stroke of a pen, the reports were nullified and her detention reaffirmed. The signature on the custodial orders was that of Dr Brian Whelehan. By placing Susan under his personal patronage he was able to circumvent all avenues of appeal.

Helena's thoughts were interrupted by the sound of her phone. Only three people knew her number. Even before the caller's code appeared on the mobile screen, she knew who it was. 'Hello, what news?' she asked.

'Treanor's dead,' a voice told her.

'Good,' she replied, and closed the connection.

An announcement from the stewardess requested all passengers to fasten their safety belts. The flight would be landing within minutes. Helena didn't need to be told; her ears popped, her stomach flipped, same sensation as taking off only worse. Her fellow passengers, including the overweight slug next to her, reacted to the plane's roar of deceleration by pressing back into their seats in anticipation of the moment when the wheels would hop, skip and thump along the runway.

Once on the ground, Helena began to give serious consideration to the next phase of her operation.

16

Emma Boylan's reputation as an investigative reporter cut little ice with Niamh O'Flynn. She cast Boylan as one of the hated 'trial-by-media' brigade. Suspicious by nature, O'Flynn smelt a rat. There had to be more to it than the flimsy excuse put forward over the phone for an interview: the *Post* was sourcing articles on ex-government ministers, examining how the loss of power affected them. *Bullshit!* O'Flynn hadn't believed a word of it. With all that had happened in the past forty-eight hours she would doubt the word of the Lord right now. O'Flynn's antenna for sniffing potential trouble led her to believe that Emma Boylan had some other agenda in mind.

She had good reason for harbouring such doubts. In the space of two days the secure world she thought she inhabited had been ripped asunder. Coming on the heels of the threatening letter, she'd been exposed to the phone connection that allowed her listen to her husband fornicate with a woman in Brussels. Bill had rung a few hours later, had the gall to claim mitigating circumstances. She had to give him full marks for brass-neck defence. 'It was entrapment,' he'd insisted.

'What, she held a gun to your head, that it?' she'd retorted, in no mood for reconciliation. The conversation had gone steadily downhill after that with recriminations hurled in both directions. She'd warned him not to come home. 'I'm having the locks changed,' she said, 'and I'll have a barring order issued if you so much as poke your nose within sniffing distance of the house.' She'd slammed the phone down after that.

She never wanted to see Bill Quinn again, of that she felt certain, but things were never quite so simple. Joan adored her father, no question about it; she idolized the man. If it came to a choice between staying with either of them Joan would, most likely, choose her father. But Niamh still hadn't decided whether or not to tell Joan about her father's carnal escapade in Brussels.

As matters stood Bill could march back into the house if he had a mind to and there wasn't a whole lot she could do about it. He would know that she couldn't obtain a barring order without giving the authorities a reason. And right now she was weighing up the options. How would it play in the press? What would her electorate think? How would Joan react? What kind of a story would Bill concoct?

And, as if that weren't enough, Dr Brian Whelehan had crawled out of the woodwork. He'd phoned her half an hour before Emma Boylan's call. Back when her party was in government Whelehan held the Arts and Culture portfolio. They were colleagues in government, but they'd crossed swords on just about every piece of legislation being enacted. Whelehan was a bright scholarly man but he was not averse to using dirty tricks to get his way, a factor she'd learned to her cost. It never bothered him who he walked over on his way up the political ladder. During Niamh's tenure as Justice Minister he had forced her to compromise on a particular aspect of parliamentary business. The compromise had backfired badly, costing her a seat in the subsequent election. Whelehan had come out of the affair smelling of roses and had been promoted to party leader.

And now, having avoided each other for the best part of a decade, he had called her. He'd sounded worried. 'I think we ought to meet,' he'd said without preamble, 'something's come up that could mean serious bother for us.'

'Could you be more specific?' she asked acidly.

'Goes back to the time we were in government.'

'That's a period I'd prefer to forget.'

'We're both in danger from actions we took back then.'

'Bit late in the day to be bothered by scruples now, wouldn't you say?'

'Niamh, will you for God's sake let me talk.'

'OK, spit it out.'

'It's a delicate situation. Can't say over the phone but . . . but let me ask you a question.'

'If you must,' Niamh said, snorting with derision.

'Have you received any threats recently?'

Niamh swallowed her breath. 'Threats? What . . . ?'

'I think you know what I'm talking about. It would be of mutual benefit to meet, believe me. You see, I know who's behind this whole thing.'

'I'm sorry, Brian, but I haven't the foggiest notion what you're on about. Now if there's nothing else I'd like to get on with my work.'

'Fine Niamh, if that's the way you want to play it. You always were a stubborn mule . . . nothing new there. But if you change your mind you know how to contact me.' Whelehan hung up.

Niamh wondered if she'd been right to play hardball. She didn't trust Whelehan. He'd seriously damaged her career once before; she wasn't about to let that happen again. And yet, another part of her wanted to admit to him that she had, in fact, been threatened. If she'd played it differently she might have found out who or what lay behind the threats.

Her thoughts returned to Emma Boylan, the journalist she'd agreed to meet in the Lansdowne Palace Hotel. In her present frame of mind she was in no mood to be manipulated into talking about some phoney subject by a journalist with a different agenda on her mind. *I don't take prisoners,* she told herself, *never have and don't intend to start now.*

* * *

Like a rabbit caught in the beams of an oncoming car, Dr Brian Whelehan sat in front of his computer, staring at the screen. It was mid-afternoon, the same time that he locked himself in his library most days. This was his place of refuge, the place where he indulged the wildest fantasies of his over-fertile brain. In the third year of his retirement, living alone in his bachelor pad in the posh Ballsbridge area of the city, his commitment to aesthetic indulgence had of late become obsessive. He protected the seclusion offered by the four walls of the real estate with zeal and vigour.

The titles on the shelves reflected the predictable academic studies in psychiatry. Yet, tidily shelved behind a glass-doored section, books of a different kind were housed. For years these volumes had represented the touchstone for his auto-erotic adventures but more recently the wonders of modern technology, in the shape of the internet, had all but replaced the printed page. He had, however, some misgivings in regard to the new technology; going on-line was, in his opinion, a form of Russian roulette; any one hit could prove fatal.

On top of that, law-enforcement forces around the globe were pursuing Operation Amethyst, a major investigation into internet child pornography. Recent raids had netted judges, solicitors, bankers, teachers, celebrities and dozens of so-called pillars of society. Whelehan had no sympathy for those who'd been caught. They were perverts as far as he was concerned. The material he liked to watch was, to his mind, of a different order entirely. His was the high art of erotica, to be appreciated by like-minded connoisseurs. In accord with Wilde, one of his literary heroes, he believed that good writing, like good art in all its forms, produces a sense of beauty whereas bad writing, like bad art, produces a sense of disgust. That he could possibly get caught up in Operation Amethyst, an investigation operated by illiterate bully-boys looking into the sordid goings-on of uncouth philistines, was a source of great annoyance to him. It was this lack of protection that exercised his temper now.

Over the past few days a number of e-mails warning him that his days were numbered had come down the line. The first e-mail simply said —

YOUR PAST IS NOW YOUR PRESENT.
SEE ATTACHMENT.

What he saw was a legal document with his signature at the bottom. It was a Form of Committal Order for The Mother of Perpetual Succour Private Psychiatric Hospital. He didn't have to think twice about the identity of the patient in question because he knew all about Susan Furlong. Her name alone was enough to conjure up one of the darkest periods of his life.

At the time, he'd been under immense pressure from his government colleagues, a pressure spearheaded by Niamh O'Flynn. Word of his complicity in the unlawful detention of Susan Furlong had reached the party leader. In a newspaper article a cub reporter named Emma Boylan had hinted at his involvement. Calls for his resignation had come thick and fast. The pressure had been intolerable so he'd sought refuge in the security of his library. There, he indulged in a spot of self-gratification, the one proclivity that never failed to enliven his spirits. Not a ladies' man or a fancier of his own gender, the concept of physical sex with another person was abhorrent to him. So, to satisfy his over-active libido he had devised his own particular methods for sexual release.

It wasn't that he didn't attract admirers; this kink in his personality did nothing to impede the attraction others saw in him. He had a captivating smile that worked wonders when canvassing votes. Women and men, equally, fell for his superficial geniality. The slightly bumbling, fawning image he pro-jected contrasted sharply with the bright scholarly intellect he possessed. His tweed jackets, cardigans and bow ties fitted in with a kind of persona one associates with a country doctor, yet he had forsaken his psychiatric practice in favour of politics.

His perverted little secret would have remained underground had he not pushed his auto-erotic pleasure threshold a step too far. He liked to use a neck compression to disrupt the arterial blood supply so that less oxygen got to the brain. By doing so he heightened the sensation and enhanced the act of sexual solitaire but on this occasion he'd miscalculated. He suffered a brain haemorrhage in the process. When he failed to turn up for an important parliamentary meeting two policemen were dispatched to his house. Getting no response, they forced an entry and discovered him barely alive and in a most compromising position.

Niamh O'Flynn and her colleagues were appraised of the shameful deed and its consequences but, because a general election was imminent, the incident had been hushed up. Perversely, the party spin-doctors used his enforced hospitalization to proclaim his virtuous nature, claiming that the haemorrhage had been brought about by the tireless effort he'd undertaken on behalf of his constituents. His approval ratings shot to an all-time high.

All would have been well except for a small matter of blackmail. Detective Larry Lawlor, one of the officers who discovered his body entangled in an auto-erotic contraption, decided to capture the squalid scene on video.

All that had happened ten years earlier.

It wasn't until Lawlor's recent death that the ever-increasing extortion being paid to the ex-cop ceased. But just when he thought the time had come to celebrate his deliverance, the current cloud appeared on the horizon. E-mails reminding him of his role in Susan Furlong's unlawful detention made their appearance on his monitor.

Before contacting Niamh O'Flynn, he had used his secret password and user-name to log on to one of his chat-room sites. Of the three erotica chat rooms he participated in, the 'Velvet Box' was the one that brought him most pleasure, its erotic content, what most people would call hard-core, strong enough to have sickened Caligula and his Roman cohorts were it available back then. On this occasion, however, it was immediately obvious to Whelehan that an uninvited user had somehow managed to hack into the site. Two words filled the screen.

DEATH ROW

Not knowing what to expect he clicked the mouse. Three rows of small black and white portraits appeared on screen, nine pictures in all. One of the head-and-shoulders shots was that of himself. It was a recent snapshot but one he hadn't seen before. It appeared to have been taken outside his house. He felt a chill in the pit of his stomach. How had someone photographed him without his knowledge? More importantly, why? He glanced at the other eight portraits. He knew most of the faces staring out at him. They were: Caroline Andrews, Jim Andrews, Niamh O'Flynn, Bishop John Treanor, Grace McCormick (aka Sr Dympna), Emma Boylan, Vinny Bailey and Detective Larry Lawlor. Four of the pictures, those of Caroline and Jim Andrews, Bishop John Treanor and Larry Lawlor had large red Xs imposed on their faces.

He clicked his own image to enlarge the picture and display the caption beneath it:

Dr Brian Whelehan, former government minister and chairman of The Mother of Perpetual Succour Private Psychiatric Hospital. Responsible for unlawfully detaining Susan Furlong in that institution and guilty of bringing about her untimely death. For these crimes, the sentence is DEATH.

He read the caption a second time not wanting to believe the implication. '*Sweet Jesus*', he hissed through his teeth, reading the caption yet again. Nervously, he reverted to the nine smaller pictures. He brought up the enlarged photograph of Larry Lawlor. The caption beneath it read:

Detective Inspector Larry Lawlor, directly responsible for bringing about the death of Susan Furlong. EXECUTED!

In a state of shock he looked at the remaining images. The four with Xs had captions that ended with the word *EXECUTED*. By now the images on the monitor seemed to shimmer like a hot summer haze but as far as he could ascertain the remaining names, like his own, contained the words — *the sentence is DEATH.*

17

Set back from the hustle and bustle of Ballsbridge, The Lansdowne Palace represented the kind of establishment people still referred to as 'a relic of old decency'. Synonymous with quality and style for decades before the plethora of new 'super-luxury' hotels sprang up in the neighbourhood, the Palace espoused the old values, and not a little snobbery to boot. Amid this opulence, Mary-Jo Graham sipped tea from a china cup that had been served by a waiter who looked as though he'd arrived, fully formed, from the pages of a P.G. Wodehouse novel.

Before ordering, Mary-Jo had taken time to find a position that suited her purpose in the hotel's lobby-cum-tea rooms. A low partition wall concealed her presence from the central seating area. Trays of foliage sat atop the truncated wall, providing camouflage between her and the people sitting on the other side.

On the wall opposite to where she sat, an ornate, gold-framed mirror allowed her to observe the people sitting in the chairs behind her without those people being able to see her. She could also see her own reflection in the mirror, an image she felt blended with the rarefied surroundings. With laptop opened, she looked the perfect high-flying executive.

But her role today was that of cub reporter. She was here to do a job, a job that entailed listening to the on-going conversation between two women on the other side of the partition. Unobtrusively, she used her mini digital camera, little bigger than a cigarette pack, to capture a pictorial record of events.

★ ★ ★

'Drop the silly banter and get down to brass tacks,' Niamh O'Flynn demanded, flashing Emma a chilling smile. Emma flinched inwardly. Sitting in the hotel's front lobby, sipping coffee, she could see that O'Flynn was hell-bent on confrontation.

'As I explained over the phone,' Emma began defensively, 'I'd like to discuss your current day-to-day activities as opposed to the role you played when you were — '

'Hold it right there,' O'Flynn cut in sharply. 'I *know* what you said earlier. That's why I asked you to cut the crap. Now please, Ms Boylan, don't insult my intelligence. Tell me what this is about right now or I walk.'

'I'm sorry.' Emma said, sounding as though

she meant it. 'I should have been frank with you from the start.'

'Yes, you should have,' O'Flynn snapped, sitting back in her seat, triumph in her eyes. 'So, Ms Boylan, what is it you wish to talk about?'

'The death of Susan Furlong . . . her suicide.'

The expression on O'Flynn's face changed to one of bafflement. 'What's this? Susan Furlong? You're serious? You've dragged me here to talk about an incident that took place, what, eight, nine, no, ten years ago?'

'Yes,' Emma replied.

'Christ Almighty, life's too short for this! I can't see any point in — '

'If you'll just let me explain. I think there could be ramifications from that episode, ramifications that could affect all of us who were involved.'

'Doesn't affect me. I had nothing to do with — '

'You were Minister for Justice at the time.'

'So what . . . ?'

'You knew Susan Furlong was detained unlawfully. Got saturation coverage in the media at the time.'

'Indeed it did, and if memory serves, you, Ms Boylan, were at the head of the posse, like rabid dogs, all of you, baying for blood.'

165

'That's hardly fair,' Emma replied, determined to hold her cool. 'A great injustice was being perpetrated; it was my job to report the facts.'

'Yes, I remember, you led a one-woman campaign. Balanced reporting flew out the window: you just went ahead with reckless abandonment and pointed the finger at those *you* considered guilty.'

'Well, if you read my articles, you couldn't have failed to notice that one of your fellow ministers was accused of issuing the committal order?'

The ex-minister no longer looked so sure of herself. 'You can hardly expect me . . . expect me to remember the details of cases that far back,' she said, her usual practised, well-modulated voice now hesitant, 'but yes, you're right, proper procedures were disregarded by one of my fellow parliamentarians. That said, I have a clear conscience on the matter.'

'Your department could have put a stop to the injustice.'

'I only found out about this Furlong person after she'd escaped from the mental hospital. Too bloody late to do anything by then.'

'True, but when she escaped, she demanded a full inquiry into her illegal detention. You refused to accede to her request.'

'Had no choice. She'd broken the law by then. I was confronted by a mentally unbalanced woman, a murder suspect no less.'

'You could've given her a hearing. She offered to turn herself in. Her only demand was that she be given a full judicial inquiry.'

'As I recall, she had quite a *few* demands, one of them being that her child be returned. We couldn't accede to that because the woman was in no state to look after an eleven-year old kid.'

'Yes, I can see that, but she should have got the inquiry. The trouble was, your party feared the fall-out that would result from such exposure.'

Niamh O'Flynn nodded thoughtfully.

A young waitress approached their table and asked if they would like some fresh coffee or scones. O'Flynn dismissed her with the kind of hand flick one might use to get rid of a fly before replying, 'Politics was a dirty business back then Ms Boylan; pulling strokes the order of the day. Everyone was in someone else's pocket; the currency conducted in brown envelopes. The Furlong woman's case fell between the cracks. The question I ask you is this: why dig it up now?'

'Someone's threatening all those who had

anything to do with the affair.'

The ex-minister looked startled. 'You have evidence of this?'

'Evidence? Yes, I've got evidence. A number of people have already met with untimely deaths.'

O'Flynn flinched. 'Like who for instance?'

Emma listed the names of those she believed had met their deaths.

Niamh O'Flynn shook her head in dismay. 'What you're saying Ms Boylan, is fantastic, utterly fantastic. I mean, if all these people have been killed as you claim why haven't you written about it? Can't imagine you passing up an opportunity like that to grab headlines. And another thing: why haven't the police set up a manhunt? Why isn't there a hue and cry from the public? Why?'

'As it happens, there's quite a lot going on behind the scenes. I haven't written about it yet because I don't have proof. Right now the police forces in London, Malaga and this country are working together to establish a link between the deaths. In spite of what you might think of me I am a responsible journalist; I want to prevent any more people meeting a similar fate.'

'And you seriously think that's a possibility?'

'Yes, I think it could happen. I've been

threatened. My husband and both our families have been exposed to intimidatory tactics. So, you see, this is not just a headline-grabbing exercise. Right now, I'm trying to establish whether there's anyone else in a similar situation. That's why I'm talking to you.'

From the look in Niamh O'Flynn's eyes, Emma knew she'd hit a raw nerve. Connolly had told her about the threatening letter O'Flynn had received but she couldn't admit to such knowledge; to do so would cause problems for the detective. The ex-minister would have to volunteer this information of her own volition. The once powerful woman sitting opposite her looked troubled, evaluating what she'd heard. A porter, pushing a brass luggage trolley towards the lifts, acknowledged O'Flynn's presence with a smile. She returned a brisk politician's smile before looking directly into Emma's eyes.

'I would like to help you, Ms Boylan, but right now is not a good time. I appreciate that you've been candid with me but — '

'I'm sorry,' Emma said, cutting her off, 'but it's imperative that you level with me. What you tell me will be off the record. You have a daughter and a husband; has anything unusual happened to either of them?'

A pained expression flitted across O'Flynn's

face. 'Yes, I'm afraid something has happened. I've had an anonymous letter accusing me of knowingly allowing the perpetrators of injustices go unpunished. Until now, until talking to you, I hadn't connected it to the Furlong affair.'

Emma felt better now; she'd got O'Flynn to admit she'd received the letter. It allowed her to probe deeper. 'Apart from this threat has anything else happened, anything that seemed unusual, suspicious . . . out of the ordinary?'

'No, thank God, nothing has happened out of the ordinary.'

Emma sensed that O'Flynn was lying but let it pass. 'We need to find out who's behind this intimidation.'

'I might be able to help,' O'Flynn said. 'I had a telephone call earlier today from someone who appears to know the source of the threats; he wanted to know if I'd been threatened.'

'Can you give me a name?'

'I'd prefer not to say.'

'I really need that name. It's important.'

O'Flynn gave a theatrical sigh. 'I think we both know I'm referring to Dr Brian Whelehan. You mentioned his name earlier; he's the one who signed the committal papers for Susan Furlong.'

'How in God's name was he allowed to get away with it?'

O'Flynn made no attempt to answer the question, offering instead the bored smile of a person who thought the answer so obvious as to need no reply.

Emma wanted more. 'So, Whelehan's been threatened?'

'Yes. Someone's put the fear of God into the old bastard. He told me to get back to him if I changed my mind.'

'I think you should,' Emma said.

'Contacting him is out of the question.'

'Can I make a suggestion?'

'Let me guess, you want to contact him yourself.'

'Yes, that's exactly what I'd like to do.'

'Well, I can't stop you, I suppose.'

'No, you can't, that's true, but you could make life a bit easier for me.'

'Just how do I do that?'

'You let me act on your behalf. I could — '

'No!'

Undeterred, Emma continued, 'I could find out what he knows. He won't talk to me if I turn up cold. But if he knows I'm acting on your behalf . . . '

'You really are a pain in the arse.'

'Does that mean we have an understanding?'

Niamh O'Flynn allowed a small smile to surface. It seemed genuine. 'Yes, I suppose it does. Let's talk a little more about the details. And I think we could do with a fresh pot of coffee.' She glanced around her. 'Never a waiter around when you need one.'

18

Candlelight flickered in front of the statuette of the Virgin Mary, its dim glow illuminating Grace McCormick's face as she knelt by the bedside. Silently mouthing her prayers, she allowed her fingers to knead the beads of her rosary. Observance of this ritual never varied. Last thing every night before getting into bed she paid homage to God and His holy mother, the angels and saints. Her head bowed, she completed ten *Hail Marys*, added a final *Glory Be to the Father* and blessed herself.

Time to extinguish the dim flame.

It would take an hour, maybe two, before she fell asleep. Having difficulty nodding off didn't bother her; it gave her time to think about things that mattered. Recent events had taken their toll and tonight she felt particularly drained. There just didn't seem enough hours in the day anymore to do all the things that needed doing. She had promised Emma Boylan to review the notes she'd made during her sessions with Helena Andrews and today had been the first time she'd been able to make good the promise.

All the ugly images flooded back. She'd already told Emma many of the circumstances that shaped Helena's life but she had held back certain dark deeds. Laying her head heavily on the pillows, she allowed these deeds, once so hesitantly recounted by Helena, to re-emerge.

— Aged seven, Helena had just celebrated her First Holy Communion and to mark the sacrament she'd been allowed to accompany her adoptive parents on a three-week holiday to Spain. They stayed in an apartment in Fuengirola, just a short stroll from the seafront. It had been Helena's first time abroad and she was determined to enjoy herself. She loved the sunshine and spent most of her time on the beach. Walking back to the apartment one evening she felt an irritation between her legs where grains of sand had lodged. Her father noticed her faltering gait and asked what was wrong. She told him.

Inside the apartment, he offered to apply some cream to ease the irritation. Showering together, Andrews hunkered down in front of Helena and used his fingers to probe the area where the particles had lodged. At one point his finger hurt her and caused her to cry out. He ceased the action immediately, stood up and said he was sorry. He then placed his arms around her shoulders and held her to his stomach. She sensed something was wrong when she felt his private parts press against her chest. She pulled away and ran to her room. When her mother returned — she'd been shopping at the time — Helena wanted to talk about what happened but she couldn't think of a way to express the sense of unease she felt.

It would be a full two years after this incident before Jim Andrews interfered with Helena again. Caroline Andrews had gone to London for a charity reception and had left Helena with her father. It wasn't a situation that gave the 9-year-old cause for concern. Before going to bed, her father kissed her in the normal way, giving her a friendly hug and telling her to sleep tight. Helena gave the familiar response — don't let the bugs bite. She'd been asleep for some time when the sound of thunder awoke her. She hid beneath the bedclothes but she could still see the bright flashes of lightning coming through her window. She began to say her prayers, whimpering, asking God to please make the storm go away. She screamed when a particularly ear-piercing clap appeared to rock the very foundations of the house. She bolted upright, letting the sheets fall from her face. In that moment she saw her father enter the room, his shape outlined by the brilliant white flashes. Shaking with fright, she'd never been so relieved to see anyone.

He got into the bed and snuggled up beside her. With his protective arms around her, she no longer felt afraid. She had begun to drift off to sleep when a new sensation stirred her into full wakefulness. Her father's hand had moved down to the top of her stomach, his fingers sneaking beneath the elasticized band of her pyjamas. She held her breath, too dazed to move as his fingers probed between her legs. After a while his movements became more pronounced. All the time he was making guttural noises, breathing heavily, saying things like — I love you sweetheart; Daddy loves his very own little sweetheart. She could feel his hips moving against her backside, feel his hardness press against the small of her back. And then, with a loud gasp, the activity ceased. She could feel an area of dampness on her skin. Her heart thumped wildly but she couldn't move a muscle, afraid even to breathe. She was aware of her father getting out of her bed but refused to open her eyes, too scared to look at him. Half an hour later she crept slowly to the bathroom.

The following night he came to her bed again. When she told him that she didn't like what he was doing he offered to return to his room, saying he'd understand if she didn't love him. Helena felt a pang of guilt and assured him she did love him. That night he taught her different ways to pleasure him.

Some months after she'd witnessed the death of Susan Furlong, full penetrative intercourse occurred. By that stage she had developed a method of shutting her mind off from what he was doing. In the make-believe world she'd invented, her real mother hadn't killed herself; she wasn't jerking her father off, and her parents loved her. The denial actually worked for a while. Her school grades were fine and she made some friends of her own age in the neighbourhood.

Then, one evening when Helena returned from school, she discovered that her mother had gone to the country on one of her charity jaunts. She had a meal and studied her lessons before embarking on a rampage of self-loathing. She sat in front of her mother's dressing-table and plastered lipstick around her mouth, applied mascara and eye shadow and put on her mother's jewellery. She posed in the mirror, telling herself what a truly wicked person she was, when suddenly she saw her father's reflection in the glass.

He looked shocked. After a moment of silence he grabbed her by the hand and dragged her to the viewing-room. This was a room fashioned in the style of a cinema, built on to the house for screening commercials and documentaries that Andrews produced for various television companies. It had a small raked auditorium, plush seating, and a screen with curtains that pulled back. Helena was dragged to the space that separated the screen from the first row of seats.

'You look like a little whore with all that muck on your face,' her father yelled.

'*Isn't that what you want?*' she screamed back.

He slapped her across the face, almost knocking her off her feet. She refused to cry. She didn't fully understand then what a whore was but she knew it was bad. He pulled her to the floor and forcefully removed her clothes. Full penetrative sex occurred for the first time.

After that episode he continued to have full intercourse whenever the opportunity allowed. Each time it happened he made her plaster make-up on her face and called her his little painted whore.

During this period the school doctor referred Helena to the local GP. Caroline Andrews brought her to the surgery and waited in the reception area while Helena underwent an examination. When the doctor was finished, he called Caroline into his surgery and told her that her daughter showed signs of sexual activity. Caroline demanded an explanation. Helena was forced to make up a story. Her father had foreseen the possibility of disclosure and had warned her that if anyone found out, she'd be put in an institution or jail. Helena told her mother that she'd read an article on sex education and had become curious about her body. Through tears, she blurted out a story about experimenting with objects.

Shortly after this crisis she missed a period, but the thought that she might be pregnant never entered her head. Three months without a period went by before the awful truth emerged. She'd come home from school for the weekend and was feeling out of sorts. She went to bed in the afternoon and dozed off but woke up with an acute pain in her stomach. Terror consumed her when she discovered that the sheets beneath her were soaked with blood. Waves of pain shot through her stomach. She went to the bathroom and sat on the toilet, doubled up with pain, in no doubt that something peculiar was taking place in her body.

While this was happening, her mother began banging on the bathroom door. She'd heard the commotion and seen the trail of blood leading from the bedroom. When Helena saw what she'd passed, she screamed a wild piercing scream. Her mother had by now barged her way through the door. She too, screamed when she took in the scene. The expression of concern for her daughter quickly turned to one of horror when she realized that Helena had just had a miscarriage. With a howl of anguish she bundled Helena from the bathroom.

In the bedroom, Helena lay face down on the bed, her body convulsed in sobs, her fingers clenched tight enough to draw blood from where her nails cut into her palms. She could hear the toilet being flushed in the bathroom over and over again. Some time later her mother came into the room. 'Who did this to you?' she asked in a hoarse whisper.

Helena was incapable of lying any more. 'Dad,' she said. 'Dad did it.'

Caroline froze for a moment, then something seemed to snap inside her. She walloped Helena across the face. 'You liar; you filthy little lying bitch,' she said repeatedly, her voice rising in ferocity. Helena didn't want her mother to stop. At that moment she would have welcomed death.

★ ★ ★

Grace McCormick turned to her left side in the bed. The awful account that Helena had told her over a series of four or five psychiatric sessions still had the power to upset her. Pondering these events had made her feel unusually weary. In less time than was usual, sleep overtook her.

19

Emma retraced the same steps she'd first made a decade earlier, the feeling of *déja vu* inescapable. Curiosity and a desire to tie up loose ends had got the better of her. She'd decided to visit Bernadette Maxwell. The meeting would, she hoped, eliminate Maxwell from the list of suspects.

The Mother of Perpetual Succour Psychiatric Hospital building was exactly as she remembered it, a large brooding mansion surrounded by formidable granite walls and ornate wrought-iron gates. The wash of steely winter light on the building's coarse-grained walls conjured up the malevolent presence of former ghosts. It had been built, so the story went, by the Earl of Duncavan for his favourite mistress, Lady Sarah Widdenham who, by all accounts, went mad in the place and hanged herself from the balusters at the top of the staircase. Later, the building was used as a sanatorium before finally, after being abandoned for several decades, been taken over by the Sisters of Perpetual Succour.

The medical director's office remained

much as Emma remembered it. Only the paintings had changed; the stately portraits of bishops and mother superiors had been replaced by a series of insipid abstract works. That apart, the place looked familiar. The medical director, a thin, dapper man in his forties, received her with courtesy, a cup of coffee and a chocolate digestive biscuit. Speaking in low modulated tones, he informed her that Maxwell — or Joan of Arc, as he called her — was no longer a resident.

'Oh,' Emma said, taken by surprise, 'she's not . . . dead, is she?'

'No, no, indeed not, she's still alive; her general health is quite stable, her mind, however, remains greatly impaired.'

'But you said she's no longer here?'

'That's right. Her friends — the ones paying for her upkeep — decided to take her into their care.'

'When did this happen?

'A few months ago.'

'Why? Could they no longer afford to pay?'

A half-hearted smile crossed the medical director's face. 'No, Ms Boylan,' he said snidely, 'finance is not a problem for her friends.' He paused, looked at her to see if she'd picked up on the innuendo. Emma knew exactly what he was getting at. She was aware that Bernadette Maxwell had been a leading figure within the Irish Republican paramilitaries. Because of her services to that organization the godfathers at the top saw to it that she lacked for nothing.

'Bernadette, or Joan of Arc as she insists on being called these days, is now in her early sixties,' the medical director said, 'and when we were informed that she was to leave our care, we had no objections. In truth, there wasn't a whole lot more we could do for her.'

'Can you tell me where she is now?'

''Fraid not.'

'Look, it would really help matters if you — '

'No, no, you misunderstand me. I'm not refusing to tell you; I simply don't know. Her minders refused to give any information in that regard.'

'You saw who collected her?'

'I did, as a matter of fact. I talked to two men who came for her; heavies they were, straight from central casting, only things missing were the shades and berets. Their conversation with her was conducted entirely in Gaelic. Couldn't understand a blessed word. I did attempt to elicit some information in regard to their plans but they remained tight-lipped.'

Emma stood up to leave. 'Just tell me one thing before I go: is Joan of Arc capable of rational thought — I mean mentally, is she competent to engage in normal everyday relationships with those around her?'

'No, she is not. Most of the time she is barely lucid and when she does talk, her mutterings make no sense at all.'

'So, in your opinion, she's no longer a threat to anyone?'

'I'd say that's a fair assumption.'

20

Emma fanned her fingers in front of her mouth to stifle a yawn and switched on the small television set in the kitchen. It was 7.30 a.m. A glass of orange juice in one hand, she sat at the table and watched the screen flicker into life. It was one of those old models that seemed to take forever to warm up. Mary-Jo Graham, the journalist who shared her work station for the past few weeks had written a novel and had wangled a slot on 'TV AM' to plug it. The fact that she'd written a book came as a surprise to Emma. Bob Crosby hadn't said anything about the fledgling journalist being an aspiring author, nor indeed had Mary-Jo herself made any mention of the fact. At least, not until yesterday.

They'd been lunching in the *Post* canteen when Emma happened to remark on the world-wide success of Irish female authors. The comment had prompted Mary-Jo to bring up the subject of her own entry into the world of publishing. Her public relations people, she'd informed Emma, had secured a spot on morning television. And now, large as life, her face filled the screen. At 22 she gave the appearance of being totally at ease in front of the cameras; she looked comfortable, sophisticated, bright and sexy, all at the same time. A Ferrari-red silk blouse, partially unbuttoned at the top as though by accident, ensured that the swell of her breasts and cleavage impacted on the screen. Her black skirt rode provocatively up her thighs, encouraged by legs that were casually crossed at the knees. The camera loved Mary-Jo and Mary-Jo loved the camera. She spoke earnestly to the interviewer about her book insisting, rather snobbishly Emma thought, that she was not part of the 'chick-lit' crop of writers. Throughout the exchange Mary-Jo's full wattage smile beamed with maximum intensity.

The interview was coming to its conclusion when Vinny arrived with two mugs of steaming coffee. It was Vinny, not Mary-Jo Graham, who'd been responsible for Emma's early start. Vinny had set the early alarm because he'd made an appointment to view some paintings in Cobh, Co. Cork at noon that day.

'I'd best be on my way,' he said, putting his coffee aside. 'I just pray to God this is not a wild-goose chase.'

'Why go then?'

'It could be on the level and I'd hate to miss out on a chance to get hold of two Nano Reid paintings.'

'Never heard of her . . . or is it a him?'

'Not a him, Nano is, sorry was, a *her*; she died back in the '80s. In her day she was described as a poetic visionary. I happen to agree.'

'What makes you think it might not be kosher?'

'The two works don't appear on any catalogue I've ever seen.'

'Wouldn't some of your fellow traders know whether the vendor was genuine or not? Why not ask around?'

'If I did that, I'd be tipping them off to my discovery. The price would shoot through the roof. No thanks, I'll take my chances.' Vinny kissed her and headed for the door.

'What time do you expect to get back this evening?'

'Haven't a clue,' he said with a shoulder shrug, 'but I'll phone in the afternoon, let you know if I managed to get up close and personal to Nano Reid.'

'Oh, so now it's necrophilia, is it?' Emma said, playfully pinching his backside. 'But listen . . . Vinny, I know I sound like an old woman but, well, I want you to be careful, OK?'

'Ah, come on, Emma, give me a break; you don't seriously believe that Helena Andrews is out there waiting to pounce?'

'No, but people have died. We have to take it seriously.'

'Yes, but I don't buy all that weird shit from Grace McCormick about Helena Andrews being involved in her parents' deaths.'

'That's because you remember Helena as a frightened child. Well, she's a young woman now and, by all accounts, a pretty mixed up one. She's been inside at least two psychiatric homes . . . and she's had electro-convulsive therapy.'

'Yeah, I remember Grace mentioning that . . . I thought all that sort of thing finished when Jack Nicholson flew over the cuckoo's nest.'

'So did I, but Grace says ECT is still around. It's sanitized nowadays and the patient feels no pain. It's only used in rare cases . . . like suicidal depression and the like. If we're to believe Grace, it can work in instances where more conventional treatments fail.'

'Yeah, I'll bet,' Vinny said, 'bit like thumping a television set with your fist to get a clear picture.'

'I doubt any psychiatrist would use that

particular analogy. But look, the thing is, we've no way of knowing what state her mind is in so, yes, I do believe she could pose a threat. All I'm saying is, be careful, Vinny.'

'Advice duly noted. Call you later, OK?' Vinny tugged his forelock in mock salute. 'I promise to be careful.'

'Yeah, right. Hope you get the paintings.'

'So do I.'

★ ★ ★

Vinny had only been gone five minutes when the telephone rang. Emma, thinking he'd called her to say he'd forgotten something, answered with a warm hello.

'Do you always sound so chirpy this hour of the day?' the voice asked.

She recognized Connolly. 'Hello, Jim. Where are you? I thought you'd gone abroad. Aren't you supposed to be in England or Spain? Don't tell me you're back already?'

'Just come from the airport. Trip took less time than I thought.'

'Useful, was it?'

'Got damn all in Spain, but London was worthwhile. Thought we might put our heads together if you're free at any stage today?'

'I'm free right now as it happens. Vinny had to leave early so I'm all on my ownsome. Why

190

not pop over to my place. Bet you wouldn't say no to a spot of breakfast.'

'Breakfast? What's that?' Connolly said with a laugh. 'I seem to recall something of that nature in the dim and distant past.'

'You're wasting your time looking for sympathy from me. You coming over or not?'

'See you in ten.'

'Good, I'll put the kettle on.'

21

True to his word, Detective Inspector Connolly planted his policeman's feet — shod in burnished leather Hugo Boss size nines — beneath Emma's kitchen table ten minutes after his phone call. He seemed totally at ease.

'Winter sunshine,' he proclaimed, indicating the light streaming into the room, 'is like a false lover.'

'How'd you make that out?' Emma asked, raising an eyebrow.

'It provides the illusion of warmth without actually delivering.'

'Wow! That's deep for this time of morning,' Emma said with a wry smile.

A waft of toast and strong coffee danced a hazy effervescent ballet in the steely-bright beams of lights. Emma's welcoming smile appeared to infuse Connolly with a new and enlivened enthusiasm for life. In marked contrast to his recent appearance in The Turks Head, he'd reverted to his more perfectly groomed persona: gleaming white shirt, suit pressed, cleanly shaved and not a hair out of place. Even his eyes seemed to have regained their enigmatic sparkle. Emma enjoyed watching him devour the light breakfast. Spreading marmalade on his toast with a refined co-ordination of movement, he'd never before appeared quite so alluring to her.

The detective was on his third coffee top-up when Emma realized that she'd been staring at him with a kind of giddy wonderment. The feeling of intimacy she'd experienced during their meeting in the pub began to reassert itself. Aware that this represented forbidden territory, she eased the conversation away from inconsequential chatter.

'Went to see Joan of Arc yesterday,' she said.

Connolly grimaced, reluctant to switch to serious matters. 'And there was me thinking that Joan of Arc had been burnt at the stake all those years ago.'

'You know exactly who I'm talking about — '

'Yeah, our very own mad revolutionary, Bernadette Maxwell. I already told you she's no danger to anyone while she's locked up.'

'Except, she's not locked up.'

'What?'

'She's no longer there. Her republican friends have taken charge of her.'

'How'd you know that?'

'Had a chat with the current medical director.'

'You *have* been busy. What'd he have to say?'

'Said she's harmless. She's old, infirm and suffers from acute brain damage. No need to worry about her.'

'My thoughts exactly. I'm just surprised that the old brigade still bother with her. I think I'll have a word with my colleagues in Subversive, see if they can throw some light on who's behind the move.'

'Maybe our hooded friends have developed a conscience?'

'I wouldn't bet on it, Emma.'

'Yeah, right. So, tell me, how were things in England and Spain?'

'London was interesting,' he said, straightening his posture. 'The CID boys let me view some CCTV footage. Most of it was excruciatingly boring but worthwhile nevertheless.'

'In what way?'

'The tapes recorded in the venues frequented by Lawlor all contain pictures of the same young woman. The officer in charge, Detective Sergeant Herbert, first noticed her face on the VT taken at the 4PLAY club ... the venue where Lawlor met his comeuppance. The woman — she looked about twenty-two or -three to me — can be seen to move towards the area where Lawlor's body was found. Unfortunately, the CCTV's coverage arc didn't include the door that led to the crime scene, which means we can't tell if she was present when the lethal cocktail was administered. But when Herbert re-examined the footage from the other locations the same face appeared in two of them.'

'Does he know who she is?'

'No, not yet. She used different names in each venue, wore different wigs, spoke with different accents.'

'How can the police tell that?'

'Herbert interviewed the people seen talking to her on tape. A man named Blackburn was with her in the 4PLAY club. Turns out he's some sort of high-flying computer nerd. Apparently, he was really smitten by our female friend, had visions of moving her into his pad. But on the night Lawlor was killed, she disappeared. The way Blackburn describes it — *one minute she was there, all charm and chat, and then, in an instant, she was gone.*'

'Presumably he told them her name?'

'Yes, Holly Appleby. We can be pretty certain that's not her real name. I mean, come on, *holly* and *apples*? I don't think so.'

'The initials, H. A. are the same as — '

' — Helena Andrews. Yeah, I spotted that. Bit of a coincidence all right.'

'Did you get a copy of the VT?'

'No, but I got some black and white stills. All I need to do is show them to someone who knew Helena.'

'Shouldn't be too difficult. You could talk to the students from Trinity who shared her flat. Better still, let me have prints; I'll e-mail them to Grace McCormick; she's seen her more recently than the rest of us.'

'Good idea, Emma, I'll have dupes made.'

'So, did you find anything interesting in Spain?'

'Not a lot I'm afraid. Dealing with the Spanish *Comisaria* is a whole different ball game. The language barrier doesn't help.'

'No CCTV footage then?'

'No such luck, but the Spanish police have interviewed a few witnesses who claimed to have seen persons acting suspiciously around the time of the Andrews's deaths.'

'These suspicious persons, were they male of female?'

'According to the *inspector jefe* in charge, a man and a woman were spotted tailing the Andrews on the night in question. But from the descriptions the Spanish gave me, the woman sounds middle-aged.'

196

'So, it wasn't Helena Andrews, or the person called Holly Appleby?'

'Apparently not. I've sent the pictures of the woman caught on the London video to the *Comisaria*. They've agreed to show them to their witnesses. Should hear from them in a few days but I'm not holding my breath.'

'I see, not a lot of joy there.'

''Fraid not. And now, Emma, tell me, did you talk to Niamh O'Flynn.'

'Sure did.'

'You were discreet I hope . . . didn't let her know I'd been talking — '

'I was the soul of discretion,' Emma assured him with a smile before outlining how her interview had gone. At the mention of Dr Brian Whelehan's name Connolly's eyebrows arched in surprise. 'So, the old reprobate's been threatened. How very delicious.'

'You don't like Whelehan very much?'

'Damn right, I don't; I don't like him one little bit. He's the kind of politician who gives his profession a bad name. He's meant to be retired but he still retains contacts with his dodgy friends. Nothing happens in this city that he doesn't know about. He remains a master tactician in the trade of half-truths, lies, gossip, innuendo, intrigue and smear tactics. Nice to know that for once he's on the receiving end of something unpleasant. Problem is, there's not a lot I can do about him unless he makes an official complaint.'

'You've got two chances of that happening,' Emma said.

'Exactly! Whelehan will keep it under-ground, get friends in high places to make enquiries, pull strings here and there, that's his way.'

'I was thinking of calling on him. After appealing to O'Flynn's better nature, she gave me permission to act as her go-between.'

'I'd be very careful, Emma. Whelehan's bad news.'

'Yeah, tell me about it, I'm aware of his capabilities. All the same I think I'll call on him. I'm a big girl, I can look out for myself. What have I got to lose?'

'Your job, maybe. Whelehan is a confidant of the proprietor of your newspaper. Rub Whelehan the wrong way and you'll soon find yourself looking for new employment.'

'Huh, I've written about him before and I've still got my job. Like I say, I can look after myself.'

Connolly smiled. 'Never doubted it for a minute.'

'In the meanwhile, get me the pictures,' Emma said, getting up from the table.

'Here, let me help you clear up,' Connolly

said, awkwardly removing utensils to the draining board. 'If you come down to Pearse Street this morning, I'll get you a set of prints.'

'You mean like, right away? I'd sort of planned to visit Whelehan, but I suppose he can wait. Maybe you could squeeze me in around ten o'clock?'

'Yes, sure, no problem at all. Here, let me help you wash up.'

'You always this domesticated?' Emma asked, immediately regretting the question, knowing she'd strayed into dangerous territory.

'With Iseult, I didn't have much choice. But here, here with you, well . . . different story. These past few weeks I don't know what I'd have done without your friendship. The whole world appears to be going to hell in a hod, coming apart at the seams, as they say, but you . . . you represent a sort of *constant*. Like here and now, this morning, Emma, the two of us sharing breakfast together, it's so good to talk . . . the way friends should . . . well, I want you to know I appreciate it.'

Emma trembled when Connolly took hold of her two hands, pulled her close to him and kissed her gently on the forehead. Contrary to every instinct in her body, she pulled away, feeling flushed, desperately trying to regain a measure of equilibrium.

'Thanks, Jim,' she said, avoiding his eyes, 'you're a good man and it's great that we have each other to . . . to lean on. I'll never forget the kindness you showed me after I'd lost the baby. You were my rock then, that's something I'll always be grateful to you for.'

Connolly's face showed disappointment. Emma read the message — *It's not your gratitude I need*. She desperately wanted to respond, let him know how much he meant to her, but hesitated. Connolly was emotionally vulnerable right now and she didn't want him misinterpreting signals. She watched as he turned away from her and headed for the door.

'See you at the station,' he said, striving to infuse a measure of authority back to his voice, embarrassed to have let his defences slip and to have exposed the need for love, affection and companionship.

Emma sighed, a sigh as much for herself as for the departing detective inspector.

22

One minute Dr Brian Whelehan was alone in his sanctum, surrounded by his beloved books, sitting in front of his computer console; next minute he was pivoting around on his swivel chair, staring into the barrel of a handgun. 'What the hell — ?' he shouted, jumping to his feet, a mixture of outrage and incredulity distorting his features. His brain laboured to find a rationale. Had he not locked the door? Yes, he always locked the library door. So, how was it that he now faced an intruder, an intruder with a gun?

'Stay where you are,' a male voice ordered. 'Sit back down, Doc. You and I need to talk. So, sit — '

'Who the blazes — ?' Whelehan began, his voice several octaves higher than its normal bass tones, his face flushed with the crimson glow that high blood pressure brings. 'Who are you? How ... how'd you get in? I locked — ?'

'Sit,' the man snapped, his instruction more appropriate to a disobedient dog than an ex-government minister. '*First*, you do as I tell you; *second*, we talk.' Using the gun barrel as a pointer he indicated the chair to Whelehan. 'Do it,' he ordered.

'I'm not doing anything,' Whelehan replied with gruff insistence, his voice regaining some of its authority. 'This is my house. I want — '

A shot rang out. A bullet exploded into Whelehan's left kneecap. The deafening din reverberated off the library's four book-lined walls. Whelehan was propelled backwards, sent sprawling along the floor, his mouth distorted in a scream. The man with the gun made a clicking sound with his tongue. 'Oh, dear me, Doc, look what you've made me do; you didn't pay attention when I asked you to. When a gun is pointed at you it's always advisable to do as you're bid.'

Whelehan squinted, trying to get the man into focus, a mixture of terror and pleading in his eyes, the pain in his shattered knee excruciating. Blood streamed down his shin, soaking his trouser leg and shoe, dripping on to the carpet. He tried to size up the gunman, figure out who the intruder was and why that person had just destroyed his knee. The eyes looking back at him, deep set beneath glowering brows, peered out from a hand-some face that showed a few days' growth of designer stubble. The man, in his late-twenties was tall, thin and wore denims and a flannel shirt beneath a stylish black leather jacket. Whelehan forced himself to speak though the pain, his eyes jumping erratically from the man's face to the gun, then back to the face again.

'Who are you?' he asked in a faltering voice.

The gunman smiled, his teeth glowing like some movie star or pop idol. 'Who I am doesn't matter all that much,' he said, 'but my friends call me Prof — that's short for Professor. I will call you Doc, if I may, and you are at liberty to call me Prof.'

'What are you doing here?'

'Always wanted to visit Dublin, see if the place has moved on since its depiction by old clever clogs Joyce in *Ulysses*. Also, I was intrigued by Louis MacNeice's poetic take on your city. You know that one, yes? It goes something like . . .

She is not an Irish town
And she is not English . . .
Fort of the Dane,
Garrison of the Saxon,
Augustan capital
Of a Gaelic nation.

Eloquent, eh? Who could resist such a description? I took it as an invocation. So here I am.'

Whelehan's expression grew more perplexed. 'I meant, why are you *here*, here in my house?'

'Ah, yes, of course. Simple explanation, I'm here because it's where you live, that is to say, my business is here . . . with you.'

'With me? What business would that be? What can I do for you?'

'Not a lot as it happens.'

'So, what's this about then? How'd you get *in* here?'

'Been watching you for some time, my learned friend. You're a man of routine. Not good, that. Makes for predictability. Makes my job easy. I took the liberty of borrowing keys from your housekeeper, without her knowledge of course. Had duplicates cut, let myself in and out of the place several times in the past few weeks. Got the measure of the place, checked the security system, browsed your Internet, looked at the books in your library. Hell of a collection if I may say so. I like to read . . . read a lot, I do. Partly why I got the name Prof. As for your books . . . hmmm, not to my taste, I'm afraid, but no matter, different strokes and all that. You've been a naughty, naughty boy.'

Whelehan tried to move his body towards the fallen chair and screamed out in pain.

'Get me a doctor for Christ's sake, you've broken my leg . . . shattered bones. I'm bleeding badly,' he said, exhausted by his effort to move.

' "Physician heal thyself",' the man calling himself Prof retorted.

'Please, look, I need — '

'You need to hold your tongue and be quiet, Doc, understand? Can't do anything until my paymaster gets here.'

'Your paymaster? What're you talking about?'

'All will be revealed in good time, Doc.'

'Who the blazes are you? You call yourself Professor but what are you: some kind of hired assassin?'

'Very good, Doc, how very perceptive. That's a fair job description.'

Whelehan's eyes looked like they were going to pop out of his head. 'You kill people, that's what you're saying?'

'Correct, provided the price is right.'

'You're not . . . not going to . . . '

' — Kill you? The answer in all probability is affirmative. To be frank, I can't think why anyone would want to waste a bullet on you. We shall just have to bide our time and see what the boss decrees.'

'But why? What am I supposed to have

done? What possible reason would you have for killing me?'

'It's a question of finance, Doc. You know what they say — if the labourer is worthy of his hire, etc etc.'

'Money? This is about money?'

'Don't knock it. Oldest reason in the world, you should know that. You've read the classics, right? Always people willing to kill for money. Why did Raskolnikov kill the old woman in *Crime and Punishment*? Why, for money, of course.'

Whelehan stared at the gunman with incomprehension. What the hell was happening here? He was on the verge of passing out and the gunman was talking about characters from Dostoyevsky. Didn't get more surreal than that.

'Who is this paymaster you're waiting for?' Whelehan asked, the muscles of his damaged leg now going into spasm, beating a tattoo on the blood-soaked carpet.

'Patience is a virtue, my friend. You'll find out soon enough.'

'Please, *Professor*, tell me — '

'Good, we're on first-name terms, but there's no need to be so formal; call me Prof. Tell you what, Doc?'

'Tell me . . . who . . . who are we waiting for?'

'No, you'll just have to hold on a little longer. You and me, my dear fellow, are mere players in this little drama. We're like Estragon and Vladimir.'

'What?'

'You know. The characters from Beckett's — '

'I know who they are. What the blazes have they got to do with this?'

'Like us they are *waiting*. According to your fellow countryman Mr Beckett, we spend our lives — *from womb to the tomb* — just waiting. Would you go along with his assertion?'

'You're mad, stark raving mad.'

'How very observant of you. You are absolutely right: I am mad. At least that's what the learned doctors concluded after they'd examined me. Being diagnosed as a paranoid schizophrenic has kept me out of prison so I have no difficulty with the description. It allows me — '

The sound of a doorbell stopped him 'Ah, this could be the paymaster now,' he said to Whelehan. 'I'd better look at your monitor, check it out.' Prof moved to the computer and worked the keyboard with the fingertips of one hand, the gun firmly held in the other. The screen flickered to a black and white view of Whelehan's front door. A woman stood outside the door and looked up to where the camera was fixed.

'Who is she?' Prof asked.

Whelehan squinted at the picture, shaking his head to clear the sweat blurring his vision. 'That's . . . that's Emma Boylan,' he replied.

'Who's she when she's at home?'

'She's a reporter . . . a journalist, works with the *Post*.'

'Why is she calling here?'

'I've no idea, could be anything.'

'I see. Well, in that case we'll just let her ring the bell until she decides you're not home, Doc.'

★ ★ ★

Emma looked at the camera above the door and grimaced. She'd been standing outside Dr Brian Whelehan's door for almost three minutes. It was cold, not exactly freezing, but near as damn it. Breathing in the sharp air, she glanced at the surrounding houses, all of them reflecting brightly in the steely November light. *Answer the bloody door*, she said to herself, hunching her shoulders and moving her feet to encourage circulation. A copy of *The Times*, the *Independent* and the *Post* lay on top of a tray that contained two cartons of milk. The presence of papers and milk led her to believe Whelehan was at home. If he'd gone outdoors earlier, surely he would have taken the milk and papers inside first? Maybe Whelehan was still in bed; he was after all a man in his sixties. She pressed the bell again, stretching her patience to the limit.

She picked up the copy of the *Post*. Her own piece on the death of Bishop Treanor had made the third lead on page one, a below-the-fold double column. It was not the kind of story that would win her the Pulitzer Prize, being more noteworthy for what it omitted to say than what it actually did. The suspicious circumstances surrounding Treanor's death had been omitted. Emma had protested to Bob Crosby, calling his restrictions tantamount to an insult to the readers. He had patiently explained how the coroner's inquiry had failed to prove conclusively that poison had been the direct cause of death. Treanor had so many damaged organs and impaired bodily functions that death couldn't be directly attributed to any one cause in particular.

Replacing the newspaper on top of the others she felt like walking away, but instinct told her that Whelehan was inside. She was annoyed with how the day was panning out. Her earlier visit to the police station had been a right pain in the arse. Connolly had escorted her from reception to his floor but getting there had been a bit like running the gauntlet. Everyone from pimple-faced rookies to hawk-eyed top brass gave her the once-over. By the time she sat in front of his desk she'd been mentally undressed, leered at, dissected, groped, manhandled, devoured and spat out again. Connolly, to his credit, looked awkward too, but Emma believed his discomfort might have had more to do with their earlier post-breakfast discussion.

Emma had looked carefully at the black and white video stills he gave her.

'Do you recognize the face?' Connolly wanted to know.

'Looks different in each shot,' she'd replied, shuffling the pictures and studying each image. 'Grace McCormick will tell us if it's Helena Andrews. I'll contact you as soon as I know anything.'

Emma had come straight to Whelehan's house after that. And now, she was about to give up on that quest. She would return later in the day if time permitted. Before walking back to her car, she looked directly into the camera perched above the door. She'd noticed it on her arrival and wondered whether or not Whelehan had seen her. It could explain why she'd failed to gain admittance. Looking directly into the lens, she mouthed the words made famous by Arnold Schwarzenegger back in his

Terminator days — *I'll be back.*

Moving away from the door she couldn't shake the feeling that someone really *was* watching her. Had her antenna been more acutely focused on the immediate environment, she might have felt the presence of the person watching her from the inside of a car, a little further down the street.

23

Prof looked away from the monitor. 'Our snoop has gone.'

Whelehan, barely conscious now, groaned. 'Need a doctor . . . losing blood . . . feeling dizzy, I'm — '

A new voice interrupted him. 'The pain you feel is nothing to the torture you inflicted on Susan Furlong.' The words sounded distorted, distant.

Whelehan hadn't been aware that another person had entered the library. He could see a blurred silhouette, the kind of defused image you might see on a steam-covered bathroom mirror. Could be anyone, a man, a woman, an alien, anyone. He wiped the sweat from his eyes with the back of his hand and squinted but his impaired senses were incapable of forcing the definition into focus. The image, like his brain, remained fogged, so much so that he wondered if perhaps he wasn't experiencing some sort of hallucination.

'Who . . . what are you?' he asked, struggling to string the words together.

He heard a cruel crackle of laughter. 'You

really thought you'd got away with it, didn't you? You thought you could destroy Susan Furlong and then live happily ever after, that what you thought?'

Whelehan couldn't hear the words properly but the meaning filtered through. He tried to ask questions but his mouth no longer worked. A second blurred outline towered above him. Was it Prof? Hard to tell. The shape of a handgun stood out in sharp relief towards the centre of the amorphous vision.

The gunman spoke. 'His other knee?' he said.

There was a flash. His second knee exploded. This time he felt no pain, no pain at all. A glorious blinding radiance lit up the whole world.

★ ★ ★

Cobh is one of Ireland's most picturesque seaside destinations, a factor endorsed by the trek of tourists who habitually include it on their holiday itinerary. However, on the 28 November, a cold miserable day, with no sunshine and a biting wind blowing in from the Atlantic, Vinny Bailey failed to embrace its virtues. Driving along the causeway that connects the mainland to the Great Island he wondered how those unfortunate immigrants must have felt when arriving at the quayside to board a transatlantic liner all those many decades ago. What thoughts, what fears crossed their minds as they set forth on their one-way voyage to the New World?

Vinny had been to Cobh previously but his visits had always been of short duration, mere adjuncts to his excursions to the Crawford Art Gallery in Cork City. Twice he'd made the twenty-four kilometre journey from the gallery to Cobh, and joined the tourist trail. He'd strolled along the quayside that had once seen passengers sail out to join *Titanic* on its doomed Atlantic crossing back in 1912. He'd posed for a photograph beside the memorial to the victims of *Lusitania*, the liner that had been torpedoed by a German submarine at the beginning of the Great War. He had walked the town's steep, narrow streets that wound up the hill above the natural harbour and photographed the pretty shop fronts and the boats as they bobbed up and down in the water.

Today, he would not concern himself with the sights. Today he was in Cobh for a specific purpose. He'd made the trip on the strength of a whisper he'd heard about two paintings. Since his student days in the National College of Art and Design he'd greatly admired the work of Nano Reid. Thought of

214

getting his hands on an original by the Drogheda born artist excited him. The source of his tip-off described the person selling the paintings as a once-posh, old-money, gentleman with a Protestant accent. The account reminded him of a description he'd once heard applied to well-to-do Protestant farmers: *they're just like Catholic farmers except they bull their own cows.* Well, whatever about bulling cows, the person he wanted to meet had had his stock investments portfolio severely dinted in recent world stock market upheavals.

He pulled his car off the road and stopped beside a field gate to consult his notepad; before setting out he'd scribbled directions to the location of the owner's house. But first he needed to get out of the car to stretch his legs. From his elevated point above St Colman's Cathedral he could see the full extent of Cork harbour and the nearby islands. The buildings and crescent-shaped terraces represented a grand dictionary of nineteenth-century architecture; a mix of clean Italianate style and ornate Gothic. In the harbour a car-ferry ploughed through the waters past Haulbowline on its way out to the Atlantic. Checking his watch, he reminded himself that he'd better make a move. He was up against a deadline, a factor underscored by the sound of the midday angelus coming from the cathedral's forty-seven-bell carillon.

A few minutes later, guided by his notes, he pulled into the driveway of an old, but well-maintained house, hidden from the road by a mature grove of silver birch, cherry and apple trees. A middle-aged man introduced himself as Jarleth Sinnott and invited Vinny to enter. He spoke with a plummy voice that to Vinny's ear sounded too good to be true. With a bald dome and hair that could have been modelled on the old familiar print of Shakespeare, he put Vinny in mind of an actor. His clothes, a three-piece tweed suit with shirt and tie, must surely have come from a theatre's costume department.

'Offer you a drink?' Sinnott asked, ushering Vinny into a drawing-room.

'No, thanks,' Vinny said, 'I'm on a bit of a tight schedule. I'd like to have a look at your collection if I may.'

'But of course,' Sinnott said, indicating the paintings on the walls.

The house itself, a perfectly maintained period residence, was the ideal setting to show off the paintings. Two-storeys over basement, all rooms with high ceilings and intricate plasterwork, cornicing, window shutters, original doors and fireplaces intact. The canvases included eighteenth- and nineteenth-century English,

French and German schools, but it was the Irish collection that really interested Vinny. Any gallery worth its salt would have been proud to own the masterpieces he now inspected, works by Hone, Lavery, Osborne, Russell, Orpen and some lesser artists of that ilk.

There was a single portrait by Nano Reid that failed to live up to Vinny's expectations. He was aware that Reid, during her formative years had out of necessity been forced to take on many portrait commissions. Sometimes the results were less than awe-inspiring. This was at a time before she had gained critical recognition for her strong and assured manipulation of paint, line and colour, the traits that were to become her trademark. None of these later works, which Vinny thought of as post-Yeatsian, were in evidence. 'Which paintings are you selling?' he asked.

'None of that lot I'm afraid,' Sinnott said.

'What? But I — '

'Sorry, let me explain. I do have a few canvases I wish to part with but the thing is, they're not insured and therefore not housed with this collection.'

'What?' Vinny said, allowing his annoyance to show. 'I was under the impression there were two Nano Reids on offer.'

'Let me explain, Mr Bailey. The revenue commissioners are under the apprehension that I owe substantial tax arrears. It's ridiculous, of course, but you can understand why I keep certain cash transactions away from their gaze. The paintings you refer to are stored in a secure location not far from here. I needed to be sure you had a genuine interest in acquiring them and that you can produce the sort of money required.'

Vinny didn't like the way the conversation was going. He could see no good reason why the paintings shouldn't be *in situ* for inspection. Something else bothered him: the house, with all its grandeur and artefacts, felt wrong, felt unlived in. There were fireplaces in several rooms and central-heating radiators in evidence, yet the place was cold. The kitchen looked as though it hadn't been used for some time. Where were the smells of food? There was no sign of life, no sign of occupancy, no cats, dogs or pets of any description, no indication of the day-to-day activities that should be evident in such a large house. Vinny kept these misgivings to himself.

'I wouldn't have come this far if I wasn't interested in buying,' he said, producing his business card. 'I am, as you see, a bone fide art dealer affiliated to the society of Fine Art and Antiques Dealers Association. Now, can we inspect the goods?'

'Just a short boat ride in the harbour — '

'You're not serious? This is not what — '

Sinnott held up his hand to stop Vinny. 'Hear me out. I have property on Haulbowline Island, near the site of the old steel works. It used to belong to the chief executive before the plant shut down. It's less than a mile out from the harbour. I store certain valuables there . . . including some paintings.'

Vinny wanted to end the discussion, tell Sinnott to take a jump in the harbour. Instead he said, 'Well then, I suppose we'd better get going. The sooner I see what's on offer, the sooner we'll know whether or not we're wasting each other's time.'

'Amen to that,' Sinnott said, a smile creasing his face for the first time. He produced a mobile from his inside pocket and pressed some numbers. 'I'll just let my man Fitzpatrick, know we're on our way, have him make ready the boat.'

24

Gulls wheeled raucously above the breeze-ruffled waters. A variety of boats remained berthed in the marina, everything from pleasure craft, motor boats, fishing boats and outboards to a few inflatables. Vinny, never a boating enthusiast and none-too-fond of the deep, picked his steps carefully. He could taste a brine-laden deposit on the tip of his tongue as all around him the mishmash of marine noises rang out, repetitive percussion-like sounds of flapping rigging and mast flags, plopping sounds of water lapped against the sea wall as it swished back and forth.

There were few people in evidence and little activity on the dock. The sky remained dense and resolutely overcast, snuffing out the sun but porous enough to allow the chill winds through.

'Ah, there's our boat,' Sinnott said, nudging Vinny's arm and pointing to a thirty-foot, four-berth pleasure craft moored below, 'and that's my man Fitzpatrick on deck.'

The man aboard, wearing oil-smeared dungarees, an Aran sweater and a black beret, waved to Sinnott. 'Come aboard,' he yelled.

Vinny followed Sinnott on to the craft with all the awkwardness of a landlubber, aware of being subjected to a head-to-toe inspection by Fitzpatrick.

'Come 'ere boy,' he said in a lyrical Cork accent, 'careful on deck, we don't want you slippin' an' slidin' an' fallin' down that open hatch behind you.'

'Sorry,' Vinny said, moving away from the hatch.

Fitzpatrick reversed the craft, which had been berthed bow-in to the sea wall, into the harbour and steered towards deeper waters. Accompanied by the cries of seagulls, they moved at five knots before gradually picking up speed. Barely half a mile out from the harbour a whipping wind caused the bow of the boat to lift and slap against the water. Vinny began to feel queasy. He tried not to think about his churning stomach, fearing he'd make a spectacle of himself by getting seasick. The boat was heading in a westerly direction and moving towards White Point when Vinny noticed a ferryboat pulling into the pier at the naval base. 'Is that where we're headed?' he asked.

'No,' Sinnott said, 'I've got my own private mooring on the south side of the island; it takes us directly to the house.'

'Just as well,' Vinny said, 'because my stomach's doing somersaults.'

Fitzpatrick drew Sinnott's attention to a boat anchored offshore from the naval base. 'We're in a restricted area,' he shouted. 'There's flags warning us not to enter this area.'

'Damn it,' Sinnott said, 'It's just some work vessel, probably laying cables or gas lines to the mainland. There's no one on deck, probably a bunch of workers having a lunch break below.'

'What d'you want me to do?' Fitzpatrick asked.

'Just ignore them. Pass as close as you can broadside.'

The sudden change of direction threw Vinny off balance. 'What's happening?' he asked, puzzled by the boat's erratic behaviour.

Sinnott didn't answer. Instead he turned to Vinny and told him there was another passenger on board. 'We have someone who's particularly keen to meet you, *Mr Vinny Bailey*.'

Vinny didn't like the emphasis on his name. Sounded ominous. Unsteadily, he followed Sinnott to the boat's forward berth, his stomach heaving in protest against the vessel's movements. It was a small triangular-shaped area that followed the contours of the bow. There was a double bunk on the port side and a stack of storage compartments to starboard. A person, wearing a long black weatherproof coat sat on the bunk giving Vinny the benefit of a triumphant smile. Vinny recognized the face straight away and thought, *Oh, Christ no, Emma's going after the wrong person.* It was the last thought he would have for some time. He felt something crash down on his skull and saw a blinding light before his world vanished down a funnel into a dark void.

Being unconscious spared him the indignity of seeing his body being stripped of all but his jocks. He remained unaware of being dragged on deck while the boat moved into the area of cover provided by the moored vessel. Even the splash he created when hitting the water failed to awaken his brain. Within seconds, his unconscious body disappeared beneath the dark waters.

25

Whelehan felt his life's blood seeping away. The stain on the carpet had increased in size, a dark-crimson rosette soaking through to the floorboards. The pain no longer registered. He'd given up hope of rescue. There would be no reprieve, no doctor, no last-minute intervention. His only wish now was that his executioner would finish him off, end his suffering, release him from the hellish netherworld he floundered in.

His accuser continued to rant but, for him, words had lost all meaning. Before the loss of blood had become critical, the diatribe had had the power to transport him back to a time when ambition was his all-consuming passion. In pursuit of success he'd sold his soul; he'd signed the committal order that kept Susan Furlong locked away. Instead of thirty pieces of silver, the betrayer's purse, he'd been handed entrée to government, given a seat of power, a seat he had no hesitation in abusing. The media back then, led by Emma Boylan, cried foul but he'd brazened it out.

Barely conscious now, Whelehan wondered

if he'd really behaved in such a callous manner. Was it all an aberration, a figment of a recurring nightmare? Some last vestige of conscience assured him he'd not been on the side of the angels. The prospect of imminent death made him face the truth, accept his culpability. He'd made mistakes, deliberately taken wrong decisions, and he was now paying the price, paying in full. His thoughts were becoming more and more disorientated. Yet, certain recollections were insistent. The spectre of Susan Furlong continued to engage the few brain cells that still functioned.

Susan had escaped after ten years of captivity. She tracked down her rapist, and separated him from his penis and testicles with the aid of a scalpel . . . and then, she'd come after him. Luck had been with him on that occasion; he'd had a miraculous escape. But now, all these years later, his life ebbing away, he realized he hadn't escaped at all. He should have kept a more watchful eye on Helena Andrews, the little girl who'd witnessed her mother's horrific death.

★ ★ ★

Ted Barry finned past the boat's mooring chain, saw how the links disappeared into the dark water below. As instructor and lead diver, it was his job to supervise and watch out for the five sub-aqua club members in the water with him. He'd received his underwater training at the naval base in Haulbowline and had eventually headed up the navy's special diving branch. The NSDB, as it was called, was dedicated to a wide range of underwater diving tasks but more specifically to mine and undertake explosive ordnance disposal underwater. He had risen to the rank of commodore before the navy had taken its decision to switch the NSDB away from the Haulbowline base. Rather than move, he had taken early retirement and now ran the local sub-aqua team.

Feeling every day of his fifty-five years, he wondered whether he ought to be plunging into freezing-cold water in a suit no more than five millimetres thick. He could, if he wished, be relaxing at home, having a drink with the lads in McCoy's, playing a game of snooker, or tucked up in his warm bed with his newly acquired partner Phyllis, a school-teacher some fifteen years his junior. But in truth he had little to complain about. He simply loved being underwater.

At first sight, he thought the dark shape in the water approaching him and his team might be a dolphin. In recent times two dolphins had washed up on the island's coastline bearing all the telltale signs of the trawlers nets that had snared them. Barry was incensed by the cruelty of it all, aware of the suffering inflicted on the mammals as they thrashed about in agony until death overtook them. It was an all too familiar story: the trawler-men, only interested in bass, would throw the dolphins overboard.

The shape in the water, he could now discern from behind his contoured mask, was not a dolphin. A boat approached from overhead, its keel slicing through the water. Damn it, he thought, there's not supposed to be any craft in this area while the dive is in progress. Whoever was sailing the vessel had ignored the flags warning them to stay out of the area. He bit hard on his breathing regulator, angry that anybody should be so lax in regard to safety precautions.

As the boat passed directly above him an object hit the water. He could not identify the shape at first but within seconds the outline of a semi-naked human body materialized. He finned towards the sinking body. It appeared to have little or no animation, the arms and legs moving limply in the currents. Reaching out to stop its descent, he could tell it was a male body, clad only in shorts. Examining the face, it was obvious that no bubbles were being expelled from the nose or mouth. Barry didn't want to jump to conclusions, but as far as he could ascertain the man in the water had ceased breathing.

26

Emma had grabbed a quick bite in the canteen and was busy putting a report together for the next day's edition when Mary-Jo Graham breezed in.

'Hi Emma, how's tricks?' she said.

'Can't complain,' Emma replied, failing to match Mary-Jo's affability. 'Had a good morning then? On the scent of a big scoop, are we?'

'I wish! Don't make me laugh,' Mary-Jo said, removing her overcoat and sitting in front of her monitor. 'Spent the entire morning at the Dunwoody Tribunal listening to arse-numbing waffle. Jesus!'

'Why were you there?'

'Our beloved editor Bob Crosby wants me to research a piece on the cost to the tax paying public of keeping all the current tribunals going. The way he sees it, the whole thing is cockeyed: the tribunals deal with politicians and state agencies that have allowed haemophilia sufferers to become injected with HIV infected blood, and children to be physically and sexually abused, yet the taxpayer is the only one singled out to foot the bill. Crazy, is it not?'

'Is a daft situation,' Emma agreed. 'Those earning the biggest bucks pay no tax and those causing the greatest damage to the rest of us get away scott-free. That's how the system works; it's criminal. And speaking of crime, I'm supposed to be down at the Circuit Criminal Court right now.'

'What for? Not your usual beat, is it?'

'No, but as a favour to Bob I'm doing an atmospheric piece on the FitzGerald murder case. I've agreed to deputize for Jim Bell who's out sick. I'm supposed to create a picture in words to dovetail with the legalistic report.'

'That could tie you up for days.'

'Jeez, I hope not. Closing arguments finished yesterday. The judge is expected to conclude his summing up this evening. I really ought to be following up on a far more interesting story.'

'Well, in that case,' Mary-Jo said, swivelling around from her computer, 'why not let me handle the court. I'd love a shot at it. Has to be more exciting than what I sat through this morning.'

'Would you really?'

'No problem. Just tell me what kind of outline you want.'

Delighted with her good fortune, Emma

briefed Mary-Jo and beat a hasty retreat from the building, determined to get away before Bob Crosby cornered her with a new assignment.

★ ★ ★

An ambulance pulled away from Dr Brian Whelehan's house as Emma sought a parking space. A *garda* officer stood in the rain outside Whelehan's door. Several people, probably neighbours, huddled in a group beneath umbrellas to one side of the house. Something's happened to Whelehan, she thought. Might explain why he'd failed to appear at the door earlier. Could have been a heart attack or a brain haemorrhage; maybe he tripped, took a tumble down the stairs, broke his neck. A darker, more insidious thought took hold: what if Whelehan had become a victim like Larry Lawlor, like the Andrews and Treanor?

She found a spot by the kerbside that had possibilities. 'Who says men are from Mars and women can't reverse cars?' she said aloud, sizing up the space. It was a tight squeeze between two poorly parked vehicles. The weather didn't help. A dozen reverse and forward manoeuvres allowed her to shoehorn the Hyundai Coupé into the space without so much as touching either of the parked cars. She hurried back to Whelehan's house, flashed her press card to the uniform on duty, a tall, broad-shouldered slab of a man, and was about to push the door open when a big hand clamped on to her shoulder. 'And just where do you think you're going, miss?'

'Remove your hand,' Emma said, thinking *this male specimen is definitely from Mars.*

The policeman smiled indulgently, removed the offending hand, pushed his square chin forward and gazed down on her. 'Don't give me grief,' he said. 'No one's permitted into the house without authority.'

'I have an appointment with Dr Brian Whelehan,' she lied, 'so, if you don't mind I'd like to get in out of this weather. He's expecting me.'

'Well in that case you're a little late; Dr Whelehan's just been hauled away in an ambulance.'

'Oh? What happened?'

'I'm not at liberty to divulge details.'

Spoken like a true Martian, Emma thought, her mind working on another approach. 'Look, you're making a mistake. I've been given authority to — '

'No one's allowed inside . . . and that includes media personnel, especially ones waving press passes.'

Emma bit her lip, getting more annoyed by the second. The rain had eased to a drizzle but she was still getting soaked. '*Please*,' she said, with a placating smile, 'I need to collect notes I left here this morning, won't be a minute.'

'You got that right; you won't be a minute 'cause you're not going in. Besides, I don't believe you left your notes here this morning, Miss Boylan.'

'What the hell is this? Who are you to say what my movements were this morning?'

'Ah, come on, there's no need to adopt a hostile attitude,' he said, giving Emma a salacious glance. 'Look, I know who you are, Miss Boylan, I saw you this morning when you came-a-calling on Connolly.'

Emma's urge to knee the man in the nuts had become irresistible. *Do Martians have nuts?* She didn't like his smug attitude, his supercilious smirk or the innuendo in his voice. She was about to give him a tongue lashing when the door opened.

'Someone take my name in vain?' Connolly asked, glaring at the officer.

Emma was first to respond. 'I was trying to tell this — '

'It's OK, Ms Boylan,' Connolly interrupted. 'Glad you're here. There's something you can help us with. If you'll just follow me, please.'

As soon as Connolly closed the door, Emma exhaled a sigh of relief. 'Thanks for saving my bacon.'

'What else could I do? Didn't expect to see you here. I'm breaking every rule in the book letting you in, but seeing as how you're here, there *is* something that genuinely concerns you.' Connolly handed Emma a pair of surgical gloves. 'We've got to be careful not to contaminate the crime scene.'

'Crime scene?' Emma queried. 'What's happened to Whelehan? He's not been . . . been — '

'Killed? Well, yes, someone has tried to kill him but he's not dead yet. Unconscious, but still alive. He's been kneecapped — both legs — lost buckets of blood. He's been taken to hospital, but I'd be surprised if he's still breathing by the time they get him there.'

'What happened?'

'Not sure exactly. His housekeeper came to the house an hour ago — it's her day off but she'd forgotten to take her umbrella from the house the day before and called to retrieve it — and as soon as she let herself in she knew something was amiss. She found Whelehan in a pool of blood and dialled 999. Her name's Mrs O'Connor; she's being interviewed by McFadden right now. The reason I'm allowing you to come in is

234

because your name has cropped up.'

'My name? What do you mean, cropped up?'

'Follow me,' Connolly said, moving down the hallway. 'Watch where you step . . . don't touch anything.' He entered the library and beckoned her to follow. Two men and a woman, dressed in white overalls were subjecting the room to microscopic examination, using tweezers and vacuum, dusting for fingerprints, bagging threads and hairs. One of the investigating team, a grim-faced young man of short stature, peered into the viewfinder of his camera and shot photographs of a blood-saturated carpet, his flash gun highlighting the freshness of the spill.

Connolly brought her attention to the computer. 'Look at this,' he said, 'whoever did the number on Whelehan left a message.' The image on the screen brought a gasp from Emma. Under a heading that read DEATH ROW, she saw a list of names that included her own name and that of her husband.

Caroline Andrews X
Jim Andrews X
Bishop John Treanor X
Larry Lawlor X
Dr Brian Whelehan X
Niamh O'Flynn —
Grace McCormick —

Emma Boylan —
Vinny Bailey X

Emma grasped the significance of the red
Xs behind the first five names immediately,
but it was the X after Vinny's name that
stunned her. 'Oh, Christ, no,' she gasped.

'I'm presuming you know where Vinny is?'
Connolly said.

Emma wasn't listening. 'I'm going to be
sick,' she said, her voice a strangled whisper.
'I need to get out of this room . . . *now*.'

Connolly took her by the elbow and
ushered her outdoors. Mercifully, the rain
had stopped. 'I'm sorry,' he said, 'I should
never have taken you inside.'

'It's all right. I'm fine now,' Emma said,
feeling nothing of the kind. 'It's just seeing
Vinny's name with that X beside it. I need to
contact him.'

'You *do* know where he is, right?'

'He's gone to look at some paintings in
Cobh,' Emma said, punching his number on
her mobile. She looked at Connolly, a
palpable fear emanating from her. 'Oh, damn
it, damn it,' she hissed through clenched
teeth, 'I'm getting his answering message.'
More urgently, she spoke into the phone,
'Vinny, ring me immediately you hear this;
your life may depend on it.'

'Shouldn't jump to conclusions,' Connolly said, 'I wouldn't go reading too much into the X beside Vinny's name. I mean, look at it this way: there's an X after Whelehan's name and he's still alive.'

'Christ, Jim, is that supposed to reassure me? You just said Whelehan's as good as dead . . . won't make it to the hospital, you said.'

'Yes, but think on this: whoever shot Whelehan was in his house little more than an hour ago. You say that Vinny's in Cobh. Well, that's the other end of the country, three, maybe four hours' drive from here. That means he's safe.'

'Safe, hah!' Emma snapped with scorn, walking away from Connolly, heading for her car. Connolly paused for a second, a look of indecision on his face. He caught up with her as she got into the car. 'Look, Emma, I really don't think you ought to drive.'

'Just what the hell am I supposed to do?' she said, a look of desperation in her eyes.

Connolly put his hands on her shoulders, squeezed reassuringly. 'I can take you back to my office . . . or we could have a little walk; there's a pub just around the corner. We could go there, have coffee or something, see if we can make sense of this.'

'I don't know. I don't know what to do; I'm scared . . . '

27

Winter darkness bore down on Emma, extinguishing what remained of her fragile spirit. Her mind was a ball of confusion by the time she'd made it back to her apartment. Connolly, who had driven her, offered to see her inside.

'No, I'll be fine,' she said, without looking at him. 'Got to contact the newsroom, flesh out the Whelehan report I sent earlier.'

'You're in no state to write anything and besides it's after six o'clock and you've had one hell of a day.'

'No, fuck it,' she said, surprising Connolly by her use of the expletive. 'I have a job to do . . . and I'm the only reporter with on-the-spot information.'

'You're not going to include the names on Whelehan's computer?'

'Bloody hell, Jim,' she said, wearily, 'give me some credit; of course I'm not going to say anything. Until Vinny's safe, and until whoever's behind this whole crazy shit is identified, I'm saying nothing.'

'Good. Only way to play it.' Connolly said, looked into her eyes, wanting to stay with her, wanting to ensure she was all right. The expression on her face spoke volumes: she needed space, needed to be alone with her thoughts and fears. He reached for her hand, squeezed gently. 'Everything's going to be fine.'

Emma responded with a reciprocal hand squeeze. 'Hope to God you're right. Soon as I hear anything I'll contact you.'

'I'll expect your call then.'

She watched Connolly drive away before putting her key in the door. Her first thought was that Vinny would be home. Blind expectation really. She wanted to believe that somehow he'd made it to the apartment, that he'd have a totally reasonable explanation for why he'd failed to respond to the phone messages. He'd laugh out loud and ask what all the fuss was about. He'd kiss her and say — haven't I gone away a thousand times before for whole days without calling you? These thoughts and hopes flashed through her mind as she hurried towards the kitchen calling his name.

A deathly silence amplified the absence of reply.

She looked into the lounge, the work den, and the bedroom; vacant spaces gaped back at her, the silence goading, the solitude mocking. Whatever faint hopes she'd entertained evaporated. 'Damn', she said, not knowing how to vent her frustration. 'Where the hell are you, Vinny?' She hit the redial button, listened to the message she'd heard a dozen times already.

Earlier, chatting with Connolly in the pub, he had tried to persuade her that everything would turn out fine. To an extent he had succeeded. But now, alone in her apartment, the ray of hope he'd engendered evaporated. Jumbled images from the day spun crazily in her head. Seeing her own name and Vinny's on the computer had thrown her. The X next to Vinny's name marked the onset of panic.

In a quiet pub — with the most inappropriate name, Savage Cabbage — around the corner from Whelehan's house, Connolly had plied her with strong black coffee. He'd contacted the police in Cobh and given them what little information he had on Vinny's visit. She'd done likewise, contacting Vinny's friends in the fine art and antiques business. None of them could help her in regard to the sale of the Nano Reid paintings.

As well as phoning Vinny's friends, she'd been able to get off a report to the *Post*, a bit like working on auto-pilot. She reported Whelehan's ordeal and subsequent rush to hospital. She instructed a *Post* photographer to get shots of the retired politician's house.

Until his retirement, Whelehan's appeal to voters had been phenomenal and he still warranted front-page headlines. He was one of those rare public figures who'd managed to avoid attracting collateral damage from the never-ending series of crises and scandals that went hand-in-hand with political life; his personal habits and private lifestyle never impinged on his constituents' perception of him as a decent, likeable man. Emma wondered if his ability to survive all adversities would see him through this, his latest upheaval.

Thinking about her conversation with Connolly in the Savage Cabbage, one item in particular intrigued her. They'd been discussing Whelehan's library and the events that had taken place there when she'd mentioned her encounter with the big *garda* officer who'd stood outside the house. 'He made some snide remarks about seeing me that morning when I came-a-calling to see you.'

'*Came-a-calling*,' Connolly had repeated, 'that the expression he used?'

'Yeah, every syllable laced with innuendo.'

'Bit of a smart-ass, that one. He wouldn't have been there at all except that today's sitting of the Dunwoody Tribunal was cancelled.'

'You sure about that?'

'Yes, he's part of the contingent — '

'No, I mean, are you sure the Dunwoody Tribunal didn't sit today?'

'Yes, of course I'm sure. It was adjourned because — '

Emma stopped him again. 'That's weird.'

'Weird . . . how do you mean, *weird*?'

'Well, according to Mary-Jo Graham — she shares my work-station — the Dunwoody Tribunal *did* sit.'

'Well, she's mistaken, this morning's session was cancelled.'

Emma hadn't pursued the subject, being more intent on checking out Vinny's associates. But now, in the empty apartment, she wondered why Mary-Jo had deliberately lied. She was still trying to figure out what lay behind the deception when the telephone rang. She grabbed it, shouted her hello.

'Emma, that you?' a female voice asked.

'Yes, it's me,' Emma answered, failing to disguise her disappointment. 'I'm sorry,' she said, 'I was expecting — '

'This is Grace McCormick, Emma. You all right?'

'Yes, yes, sorry, Grace. It's been a lousy day. Not sure whether I'm on my arse or my elbow. I thought you were Vinny. I mean, I thought your call — '

'No need to explain, Emma, know exactly

what you mean. Listen, I won't delay you; I just wanted you to know that I had a look at the photograph you e-mailed. It's definitely Helena Andrews and it means my theory's right; she *is* responsible for the deaths. There can be little doubt.'

'Certainly looks that way,' Emma agreed, 'but there's been some very disturbing developments here since we last spoke.'

'Like what?' Grace asked, apprehensively.

Emma outlined recent events, including her meeting with Niamh O'Flynn and Bishop Treanor and her experience in Whelehan's house. Grace's intake of breath was audible when she heard that her name featured on Whelehan's computer. Emma concluded with her account of Vinny's trip to Cobh and her immediate concern for his safety.

'Have the police got a fix on Helena's whereabouts?' Grace asked.

'Until today they didn't have enough evidence to bring her in. But now a full alert has gone out to the airports, seaports and the entire police network. As of tomorrow, radio and television news bulletins will include appeals to the public to come forward if they can shed any light on her whereabouts. They're treating it as a missing person enquiry.'

'That should help,' Grace said.

'Maybe so, but I still don't know where

Vinny's got to. He's not even answering his mobile. I'm going frantic.'

'I understand, Emma. Look, why don't I come across? It'll only take a few hours and I can be there.'

'No, no, I don't want you to go to all that trouble,' Emma said, touched by Grace's offer. 'What benefit would that serve? Besides, your name's on the death list; why put yourself at risk?'

'You're forgetting something, Emma, I know Helena better than anyone. I've listened to her innermost thoughts. I could make an appeal to her through the media, perhaps? What do you think? I could prevail on her to come and talk with me. It's possible I can get through to her before any more lives are put at risk.'

'Could work, I suppose,' Emma said, unable to infuse any enthusiasm into her words. 'Could be helpful to have someone who understands her background.'

'I'm glad you agree, Emma. You think I should come then?'

'That's up to you but, yes, I think it might help.'

'Good! I'll do it.'

'You'll stay here in the apartment?'

'Yes, that would make sense if you're sure you don't mind?'

'You're more than welcome. When can I expect to see you?'

'I'll catch an early morning flight. Be with you around midday. Hopefully Vinny'll be back by then.'

'I pray to God you're right.'

28

Mary-Jo Graham got back to the *Post* before 6 p.m., relieved to escape the biting east wind and glad to embrace the warmth of the newsroom. The place was buzzing with the story of Whelehan's shooting. Everyone seemed to be involved in putting the piece together. Day staff remained on after their shift, caught up in the excitement, anxious to ensure a smooth flow to their night colleagues. Reams of archival material were being sifted through, highlights of Whelehan's political career collated, photographs sourced and selected.

It surprised her that Emma Boylan should be absent from her work-station. This seemed all the more remarkable considering that the main text for the story carried Emma's by-line. She should have been in the thick of things, co-ordinating the effort, taking responsibility for every detail. So where was she? A word with the other journalists let her know that Emma was working from home, conducting her contributions on-line.

Mary-Jo set about writing her own report. She'd spent two and a half hours in the

Circuit Criminal Court taking notes. The jury had failed to reach a verdict on the FitzGerald murder case and had been sent to a nearby hotel for the night. She keyed in her account, consulting her notes from time to time, determined to capture the atmosphere that had prevailed in the courtroom. Her overriding concern, however, was that it should receive Emma Boylan's imprimatur. She checked it twice, tidied a few awkward sentences, and e-mailed the final draft. Seconds later, she phoned Emma to verify that she'd got it. Emma, without any attempt at chit-chat, confirmed that it was on her screen and said she would read it straight away.

Before Emma could hang up Mary-Jo decided to satisfy her curiosity. 'Emma, your story on Brian Whelehan is causing great waves in the newsroom; how come you're not here?'

'Something's come up,' Emma replied rather stiffly. 'Decided to work the story from home. Be back to you as soon as I've checked your piece, OK?'

Two minutes later Emma rang back. Without suggesting a single alteration or edit, she told her to pass it to editorial.

Mary-Jo felt good; the courtroom assignment had gone well and, more importantly, it had got the OK from Emma. And now, with Emma's work-station all to herself, she decided to do some work of a personal nature before heading for home. She scanned the newsroom to make sure no one was paying particular attention to her. Satisfied, she connected her digital camera to the computer and began downloading the images she'd shot over the past few days.

She'd managed to capture images of Emma's husband leaving the apartment early that morning. Shortly afterwards she'd watched Detective Inspector Connolly arrive. He'd remained there for the best part of an hour. Later, she'd lined up the Pearse Street Police Station in her viewfinder and captured Emma entering and exiting the building. After that, she'd followed Emma to Whelehan's house and watched her wait outside his door. As soon as Emma left and had disappeared round the corner, a woman got out of a car that had been parked opposite the house. Her camera caught the person's furtive glances as she crossed the road to Whelehan's door. The woman then produced a set of keys and let herself into the house.

At the time of taking the photograph, Mary-Jo had no idea of the dramatic events that were to unfold later that day in Whelehan's house. But now, the possibility that she'd stumbled on to something that could be considered serious evidence seemed more than a possibility. That could present a major problem; she couldn't allow anyone to see the digital images. To show them would be to admit she'd been stalking Emma Boylan, to admit she'd been lying about her whereabouts that morning.

Viewing the photographs on the monitor, Mary-Jo cut to a close-up of a woman's face. She studied the face intently for several seconds before realizing there was something familiar about the woman. *I've seen you before*, she thought, racking her brains to remember why the face should strike a chord. And then, in an instant, she knew the answer. Quickly she returned to the pictures she'd already viewed. She checked out the people who appeared in the peripheral areas of each shot. 'Got you' she said aloud, looking anew at one of the earlier images.

29

Almost midday and Connolly hadn't so much as ventured from behind his desk. Since getting to work at 8.30 a.m. he'd been hostage to the telephone. McFadden and Dorsett had already been to the canteen for their mid-morning break. DS Bridie McFadden had been considerate enough to return with a mug of coffee and a Cadbury Snack for him. The coffee and snack bar remained untouched.

First call of the morning had been to Emma Boylan. She'd left several messages on his answering service during the night, none of which he'd heard until his arrival in the office. He called her straight away but her *hello* let him know that the situation remained grim. She'd had no news of Vinny and she sounded like someone on the verge of physical and mental exhaustion.

Guilt consumed him as he listened to the list of contacts she'd managed to involve in the search. She'd also informed him that the psychiatrist, Grace McCormick, had made a positive ID of the woman on the video. The face belonged to Helena Andrews, no ifs, buts, or maybes. According to Emma, Grace McCormick had offered to make an appeal through the media to encourage Helena to break cover and seek professional help. He'd passed that piece of information on to Superintendent Smith. The super would get back to him in the course of the day with a decision.

He had telephoned the hospital after that to get an update on Whelehan's condition. Bounced around the switchboard like a ping-pong ball and put on hold continually, a doctor finally condescended to talk to him. 'Whelehan's in intensive care,' the doctor informed him, adding that the chances of recovery were fifty-fifty and that the patient would be confined to a wheelchair *if* he pulled through.

After his call to the hospital he contacted his colleagues in Cobh. Detective Sergeant Steve Keenahan, a man he'd met a few times at police conventions, took his call. Keenahan, a big ruddy man full of vigour and *bonhomie*, reminded him of the stereotypical Irish NYPD cops so beloved of early Hollywood movies. The Cork-based detective had put out feelers to see if anyone in the greater Cork area had been in the market to offload paintings. Apart from the legitimate art galleries and antique dealers nothing of interest had come to light. Only one private art collection, housed in the Cobh area, remained unchecked. He'd ruled it out because the owners had gone on a world cruise and the premises remained locked up for the duration of the trip.

The description and registration of Vinny's car had been circulated to every police station in the area but no sightings had been reported. No one fitting Vinny's description had been admitted to the local hospitals over the past twenty-four hours. Keenahan proceeded to give a run down of the incidents in his area that could conceivably be of interest. There had been one road fatality but the victim was a 17-year-old student. A serious stabbing incident outside a public house in Cobh had been reported but the participants had been local folk. A man had fallen overboard from a boat off Haulbowline and was recovered by a group of divers who happened to be in the area at the time. The rescued man was thought to be suffering from loss of memory. In another incident, a bull had gored a farmer. Connolly thanked Keenahan for the information, saying, 'Doesn't sound like our man is among that lot.' He was about to hang up when a thought occurred to him. 'Maybe you could get me a description of the fellow who fell overboard? Can't think why an art dealer would want to go sailing but we might as well check all angles.'

He considered ringing Emma again but hesitated. Vinny's disappearance, had forced him to evaluate his feelings for the art dealer's wife. Emma and he had been friends for several years but in more recent times he felt they had grown closer, their relationship edging towards a more emotional level. It was possible that he was fooling himself, allowing himself to see something special that wasn't there. Unless he was greatly mistaken, Emma's feelings mirrored his own, invading that emotional no-man's-land that lay between the platonic and the passionate.

His thoughts reverted to their recent tête-à-tête in The Turk's Head. The charge he felt when Emma reached out and took his hand could not be lightly dismissed. For him it had been a seminal moment. It had scrambled his brain and sent his equilibrium into a crazy tailspin. Had it meant the same for her? He wanted to believe so, wanted to trust his instincts, but making that leap of fate was difficult. Emma never gave the slightest indication that anything was wrong with her marriage. *Though shalt not covet thy neighbour's wife*, wasn't that what the Good Book said? Well, he'd smashed that commandment good and proper.

Vinny's disappearance highlighted Emma's concern for her husband. Where did that leave him? It was one thing to covet a man's wife while that man was hale and hearty, but how was he supposed to react when that man went missing and might even be dead? Somewhere in the back of his mind a dark, ugly, half-formed, malevolent thought struggled to surface. It had something to do with the possibilities that could follow (for him) should Vinny disappear from the equation but he refused to entertain the notion, ashamed that such an outrageous idea, however vague and ill defined, could seek expression.

Dismissing this quandary, he picked up the phone and was about to dial Emma's number when an internal call came through. It was Ellen Furey, to tell him to report immediately to her boss, Superintendent Smith.

Harry Smith, sitting ramrod straight in his high-backed chair, waved Connolly to a more sedate seat in front of his desk. His military-type moustache and flat-top cropped hair made him look more like an army man than a policeman. The superintendent prided himself on his sense of style and dress; in or out of uniform, he looked the business. Today he wore a three-piece suit complete with breast-pocket handkerchief, pale-blue shirt, silk tie and gold tiepin. For a man on the threshold of his sixtieth birthday he was in remarkable physical shape. Weekly workouts in the gym ensured that no extra poundage dared attach itself to his six-feet-plus frame. Married with two daughters he was a hard worker and expected no less from the officers in his charge.

'Sit down Jim,' he said, his voice resonating round his office. 'Get you a coffee or something?'

'I'm good,' Connolly answered, knowing the correct response. He rated Smith's ability highly and considered him methodical and dependable. The chief super had a common-sense approach to most problems, but sometimes ran foul of internal bureaucracy because of his hair-trigger temper and impatience with political ineptitude.

'Heard the oddest damn thing,' he said. 'Just got word from Brussels that Bill Quinn hanged himself in his apartment. You know who Quinn is?'

'Yes, yes, I do,' Connolly said, taken aback. 'He's Niamh O'Flynn's husband. Has it been established that it *is* suicide?'

'The authorities there seem to think so.'

'Bound to be questions.'

'Exactly. I expect a big flap when the media get wind of it. Normally, that wouldn't bother me, Brussels being outside my jurisdiction, but things are never that simple.'

Connolly knew what Smith meant. 'We're involved because Niamh O'Flynn came to us with the threat she'd received.'

'Right. I'm counting on O'Flynn making no disclosure about the threat or the fact that she'd contacted us.' Smith paused for a second and fixed Connolly with his deep aquamarine eyes. 'That's why I wanted a word with you, Jim.'

Connolly, wondering what was coming, waited, said nothing.

'Saw you with that reporter from the *Post*, what's-her-name . . . ?'

'Emma Boylan,' Connolly answered, even though he knew the super had no difficulty remembering Emma's name. 'She's helping with the identification of the suspect, Helena Andrews.'

'Ah, yes, of course, so you told me. Let me see if I've got this straight; through this reporter we have an offer from some psychiatrist to appeal to Helena Andrews to come out of hiding, give herself up, is that it?'

'That's right. The psychiatrist's name is Grace McCormick; she worked with Helena Andrews in the past. She's flown in from Liverpool this morning and is staying with . . . the journalist.'

'I'd prefer *not* to involve the press. Could compromise operations. We don't want leaks, tip-offs or indiscretions coming from our side of the fence.'

'Sorry? I'm not sure I follow you. Are you accusing me of — ?'

'I'm not accusing you of anything, Jim, I'm just pointing out how delicate the O'Flynn situation is. Less the press know, better I like it. I especially do not want any journalists to know about the threat to her family.'

Connolly listened with growing unease. 'I understand,' he said, aware that he'd already spilled the beans. 'Might be a problem keeping Emma Boylan out of the loop.'

A flash of annoyance rippled across Smith's face. 'Why is that, Jim?'

Connolly outlined the activities of the past twenty-four hours in some detail, stressing the importance of the link between the appearance of Vinny Bailey's name on Whelehan's computer and his sudden disappearance.

'This man Bailey has been missing for less than forty-eight hours — is that right?' Smith asked.

'That's right, but — '

'And Whelehan is still alive?'

'Yes, but — '

'And there's nothing to link Bill Quinn's suicide to any of the activities we're discussing?'

'Only the fact that Niamh O'Flynn has told us about being — '

'Yes,' Smith snapped, 'but the media are not aware of that, right?'

'Right.' Connolly lied.

'I believe Niamh O'Flynn will want to avoid the press. That means the great unwashed public whom we serve so diligently don't know diddly squat. They've no inkling that the deaths of Larry Lawlor, John Treanor, and the Andrews are in any way connected to this woman Helena Andrews.'

'What's the point you're making?' Connolly asked.

'Point is, I don't want scare headlines. I don't want a feeding frenzy in the press. We'll play this low-key until we're one hundred per cent sure of our facts. I want you to find Helena Andrews, get her in here for questioning. I don't want this shrink to get within an ass's roar of the media.'

'Well, if she's already here, offering to — '

'Damn it Jim, you're not listening; I don't care how you do it, just get her off our backs, OK? One last thing, keep Emma Boylan at arm's length.'

'That's going to be difficult considering that her husband — ?'

'I don't give a monkey's. As far as I'm concerned, Emma Boylan is a loose cannon; I want her frozen out. If something develops on the Vinny Bailey thing, we'll deal with it then, OK? In the meantime we keep her on a need-to-know basis, nothing more. Do I make myself clear?'

'Perfectly, sir,' Connolly said.

30

Getting through the letter without a break in concentration proved impossible. Niamh O'Flynn's mind involuntarily strayed from the text as she desperately sought to grasp its import. She attempted to read it one more time.

Commission Européenne, Bruxelles.

Dear Niamh
By the time you get this letter I will be no more. I seek no absolution for my deeds but do feel obligated to offer an explanation.
I was the victim of an entrapment scheme, something I should have been above. I can understand your abhorrence, your refusal to talk or meet with me, but I feel it incumbent on me to warn you of impending danger. YOU are the target of this woman's insane obsession. I believe she wants to make you suffer before she strikes directly. I happened to be convenient, easy prey. After she'd engineered the phone lines to bear witness to my stupidity,

she drugged and injected me with the AIDS virus. Effectively, she killed me.

I have no wish to endure a lingering death nor do I wish to put you and Joan through that ordeal. I can imagine the abuse that would be heaped on Joan by her schoolfriends. And then, there are your constituents to think about. Having a husband with AIDS could never be considered a good career move. I suspect this thought was uppermost in the mind of the perpetrator of this evil. All I ask is that you take care of Joan. I'd hate to see her end up as collateral damage.

Do not think too unkindly of me in death. I tried (and failed) to be a decent husband and a good father. In as much as I was capable of loving anybody, you and Joan were the only ones who ever really mattered. I thank you both for the love you showed me. You deserved better of me.

In sorrow and despair.

Bill.

The words made her head reel and rage. The rage was partially directed inwards, an acknowledgement that much of the current difficulties stemmed from a bad decision she'd made a decade earlier. Notwithstanding her own culpability, she apportioned the greater blame to Bill. His actions were anathema to her. How could a man of his undoubted intellect have been so bloody stupid? Firstly, to fall for the lure of a young woman's yawning thighs and secondly, when things got awkward, to opt for the coward's way out.

How much more punishment could she take? Like an incoming tide, one crisis overlapped another, grinding her down, ripping her asunder. She needed no mirror to see how the skin on her face had become pinched and worn. Yet, from some hidden reserve, her indefatigable spirit clawed its way to the surface, refusing to allow her to wilt beneath the pressure.

It would be some days before the authorities in Brussels released Bill's body. With no suicide note, the forensic team had to satisfy themselves that foul play was not a factor. The letter she'd received would have satisfied them on that score but she had no intention of revealing its existence. Better that they entertain doubts in regard to his death than be acquainted with the sordid truth.

Brussels would eventually give up the body, pack it in the cargo hold of a plane and dispatch it home. She was dreading that part; as the grieving widow she would be obliged to acknowledge the sanctimonious clap-trap of his colleagues. All the old clichés would be trotted out — the dedicated family man, the loyal husband, the caring father, the hard worker, and so it would go. The rituals of death would be adhered to, the whole gamut of emotions laid bare for the world to see. And then there was the media, the accursed media. Hardest to take would be their voyeuristic attention and feigned sympathies. Like ravenous rats, they would look on from the periphery, seeing all, ready to tear the cadaver to shreds at the slightest hint of impropriety, ready to devour any morsel of scandalous tittle-tattle on offer.

Chief Superintendent Smith had assured her that details of Bill's suicide would be withheld from the media. It was Smith who had informed her that no suicide note had been found, a factor that allowed the authorities to record the death as misadventure or some such phrase. That suited her. Should the sordid truth leak out, she could kiss her political career goodbye. With only one income from now on, she needed her job more than ever. She still had a daughter to feed and dress, to educate and send to university.

Joan still hadn't been told about her father's death. She'd stayed with one of her schoolfriends overnight. Niamh would have to break the news to her as soon as she got home. How do you tell a 9-year-old girl that her father is dead? Bound to be initial hysteria, and afterwards, the big questions: *how* did Daddy die? What answers would she offer? The truth? Some fanciful tale? One way or another Joan was about to come face to face with the most shattering news yet to confront her.

Another more long-term concern played on her mind: the question of Joan's safety. She knew better than to dismiss the threat that had been made: Bill's death had taught her that much. The options on offer were limited. If she talked to Chief Superintendent Smith she'd have to admit she'd received a suicide letter. That would pose a major problem. But she had no intention of allowing Smith to know that Bill had had an affair, let alone the fact that he had been infected with the AIDS virus. Oh sure, Smith would promise to keep details of the letter under wraps but she knew better than to place any store in such assurances. Within weeks, maybe days, some official or filing clerk with thoughts of monetary reward in mind would leak the information to the press.

There was another reason for not telling Smith. If he knew that Bill Quinn was infected with AIDS, he would be obliged to contact the powers-that-be in Brussels. How would they react? Send the body home in a lead-lined reinforced box? Write the words — *Danger, Infectious*, or some such warning? Have it accompanied by men wearing space suits? The press would love that. Jesus, they'd eat it up. Well, it wasn't going to happen because she would keep the letter under wraps and her mouth shut.

Before news of Bill's suicide reached her she had read about Whelehan's shooting. The two events, overlapping as they did, represented the latest catastrophe in what was turning out to be the roller-coaster ride from Hell. Whatever sympathy she might have for her husband, she could not find it in her heart to dredge up any feelings of pity for Whelehan. Did that make her the hard-arse bitch so often depicted in the press? Yes, it probably did, but it didn't bother her any more. However, the fact that an attempt had been made on Whelehan's life underscored her own vulnerability and that of Joan. The coming days, she suspected, would be the most difficult of her life.

31

Emma was rapidly going out of her mind. At least that was how she felt. Mounting chaos crowded her from all angles. Like a juggler with multiple objects in simultaneous motion, the prospect of a crash seemed inevitable. Not knowing what had become of Vinny had kept her awake during the night. This morning she felt tired and irritable. Yet a growing number of demands were being made on her. She needed to prioritize.

It had been a mistake to invite Grace to stay in the apartment; she had enough on her plate without the added complication of playing host to the psychiatrist. The *Post* needed a follow-up story on Brian Whelehan's shooting and Crosby wanted her in his office within the hour for a briefing. He knew about Vinny's disappearance, had made sympathetic noises, but felt strongly that she'd be better off surrounding herself with work. The best she could do, she informed him, was to make it to the office around midday. Crosby was far from satisfied but for once decided not to push the issue.

She was still attempting to prioritize

matters in her head when the doorbell chimed. Probably Grace McCormack, she thought. She glanced at her watch. Bit early for the psychiatrist. Could be Connolly. Another thought: what if it's Vinny? She hurried to the door, opened it expectantly. Wrong on all counts. The caller was the last person in the world she expected to see. For a moment she stood staring at the young woman, remembering her face from the images taken from the London video.

'Helena Andrews,' she said, 'I *am* right in thinking you're Helena Andrews?'

'Hello, Emma,' the woman said with a smile, 'You've been looking for me I believe? May I come in?'

★ ★ ★

Detective Sergeant Steve Keenahan looked at the blank telltale spaces where paintings had once hung. Even at first glance, it was obvious he was dealing with a major art theft. The local postman, John Lucey, had raised the alarm when he'd seen a removals van drive away from the Sinnott house. Lucey, a well-known character in the Cobh area, knew just about everything about everyone on his round. He knew for instance that Jarleth and Norma Sinnott were on holiday and had cancelled their post for three weeks. So, it struck him as odd that there should be activity in the Sinnott home.

Keenahan was in the process of inspecting the damage when Finn Lynch, the local sergeant, approached.

'Sinnott's boat is missing,' Lynch said. 'Two lads on the quays saw strangers board the boat 'round lunchtime yesterday. They were surprised to see the boat being used without Jarleth onboard.'

This revelation prompted Keenahan to recall the recent conversation he'd had with Jim Connolly. The Dublin detective had asked him to run a check on the 'man overboard' incident but he'd been too busy to follow it up and besides he hadn't seen any connection. Wrong assumption. He needed to rectify matters pronto.

★ ★ ★

Joan Quinn hopped off the bus that stopped at the end of her street and began to walk the half-mile to her house. She'd spent the night with her friend Carmel and had really enjoyed the novelty of sleeping away from home. They'd watched videos, stuffed their faces with junk and sat up talking till way past midnight. She had no school today and intended to laze around, text her friends, maybe read the new *Harry Potter*, watch the box, listen to her latest pop music downloads.

Halfway between the bus stop and her home a car pulled in towards the footpath; a woman rolled the driver's window down and waved. 'Excuse me,' the woman said, 'could you tell me which house Niamh O'Flynn lives in?'

'Yeah, sure, it's just up ahead,' Joan replied. 'That's where I'm going; Niamh O'Flynn's my mum.'

'Are you serious? What a wonderful coincidence; you'd better hop in and take me there.'

Joan hesitated, looking at the woman, not sure what to do.

'It's all right,' the driver said with a reassuring smile. 'Your mum and I are old friends, we go back a long way. We're both in politics . . . best friends.'

'Well, OK, then. It's only a tiny bit along the road.'

★ ★ ★

Vinny Bailey sat talking to Ted Barry in Ted's compact sitting room. The fisherman's house, overlooking Cuskinny Bay on Cobh's southern coastline, had been home to Vinny for as long as he could remember — which in his case was less than forty-eight hours. In that time Ted and his partner Phyllis were the only people he had got to know. The ex-navy man had rescued him from a watery grave and called an ambulance. In Cork's Regional Hospital Vinny was held for three hours in A&E before being consigned to a trolley in the corridor. Ted stayed in the hospital during this period and managed to persuade the doctor in charge to allow him to take Vinny home to his house. It was there that Ted and Phyllis had fed, clothed and pampered him for the past two days.

But Vinny Bailey could not give his rescuer his name because he had no idea who he was. Nor could he remember anything that had happened before he'd been fished out of the water. Ted and Phyllis had tried to stimulate his memory by suggesting all sorts of scenarios. Nothing helped. They were certain he did not hail from the Cork area because of his accent. Definitely Dublin, they decided. They could tell from the softness of his hands that he was no seafarer. Indeed, his general physique let them know that their mystery man didn't engage in manual labour. Equally, his pale skin told them that he didn't work outdoors. Vinny listened to all this speculation but nothing struck a chord.

In the short time that he'd spent with Ted and Phyllis a doctor had come twice to examine him. The bump on the back of the head had been responsible for the amnesia but apart from that he appeared to be in reasonably good shape. He listened as Ted talked about his life in the navy and his love of diving and what it was like to live in Cobh. Phyllis, a teacher, had gone to her school and wouldn't be back till late afternoon. Ted was in the act of opening two cans of beer and handing one to Vinny when they had a visitor.

'I'm Detective Sergeant Keenahan,' a big burly man in his fifties said, squeezing Vinny's hand with a grip of steel. 'I've had enquiries from my colleagues in Dublin about a missing person. I have reason to believe you're the boy-o they're looking for.'

'What's my name?' Vinny asked.

'Your name is Vinny Bailey,' Keenahan said, expecting a big reaction.

Vinny shook his head. 'Means nothing,' he said, sharing the detective's disappointment. 'What am I doing in Cobh?'

'Looks like you came down here to buy paintings. We think you went to a house in Carrignafoy to look at a collection owned by Jarleth Sinnott. Only thing wrong with that is this: the Sinnotts are away on holiday and the house is meant to be locked up. We think

271

someone pretending to be Jarleth Sinnott met you there. And then for some unknown reason you were taken down to the quay and taken aboard Sinnott's boat before being dropped in the drink. Hadn't been for Ted here you'd be a goner. And while you were being deposited in the sea, Sinnott's house was stripped of all its paintings.' Keenahan halted his conversation and stared at Vinny. 'Any of this ring a bell?'

Somewhere, deep, deep, in the recesses of Vinny's mind the faintest of images, like a snow scene viewed through gossamer, struggled for definition. 'What you're telling me sounds like it could be right,' he told Keenahan, 'but I can't seem to clear my mind.'

'Oh, 'tis true right enough, boy,' the detective sergeant said, 'and now if you don't mind I'm going to take your picture and get it up to Dublin, let them see you're alive and well and guzzling Ted Barry's beer.'

Vinny smiled, something he hadn't done for a while. He watched bemused as Keenahan produced a mobile phone with built in camera and aimed it at him.

'This picture is already on its way to the computer up in Dublin. They'll show it to your missus for verification. If she says you're her man, we'll make arrangements to get you back to her . . . that's assuming the good

272

woman wants you back. But before we send you packin' I'll need to bring you down to the station to show you a few mug shots of the likely suspects on the art theft, see if we can't jog that memory of yours.'

'That's fine by me,' Vinny said.

Keenahan turned to Ted and winked. 'First things first though, I wouldn't say no to one of them cans of beer.'

32

'Weren't expecting me I dare say,' Helena said, taking a seat in the lounge.

'No, I wasn't,' Emma agreed, attempted to hide her confusion, 'As a matter of fact I was expecting a mutual friend of ours.' Emma sat uneasily across from Helena, striving to regain control of the situation but fearing she'd somehow lost the plot. The person she suspected of being behind all the unexplained deaths and disappearances was now ensconced in her lounge, sitting comfortably in one of her chairs. *What the hell's going on?* Helena Andrews didn't look like she had an evil bone in her body. She was beautiful in an understated sort of way with little or no make-up and wearing simple, well-cut clothes that accentuated her super-model figure. Admittedly, she did appear a little older than early twenties and she had a world-weary look in her eyes. Her words, when she spoke, were carefully articulated, the voice of a radio newscaster or continuity announcer.

'Ah yes, Emma, you were expecting Grace McCormick?'

'That's right but . . . but how did you know?'

'How I know is of no consequence,' Helena said. 'But I *can* tell you this: she won't show.'

'What have you done to her? And Vinny? What have you done to him?'

Helena Andrews flashed a coy, cheerless smile. 'What have I done to them? Hmmm, good question. Let's see now, Grace first: I think it's a safe bet she won't be calling here for quite a while.'

Emma let that go, asked, 'What have you done with Vinny?'

'My, my, you really are a slave to your trade. Always questions. I'll answer you presently; first we need to talk.'

'We'll do nothing till I find out what you've done with Vinny.'

'Shan't tell you anything till you listen,' Helena said, an edge creeping into her voice. 'When you've heard what I have to say, then perhaps we'll talk about Vinny.'

'No,' Emma said defiantly, moving to the telephone. 'This nonsense has gone far enough; I'm contacting the police.' Emma lifted the phone and was about to dial when she heard the doorbell ring. Relief coursed through her. Could be Grace McCormick, she thought; better still it could be Connolly. She replaced the phone, moved swiftly to the door and pulled it open. A young man stood there.

275

'May I come in?' he said, looking beyond Emma.

Emma sensed Helena approaching from behind.

'Ah, the professor,' Helena said cheerfully. 'Do come in, Prof, your timing is, as ever, impeccable.'

Emma held up her hands to protest. She'd never seen the man before. Helena called him a professor but he didn't look much like a professor to Emma. To her, he looked more like one of those cheesy male models who appear in soft drinks and car commercials.

'Wooah! Hold it!' she demanded, standing firm in front of him. 'I didn't say you could come in. I want — '

The man ignored her protestations, flashed his bright white teeth in what approximated for a smile and deftly side-stepped her. His swiftness caught her unawares. Feeling incensed, she grabbed his shoulder and attempted to pull him around. His reflexes were instantaneous. He took hold of her hand and forcefully jerked her to one side, making her wince in pain and stumble off balance. As she attempted to regain her footing she noticed that the man now held a gun in his hand.

* * *

Mary-Jo Graham knew she was taking a risk. She sat at Emma Boylan's computer, inserted Emma's password and gained access to the hard disc. Searching files and checking dates for several minutes rewarded her with the item she was looking for. A black and white photograph filled the screen. Two days earlier Mary-Jo had seen Emma scan the same picture and drag it on to the screen before sending it to someone via e-mail. Looking at the image on the monitor now, she could see a striking resemblance to the person she'd photographed entering Whelehan's house.

She checked Emma's items sent box and found the relevant message: *Can you confirm that this is Helena Andrews?* It was sent to Dr Grace McCormick's e-mail address. She scrolled through Emma's in box to see if the recipient had replied. Yes, there it was: *Can confirm image is Helena Andrews. Will phone u to discuss.*

★   ★   ★

Joan Quinn opened her eyes, yawned and felt a shiver run through her. Momentarily, she thought she might be emerging from a bad dream. With something of a jolt, she realized she was lying on a carpet-tiled floor, still wearing her day clothes. Startled now, the

9-year-old looked around trying to remember how she'd got here.

She scrambled to her feet but felt a dizziness overtake her. Stretching her arms like a tightrope walker, she attempted to steady herself. After a few seconds, the swirling motion slowed down. She let her arms fall to her sides and looked around with wide-eyed puzzlement. She was in a large room that had been decorated to look like a cinema. A white screen with red velvet curtains covered one of the walls and five rows of plush seats faced the screen. She'd been lying in the space between the front row of seats and the screen. Her immediate concern was to find a way out of the room. She could see an exit sign above a curtained door to the left of the screen. She pulled back the curtain and saw a steel door locked with iron bolts and a padlock.

Anxiously, she climbed the steps by the rows of seats and headed for the top end of the room looking for another way out. A small box-like booth jutted out from the back wall. It had a row of slim windows and a narrow door to one side. She stood on tiptoe and pressed her face against one of the windows. It was darkish inside but she recognized a cinema projector and some video equipment. Joan pushed on the door but, like the exit door, it was locked.

Panic set in. 'Help,' she shouted. 'Someone let me out of here.' The sound of her own voice echoing around the small auditorium made her feel more abandoned than ever. She started to cry, her thoughts reverting back to the circumstances that had led to her present predicament. She remembered the car and the person hunkering down low in the space where the back seat should have been. She'd heard a movement behind her and had been about to turn around when an arm clamped around her throat. A hand had pressed a syringe to one side of her neck. She'd screamed and struggled for a few moments before blanking out. She could remember nothing more until waking up on the carpet-tiled floor. She had no idea who'd taken her here or how long she'd been out for.

She wiped her tears and told herself to be brave. Her mother would be looking for her, wondering why she hadn't arrived home. The police would be informed and maybe her picture would be flashed on the television. That would be cool. Once when she was seven her picture had been shown on TV3. The weatherman had wished her a happy birthday. All her friends had seen it. Maybe now they would show her picture again.

She thought about the day-trip she'd taken to the government buildings and the scruffy, cider head who'd grabbed her. Thinking about that incident, it struck her as odd that she hadn't felt half as afraid then as she did now. She banged, kicked and pounded on the door, begging for help and screaming at the top of her lungs. There was no response. It was useless. In spite of her best efforts to be brave, she began to cry again.

33

Helena Andrews yanked the telephone connection free from its socket. 'There now,' she said, as though imparting helpful information, 'no need for that.'

'What *is* this?' Emma demanded, aware that the man called Prof continued to hold a gun on her.

'Being careful,' Helena replied, taking Emma's mobile from the table and dumping it into a flower vase. Prof had positioned himself on a couch opposite Emma, his legs crossed casually at the knees, the pistol, a Beretta 9mm, held steadily in his right hand.

'You look different,' Helena told Emma, as she moved to sit next to the gunman. 'I've had this weird picture of you in my head ever since the night you killed Susan Furlong. You *do* remember my mother?'

'Yes of course I remember, but *I* did *not* kill her; I tried my level best to save your mother. I was the person who — '

Helena interrupted. 'You killed her as surely as if you'd pulled the trigger. If anything, I hold you more responsible than the others.'

'How can you say that? I did more than anybody to save — '

'If you interrupt me again I'll ask Prof to hurt you. He likes to hurt people so don't upset him. He's been institutionalized most of his life, poor darling; had all the best psychiatrists in the land try to discover why he likes hurting people. Confounded the lot of them. So, be advised Emma, don't fuck with him . . . or me. You want to know what this is about then shut your face and listen. I thought you'd want to hear my side of the story before Prof does his thing.'

'And Vinny? What have you done with him?'

'No questions. Just listen, all will be revealed.'

'I'm listening.'

'Let's keep it that way. Like I was saying, in many ways you're the most reprehensible of my mother's killers. You wrote articles highlighting the injustice of a system that could compulsorily detain a person in a mental hospital without the right of appeal. You knew the score, you saw . . . you understood the injustice, but you did sweet f.a. to rattle the right cages. You wrote moralistic-sounding articles, big fucking deal; you won journalistic kudos, but then you sat on your arse, forgot about the victims and moved on to the next story, right?'

'No, you're wrong! I brought the plight of Susan Furlong to the attention of the state. I banged on the right cages — as you call them — but nobody wanted to hear. I'm not a legislator, wasn't a whole lot I could do. I'm an investigative journalist; part of my job is to focus attention on wrongdoings, corruption and the like. Up to others to put matters right.'

'Like Pontius fucking Pilate, you washed your hands of all responsibility. And yet, when you should've kept your nose out of it, you interfered.'

'Sorry, I don't follow. What are you getting at?'

'You prevented Susan Furlong from killing John Treanor, the person I thought was my uncle, the slime ball who turned out to be my grandfather. If you'd let her kill him that would've been the end of the matter. Susan's actions would've been seen as justifiable homicide. She wouldn't have faced trial. She'd have received proper psychiatric care. But just as my mother was about to put a bullet in his head, you stopped her. Yet, when she put the gun in her own mouth, you stood there, let it happen.'

'That's not true. I — '

'Like fuck it isn't. I know, I was there for Christ's sake.'

'Yes, but — '

'Shoot her knee,' Helena said, turning to Prof.

'No, no,' Emma shouted as the shot rang out. She felt the sting to one side of her knee. Blood poured down her leg. She screamed involuntarily. She tried to jump up from the seat but had barely moved when Prof leaped towards her and propelled her back. Helena moved to stand in front of her, a look of rage on her face.

'I told you to shut your gob,' she said, hitting Emma across face with the full force of her open hand.

Prof aimed the pistol once more at the injured knee. 'Only grazed her,' he said to Helena, his voice apologetic. 'Want me to trash it?'

'No, not yet, I do believe we've got her undivided attention.' Helena patted Prof on the thigh, gave him a smile before turning her attention back to Emma. 'You failed Susan Furlong, that was bad enough, but what sort of woman turns her back on a child in peril?'

Emma wanted to ask what she meant but one look at the madness in Prof's eyes persuaded her to say nothing. Helena and Prof looked at her expectantly as though wanting an excuse to harm her further.

'You and Vinny Bailey came to my house

after my mother's death,' Helena said, after a short, tension-filled pause. 'I'd just turned twelve at the time and was naïve enough to think you'd come to rescue me from my adoptive father's sexual abuse. I used my eyes to communicate my desperation but you chose to ignore my plea. All it took was a little discouragement from my father for you to walk away. I was left to the mercies of a child rapist. You never had my interest at heart; you just wanted to tell your readers what a wonderful caring individual you were. Truth is, when you and Vinny walked away, you condemned me to a fate worse than death. I blame you for what — '

'You're wrong,' Emma cut in, unable to listen to any more. 'You're twisting every-thing, putting constructions on things that simply aren't true. I never — '

'Don't you dare contradict me. I've lived with the truth for all these years and I've had enough, you hear, enough. I've decided to even things up. It's time people paid for what was done to Susan Furlong . . . and me.'

Prof nodded and looked to Helena. 'You want me to inflict a little pain in her other knee?'

'No, I want you to put the pistol in her mouth. I want her to know what Susan Furlong's last moments felt like.'

Prof grabbed Emma by her hair and jerked her head backwards. 'Open,' he ordered.

Emma started to protest but found her mouth blocked by the barrel of the Beretta. She felt the coarse metallic weapon push all the way to her throat. A gurgling, choking sound accompanied her effort to avoid retching. But even as death beckoned she was aware of the man's after-shave and thought it smelled like the subtle fragrance her father used. Why this thought should occur to her at such a critical time puzzled her. Had it something to do with the fact that she could leave this world without saying goodbye to her father and mother? And what of Vinny? What of Connolly? She thought of them as her eyes darted from Helena to the man holding the gun in her mouth. A tremor of fear shot through her body. The certainty that she was about to die overwhelmed her.

34

Connolly couldn't get through to Emma Boylan; no response from either landline or mobile. He was anxious to let her know the good news: Vinny was alive and well. Admittedly, there was a down side; he was suffering from loss of memory but that represented a minor problem compared to the darker fears they'd harboured earlier. Detective Sergeant Keenahan was in the process of driving Vinny back to Dublin.

Amid this activity, Connolly heard from his colleagues in *subversive* — the unit charged with monitoring paramilitary activities. They had traced Bernadette Maxwell's whereabouts to an IRA safe house in Monaghan. High-ranking officers of that illegal organization had been seen to visit her in recent days. A discreet watch was being maintained and he would be kept abreast of developments.

His concern right now lay with Emma's welfare. The absence of a response from her phones prompted him to contact the *Post* on the off-chance that she might be at her desk. Word from that quarter was no better; she hadn't come in yet. He was all set to go to

Emma's apartment when a call came through from Chief Superintendent Smith. Niamh O'Flynn, he was told, had reported her daughter missing. 'According to O'Flynn,' Smith said, 'her 9-year-old stayed overnight with a friend and had failed to show up this morning.'

'She's checked with the people the child was staying with, I presume?' Connolly asked.

'Yes, first thing she did. Joan — that's her daughter's name — had left for the bus an hour earlier. The journey between the two houses shouldn't take longer than half an hour. O'Flynn drove to the set-down stop but there was no sign of the girl. She waited for an hour, then returned to the house and called me. Giving what's gone before, I want you to drop whatever you're on and give this top priority.'

Connolly briefed McFadden and Dorsett and was about to try once more to contact Emma when a call came through from the front desk. Mary-Jo Graham wished to speak to him. 'I'm too busy to talk to anybody,' he told the receptionist. A second message followed immediately — Ms Graham insists on meeting you. She says it concerns Emma Boylan.

'Send her up,' he said.

She was young; she was pretty, Connolly

noticed first, but the look of concern in her eyes was unmistakable. 'I'm told your visit concerns Emma Boylan?' he said.

'Yes,' she replied. 'I'm worried about her.'

'Why so?'

'Well, I work alongside Emma. I saw the picture you gave her to scan, the picture lifted from the London CCTV.'

Connolly frowned. He didn't believe Emma would allow others to see the image but he let it pass. 'What about it?' he asked.

'The woman in the picture, her name's Helena Andrews, right?'

'Yes,' he replied, his annoyance growing. 'Where are we going with this?'

'I've seen Helena Andrews. I've managed to photograph her.'

'Where have you seen her?'

'Spotted her going into Dr Whelehan's house after Emma failed to gain entrance. And half an hour ago I watched her enter Emma's apartment.'

'How did you see all this?' Connolly said, with undisguised scepticism. 'Why would you be watching Emma's apartment?'

'Does it matter *why*? The point is, I think she's in trouble. After Helena Andrews went into the apartment, a man called at the door. I'd gained access to the building and was walking back and forth on the third-floor landing, pretending to be heading for the next floor. I saw the man force his way past Emma. I couldn't hang around so I tried to contact her on the mobile but couldn't get through; same story with the landline. I got a bad feeling that something's wrong and hurried straight to you.'

'If what you're saying is true, I'd better get over there straight away.'

'It *is* true . . . why would I lie?'

'Why indeed? But if this is some sort of game, you're in deep shit.'

'Look, I'm telling you the truth. I'll go with you if you don't believe me.'

'Won't be necessary,' Connolly said, her offer reassuring him. 'I'll check it out myself.'

★ ★ ★

Keenahan had made the journey from Cork to Dublin in just over three hours, stopping just once to take an unabashed nature call against a roadside gatepost. Driving in an unmarked police car, paying scant attention to lane discipline or speed limits, he'd chatted amicably to Vinny throughout the journey. Vinny, more reticent, added little to the conversation, content to listen to Keenahan's loquacious take on life. As matters stood, his life's experiences could be written on the back of a cigarette pack.

'I love coming to Dublin,' Keenahan was saying, pointing to a lock-gate on the Grand Canal, 'best city in the world.' They were now caught up in the traffic crawling along Grand Parade, moving in the direction of Leeson Street junction. 'In spite of the drugs and binge drinking and god-awful traffic, it's still a wonderful spot. No problem pullin' young ones in this town, I tell you, they're horny as hell . . . laugh at your best, they would, then beg for more.' Keenahan looked at Vinny for reaction, got none. 'Been to the night clubs here?' he asked.

'I wouldn't know,' Vinny replied, 'could have been for all I know. Would I enjoy it, d'you think?'

'Well, if you ignore rip-off prices, crap plonk, jungle music and the whiff of body odour, you'd have a ball . . . if you like getting your rocks off, that is.'

'Yeah, right,' Vinny said with indifference.

Keenahan had moved on to Mespil Road when he pointed to a sculpture by the canal side. A life-size bronze figure sat on a bronze bench. 'Isn't that y'ur man, the poet, what's his name . . . ?'

'Kavanagh,' Vinny said. 'That's Patrick Kavanagh, a cantankerous genius if ever there was one. A thorn in the side of the literati back in the swinging sixties. Wrote *The Great Hunger* and *Raglan Road*. Fair man to knock back a pint of the black stuff.'

'Jesus!' Keenahan exclaimed, pulling the car to the side of the road. 'How'd you remember that, Vinny? You've just remembered something.'

Vinny's eyes misted over. 'Hey, you're right, I know who I am. I'm getting flashes from my past. There's a whole jumble of stuff pouring into my head. I don't believe it, it's great, a miracle, a bloody miracle.'

'I don't know how it happened,' Keenahan said, clapping Vinny on the shoulder, 'but I'm fecking delighted because now maybe you can direct me to where you live.'

'We're almost there,' Vinny said, looking around excitedly, 'continue on through the next junction and swing left into Percy Place. You'll see the building from there.'

Within a matter of minutes, Vinny, accompanied by Keenahan made his way into the apartment block. They were waiting for the lift doors to open when Detective Inspector Connolly came through the front entrance and hurried towards them. Keenahan and Connolly greeted each other briefly. Vinny explained to Connolly that his memory had returned but that he needed to be appraised of the latest developments.

'I'll fill you in on all that's happened presently,' Connolly promised, 'but first, we might have a problem on our hands.'

'What do you mean?' Vinny asked.

Connolly told him what he had heard from Mary-Jo Graham.

'You think Emma could be in trouble?' Vinny asked.

'If what I've been told is right, we've got to be careful.'

'Well, let's get in there,' Vinny said, 'no point hanging about.'

'Might not be such a good idea for all of us to rush in together,' Connolly cautioned, 'we've got to think about this.'

Vinny dug his hands into the pockets of his borrowed trousers. 'Damn it, I don't have keys. My keys and my clothes and car are missing, lost in Cork.'

'Is there another way into the apartment?' Connolly asked.

'Well, there's the fire-escape. We could get in that way but we'd have to get into the apartment directly above or below to gain access.'

'Worth a try,' Connolly said. 'Let's sort out a plan of action fast.'

35

With the barrel of Prof's 9mm pistol pushed awkwardly into her mouth, Emma had little choice but to listen to Helena Andrews's diatribe. Prof remained mute throughout, an enigmatic expression on his face. What was it Emma saw in his eyes? Impatience to use the gun? A desire to hurt her? Hard to say. One thing was certain, staying alive depended on the pressure his finger exerted on the trigger.

And yet, in spite of this racket, Emma sensed another presence in the apartment. Apart from Helena and Prof, she felt sure someone else had entered her home. Living in the same space for nine years had given her an acute sense of the place. The apartment had its own unique traits, sounds and smells familiar as a second skin. Right now her antenna registered a disturbance in the utility room, an area adjacent to the kitchen, tucked away at the back of her apartment and next to a balcony overlooking the canal.

For direct access to that particular area, one had to enter from the front door and move through the hallway that led to the kitchen area. Were someone to use that approach they would be in full view of Emma as well as Helena and Prof. There was a second more circuitous route. It was possible to access the utility room via the fire-escape, but to do so would necessitate entering the floor above or below her apartment. Emma's hopes were raised; could it be that someone was using that route to get to her? Was her imagination playing tricks? No, surely not; there *was* movement in the vertical strips of the blind that served as a screen between kitchen and utility room. Doubts assailed her: had she left a window open? No, she felt reasonably sure she hadn't. She'd always ensured that the back windows and doors were locked.

Helena had by now moved on to a vitriolic onslaught on John Treanor, her outpouring rising several octaves to earpiercing levels. There was little new in what she had to say. Equally, her verbal onslaught on Brian Whelehan yielded nothing that Emma hadn't already known. Helena pronounced both men guilty and had moved on to Niamh O'Flynn when she stopped in mid-flight. 'What was that?' she asked.

'What was what?' Prof asked.

'Thought I heard something at the door.'

'I don't hear a thing.'

Helena pressed an index finger to her lips,

'Shush,' she said, 'listen.'

Silence followed. Emma strained to hear if there was a noise. Ten seconds passed before she heard it: a scraping noise on the marble floor outside her front-door landing. Sounded like a foot grinding the butt of a cigarette. Emma's sense that someone was present in the utility room remained fixed in her mind but this sound was coming from the opposite side of the apartment. Why would anyone pause outside her front door to stamp out a butt?

Helena and Prof nodded to each other. 'We got company,' Helena said, her voice now reduced to a whisper.

'I hear it,' Prof acknowledged.

Helena faced Emma. 'Got a spy-hole in your door?' she asked.

Emma made a gurgling noise, indicating with her eyes that she couldn't speak while the gun remained in her mouth.

Helen turned to Prof. 'Remove the gun but keep it on her.'

Emma found it awkward to speak after her enforced silence. The oily metallic taste on her tongue remained suffocating. 'Yes, there's a spy-hole,' she managed to say.

'Give me the gun,' Helena said to Prof. 'See who's outside the door.'

Prof hesitated a moment before parting

with the weapon. He waited until it was trained on Emma before moving into the hallway and out of sight. Helena held the Beretta mere inches from Emma's forehead. 'Make the slightest sound,' she warned, 'and I won't hesitate to pull the trigger, understand?'

Emma nodded.

Helena turned, her eyes following the direction Prof had taken. 'Can you see anything?' she called out to him.

'Difficult to see through this thing,' Prof replied. 'Don't see anyone . . . can't see to the extreme left or right . . . could be someone there I suppose.'

While Prof spoke, a movement behind the blinds caught Emma's eye. Helena missed this activity, her attention being concentrated solely on the opposite side of the room. 'Open the door,' she called out to Prof, 'take a look outside.'

'Will do,' he called back.

Emma could hear Prof turn the lock and open the door. Silence followed, then shuffling sounds. Without visual contact it was hard to tell what was happening. She heard Prof wheeze. It sounded as though someone had clasped a hand over his mouth. A struggle appeared to be in progress, the landing echoing to the sound of scuffling footsteps. The activity ended with a loud gasp.

Helena inched away from Emma and moved into the hallway. 'Make a move,' she warned, 'and I'll shoot.' Her gun hand remained extended in Emma's direction. A movement in the kitchen area caught Emma's eye. She stifled a gasp of astonishment as Connolly eased his way through the blinds. She swallowed her breath, terrified in case she alerted Helena to his presence. Connolly looked at her and formed a shush shape with his lips. He pressed his back to the wall and slowly manoeuvred his way towards the hallway entrance. He could see the barrel tip of Helena's pistol pointing at Emma. The sound of Helena's voice halted his progress. 'Unless whoever's out there comes in here in the next few seconds I'll put a bullet in Emma's head.'

No response.

Connolly brushed away the trickle of sweat from his forehead. His plan was to disarm Helena but he couldn't see enough of the gun to do so in safety. Emma, understanding his strategy, knew that should anything go wrong she was in the line of fire.

'OK out there,' Helena yelled, 'I'm going to count to five. If whoever's out there doesn't come in with their hands up by then, I pull the trigger.'

After a short pause she began counting.

'One . . . two . . . three . . . four . . . '

Before Helena got to five, her arm protruded further into the room, her finger ready to depress the trigger. Connolly saw his chance and swung his hand in a downward arc, catching her wrist with a forceful blow. The gun remained in her hand; her finger pressed home on the trigger. Emma saw a flash and felt the vibration of the blast. She screamed. A bullet, deflected from its intended trajectory, ploughed into the carpet inches from her feet.

In a state of shock she saw Connolly wrestle Helena Andrews to the floor and kick the gun out of reach. Relief flowed through her as she watched a handcuffed Prof being led into the room. A big burly man with sparse ginger hair and a 'blood-pressure' complexion accompanied him. A policeman, Emma thought; even in civvies, you could always tell.

Connolly continued to grapple with Helena. He planted a knee in the small of her back and pinned her to the floor before securing handcuffs. Glancing sideways, he acknowledged the arrival of the ginger haired man and his prisoner. 'Nice work, Steve,' he said, 'your timing couldn't have been better.'

'Looks like we both done good,' the man said with a pronounced Cork accent. 'We'd best call in the cavalry, get some uniforms to take these jokers into custody.'

Connolly nodded his agreement as he lifted Helena Andrews bodily off the floor and stood her in front of him. She had a bloody nose and lip and looked dazed. Her jaws struggled to formulate words but all that emerged was a croaking sound in her throat. Connolly ignored her plight and turned to Emma. 'You all right, Emma? Christ, you're bleeding!'

'Yeah, bullet grazed my knee,' Emma said, trying to sound brave but still shaking with shock. 'Surface wound . . . nothing serious, could have been a whole lot worse.' She pointed to the burly man with Prof. 'Who's this?'

'Sorry Emma, didn't get a chance to introduce you to my friend Detective Steve Keenahan from the Cork division. Couldn't have got through your back kitchen without the distraction he caused out front.'

'Pleasure to meet you, Emma,' Keenahan said, nodding in her direction. 'I brought you a little present from Cork. You can come in now Vinny, everything's under control.'

'Emma!' Vinny cried as he entered the room. 'You all right?'

Emma, speechless for once, allowed him to bear hug her.

'You've been injured,' he said, releasing her from his grip, looking down at the blood on her leg. 'We need to get you to a doctor.'

'It can wait,' she said, taking a good look at him. 'What the hell happened? You had us all worried sick.'

'It's a long story. Some of it's still vague. Tell you about it later, OK?'

The sound of police sirens interrupted their conversation. Keenahan escorted Prof into the hallway in readiness to hand him over to the uniforms. Connolly shunted Helena towards the door. Passing Vinny and Emma, she stopped in her tracks. 'Don't either of you think you've escaped,' she snarled. 'You've just got a reprieve, that's all.'

Connolly pushed Helena ahead of him. 'Where you're going,' he said, 'you'll be in no position to do anything to anybody.'

'You think so, huh?' Helena snapped, 'Well you can think again. I'll get them all, you hear me. You think Niamh O'Flynn and her little brat are safe, huh? That what you think? Haaaaah, well, you're wrong. I'm the one pulling the strings, so fuck you, Mister high 'n' mighty Detective Inspector. Fuck you all.'

'You're wrong,' Vinny said, confronting Helena. 'You're not the one pulling the strings, you're just a pawn in this; you're being *used*.'

'Like fuck I am. I'm — '

'You're being manipulated,' Vinny insisted. 'You might not know it but you've been brainwashed into doing exactly what your mentor wants.'

Helena spat at him, landing her spittle between his eyes. She tried for a head-butt but Connolly managed to restrain her.

'What are you talking about?' Emma asked. 'What makes you think she's not behind all that's happened?'

'I've met the person who's running the show, the same person who tried to drown me in the sea at Cobh.'

'What?' Emma asked. 'Who tried to drown you? What are you on about?'

'I came face to face with the person who's organizing all of this . . . stood in a boat in Cork harbour, saw the person who's responsible for the subterfuge, deceit and death . . . the person who put our death notices in the papers and tried to frighten our parents. Before I was walloped over the head and thrown overboard I realized what had happened. I knew who the killer was.'

'Who, for God's sake, Vinny?' Emma asked almost screaming. 'Who are you talking about?'

'I'm talking about Grace McCormick; she's running the show.'

36

Central heating was cranked to full blast yet the house felt cold. Flurries of winter rain swept against the windows. Another miserable day in the upper-crust enclave of Castleknock. Grace McCormick thought about lighting the fire, glanced at the logs and coal sitting in the grate and decided against it. Too much smoke. Too much bother. Pacing the main reception room, she stopped momentarily and stood in front of the big picture window. She stared absent-mindedly at the grim architecture surrounding the house, neo Georgian two-storey glorified boxes that harked back to more grandiose times but displayed all the brashness of today's superficial values.

Yet, the bleak weather and the conformity of the housing did not dampen her spirits. What she felt was a mixture of excitement and apprehension. She caressed the rosary around her neck, her fingertips gently rolling the recent additions to the necklace: black beads that represented acts of completion. Soon she would add the final stones to the chain, tangible evidence that she had honoured her debt to Susan Furlong. She unhooked the chain's clasp and took the small crucifix in her hands. She pressed it reverentially to her lips and kissed the figurine of the crucified Christ, all the time mouthing an invocation . . . *pray for us sinners, now and at the hour of our death.* A contemplative expression settled on her face as she replaced the chain on her neck. She moved to the open fireplace, eased herself on to the couch and allowed her mind to wander back to events that had led to this moment.

The death of Susan Furlong had turned her world upside down. Until that life-altering crisis she had lived a lie. Of course, back then she hadn't known it was a lie. On the contrary, she had total belief in herself, confident and assured of her own worth and usefulness.

Earlier still, as a 17-year-old girl she'd taken her sacred vows. Married to Christ . . . a higher calling . . . at least that's what she'd believed then. Fifteen years later, after she'd qualified as a psychiatrist, she insisted on wearing sombre clothes and being addressed as Sister Dympna rather than Dr McCormick. She'd been confident in her vocation, secure in her beliefs. Working in the rarefied atmosphere of The Mother of Perpetual Succour Private Psychiatric Hospital, her eyes and her mind had been exposed to facets of life on the outside. Her association with one patient in particular had a profound effect. That patient's name was Susan Furlong. She'd seen Susan as a broken angel. As her therapist, she believed that she alone was equipped to put the pieces back together again. In doing so she came to love the patient. It was a love that blinded her to all the tenets of her profession. She'd convinced herself that it had nothing to do with carnal desire, believing then that the pleasures of the flesh held no attraction for her. The love of God was enough, a gift far more fulfilling than any worldly intimacies.

The sin of pride compounded by a remarkable display of imprudence, arrogance and self-deception corrupted the purity of her motives. Through Susan's dark journey into uncharted realms of madness, she looked after her in a way that, even then, she realized was less than professional. Susan's enemies had become her enemies. A sharing of deep hatreds evolved; a trust developed between them. For Grace, that trust equated to love.

Susan's first attempt at suicide marked a significant shift in their relationship. After cutting her wrists, Susan refused to respond to anyone. It was then that Grace appointed herself Susan's exclusive minder and round-the-clock therapist. She'd spent long hours talking to her unresponsive patient, marvelling at the beauty and serenity evident in the stillness of her repose. Each night she helped place Susan's emaciated body in bed. Before leaving she would tend to the dressings, wash her face and press her tangled red tresses into shape. She would then place a kiss on Susan's unresponsive lips and whisper her favourite prayer, '*Hail Mary, full of grace, the Lord is with thee. Blessed art thou amongst women and blessed is the fruit of thy womb . . .* '

Two months into this ritual, when she'd placed her kiss on Susan's lips, the patient's hand reached out and held her head. Grace felt a response in Susan's lips, saw her eyes open, knew that a new relationship had evolved.

And now, all these years later, she wiped a tear from her eye. Thinking about the time she'd spent with Susan Furlong brought mixed feelings. The happiest and saddest moments of her life had sprung from those times. They had become lovers. It had been a bittersweet relationship, for the most part sad, neurotic, and tragic but there had also been moments of sublime happiness, extraordinary beauty and passion that more than outweighed the bad aspects.

Back then, Susan Furlong had a foreboding that she might not be around to see her

306

daughter Helena mature to adulthood. On several occasions she'd asked Grace to care for Helena's welfare should anything untoward happen. Nothing mattered so much to Susan as her child. She'd been prepared to go to any lengths to reclaim Helena. And for a few hours, that dream of reunion had become a reality. Tragically, it had ended with Susan's self-inflicted death.

Grace had renounced her vows after that. A light had gone out in her life. Depression set in. She experienced the darkest hour of her life but from that darkness came salvation. For the first time in her life she felt touched, *really touched* by the greatest power in the universe. She felt herself elevated above the trappings of organized religion and at one with a higher deity. At first, when the voices spoke inside her head, she thought she was going mad. She had wanted to reject the whole idea that she could be a receptacle for spiritual communication. Only when the voices instructed her to avenge the wrongs meted out to Susan Furlong did she accept that she'd been selected as the Lord's instrument in a quest for justice. She became His most willing disciple.

Her first task had been to draw up a list of those who'd stood by and watched Susan destroy herself. None of them appeared to accept their culpability. None of them had the decency to attend Susan Furlong's burial. None of them considered it worthwhile to place a death notice in the national dailies.

Guided by this higher power, it had taken her ten years to pay the debt owed to Susan Furlong. Obeying the voices, she had systematically gone after Susan's detractors. For each individual she'd conceived a plan that dealt in kind with the injustice visited upon Susan.

She had worked hard to forge a relationship with Helena. Through patience and understanding she had eventually won the love and respect of the younger woman. As part of that arduous journey it had been necessary to submit Helena to a course of intensive psychoanalysis. These sessions had been a virtual trip to Hell and back for both of them. Old wounds had been opened, exposed, probed, inflamed and bled dry before being soothed once more and calmed into a limbo state of tranquillity. She had taken Helena on a guided tour of the various psychoses that had blighted Susan's life. It was a journey that Helena felt drawn towards. Insanity, she had discovered was like a drug, its pull insidious. It coaxed you in, then obscured the exit. Once inside you adjusted to the darkness to such an extent that after a while you didn't think about the dark anymore.

For Grace, the re-enactment of Susan Furlong's descent into madness brought about new insights into the persecution and injustices that had been inflicted on the doomed woman. Susan's demons took shape and became infectious. Like some contagious disease, the malaise that once drove Susan Furlong to destruction now infected her and infected Helena in turn. All the hatred and animosities found a new, dual berthing place.

Agreement had been reached in regard to the type of justice to be doled out to each of the targeted individuals. They were in accord on all the objectives except for one aspect: taking Caroline and Jim Andrews out of the picture created a measure of conflict. Helena balked at the idea, but eliminating the Andrews had been a prerequisite to everything Grace had planned. The overall operation would require a substantial input of cash. As heir to the Andrews's fortune, Helena held the solution to the problem in her hands.

It only required that Caroline and Jim Andrews die.

Grace decided to personally oversee this first phase. She used her own money to cover expenses. Her life savings had been swallowed up in the venture. The services of one of her ex-patients — a killer suffering from paranoid psychosis who'd been sent to her for evaluation after the courts accepted an insanity defence — had not come cheap. The man, Gerard Dean, was volatile, a virtual time bomb ready to explode at any moment. But she could count on his unswerving loyalty and he knew how to handle himself in a fight. He was also a pro when it came to using a gun.

After much persuasion, Helena provided the necessary background information for this first segment of the operation. She supplied a detailed layout of the Andrews's Spanish holiday home and the surrounding area. The operation that followed had been painstaking but the outcome well worth the effort. Helena believed that Grace McCormick had done the deed for her. From that point onwards, Helena's loyalty and subservience was total. Helena was now rich. The trust fund that the Andrews had opened for her on the day of her adoption matured on Helena's twenty-first birthday. On top of that, she was able to secure bank loans on the strength of the wealth that would transfer to her as soon as probate of the Andrews's will was granted.

The plan had gone like clockwork. Helena

followed instructions to the letter, never once letting her down. The use of ex-mental patients worked extremely well. Gerard Dean was upstairs resting in the master bedroom, his big ungainly body sprawled on top of the king-size bed. Having him with her was a calculated risk but she needed backup to take care of the business that lay ahead. If Dean saw anything of a threatening nature he would shoot first, ask questions later. It was this kind of protection that made her feel safe.

Grace waited impatiently for the phone to ring. She expected Helena to tell her Emma Boylan had been taken care of. That would only leave Niamh O'Flynn to be dealt with. Helena and Grace had agreed they should both witness the demise of the ex-minister.

Grace looked at her watch. It was time to bring Joan Quinn in from the cinema room. Keeping the 9-year-old separated from Gerard Dean had been a precautionary measure. One of Dean's earliest victims had been a young boy in Leeds. He'd killed the boy for no other reason than to watch him react to pain. Grace could not afford to take any chances with Joan, at least not at this stage. The child was an integral part of the plan to entice her mother to the house. Isolating Joan in the same room where

Helena had once suffered at the hands of her adoptive father would, she hoped, instil a degree of fright in the child. Leaving Joan there on her own would ensure that when she spoke to her mother on the telephone the child's panic would be evident.

She looked at the telephone again and wondered why it remained silent.

37

Connolly swivelled Helena around to face him. 'I want answers,' he demanded. 'Where's Grace McCormick? Has she got Niamh O'Flynn's child with her?'

An insolent smirk flitted across Helena's face. 'Even if I knew, why should I tell you?'

'Things might go easier for you if you co-operate . . . even at this late stage.'

'What? I betray my friend? I get more favourable treatment? That it? I'll get the same justice my mother got?'

Connolly shrugged his shoulders. 'What happened to Susan Furlong had nothing to do with me. What can I say . . . shit happens; all I can do now is ensure it doesn't happen again. You help us, I'll see you get a fair hearing.'

'You expect me to believe that?'

'Believe what you like: it's your call.'

Helena's eyes challenged Connolly. 'No,' she said bitterly, 'I could never trust you lot.'

'Take her away,' Connolly ordered, handing her to the two officers. Emma and Vinny, who'd been listening to the exchange, followed Connolly into the hallway. Detective

made to move her forward, she angrily jerked her handcuffed hands and stood her ground. 'OK,' she said, 'I'll take you to her but I want you to remove the cuffs first.'

'No can do,' Connolly said.

'In that case we don't have a deal,' Helena shot back.

'Tell you what, we'll remove the cuffs when you get in front of Grace McCormick. That's the best I can do.'

Helena hesitated a second, then said, 'Yeah, all right then.'

'Good, now tell us where we'll find her?'

'You must be joking. I tell you where she is and you whip me off to the clink. You can stuff that! Here's how we play it: put me in the car . . . I'll lead you there.'

'Right,' Connolly said impatiently, 'let's move it then.'

★   ★   ★

Niamh O'Flynn headed for the address she'd been given. Just when she'd thought nothing worse could happen Joan had been kidnapped. The caller had warned, 'You won't see your daughter alive again if you contact the authorities.' Hearing Joan's terrified voice on the phone had left her in no doubt as to the action she must take.

315

Getting to the location had taken less than half an hour. She was familiar with this part of the city, had friends there. The Georgian Village, Castleknock, one of Dublin's more desirable addresses was for the most part populated by people who had 'made it' in what passed for posh society in Dublin. She drove slowly along Willow's Drive until she came to number 8. Like the surrounding houses, the front lawn had that groomed, cultivated look with neat borders and manicured shrubbery that somehow managed to look good even in winter. She pulled in behind a Volvo that was parked in the driveway, got out of her car and headed for the front door.

★　★　★

Emma and Vinny followed the squad car as it sped away from their apartment block. Vinny had wanted to drive but Emma was having none of it. Behind the wheel, she stuck doggedly to the squad car as it headed along St Stephen's Green South, past the bottom of Harcourt Street and on by the corporation flats in Cuffe Street. Reaching for the gear stick, she noticed the dried, caked blood on her knee where the bullet had grazed her earlier. The adrenaline pumping through her body refused to allow her to dwell on the wound.

Vinny insisted on bringing her up to speed with all that had happened on his Cork adventure. His memory had been fully restored, his vocal output back to full fluency. Missing out on the Reid paintings had, it appeared, upset him more than the fact that he'd almost ended up in a watery grave. His moan about the paintings was getting to Emma, but she made sympathetic noises while keeping her mind focused on the Ford ahead.

'Frig,' she hissed, caught out when the squad car jumped lanes without warning, forcing her to bully her way on to the same lane in response. The negotiation was accompanied by a blaring of horns from irritated motorists. Her rear-view mirror reflected a car flashing its main beams while the driver gave her the universal one-fingered gesture of contempt. Skirting the high wall that protected Guinness's brewery along Victoria Quay, the squad car picked up speed and bridged the River Liffey before veering into Parkgate Street. With some fancy driving of her own she was now sitting on Connolly's bumper. It was only when the car entered the Phoenix Park and headed along Chesterfield Avenue that she guessed its destination.

If she was right, it meant Grace McCormick

was staying at the Andrews's residence. It meant that the two women were in league with each other. It put a new complexion on everything. But how long had Grace McCormick and Helena Andrews been working together? Emma remembered the stories Grace had told when she'd stayed overnight. How much of that had been the truth? Very little, it would appear. One thing was certain; right from the start Grace had been the one directing operations. She'd been responsible for the death notices. She'd made an appearance at the phoney wake, put herself forward as a victim and produced a 'death' sympathy card to back up her story. Later, when the psychiatrist's name appeared on Whelehan's computer, it never occurred to Emma that the person creating the list was none other than Grace herself.

The more Emma thought about it the angrier she became. She should have twigged Grace McCormick's act, examined all the angles, checked to see the psychiatrist really had flown in from Liverpool and made sure she'd boarded a return flight. She was still fuming with herself as she watched Connolly's car turn into Castleknock Georgian Village. *Well, at least, I got something right*, she thought, allowing herself a satisfactory sigh.

38

Grace McCormick stood with her back to the fireplace, a grizzly bear of a man to her right. She called him Gerard. A crop of silver-grey hair, not unlike an exploding Brillo pad, crowned the man's head. His facial features resembled those of the old, tough guy actor Charles Bronson, except that in Gerard's case the combination of hair and features looked a whole lot uglier and twice as menacing.

Joan Quinn was bound to a chair, a gag in her mouth, her eyes red from crying. The chair she sat on, a walnut carver, had been borrowed from the dining-room. Hovering behind the child Gerard appeared giant-sized. He held the tip of a handgun to her temple, his gaze fixed on Grace. To Grace's left, bound to another carver, Niamh O'Flynn sat uneasily. Gagged like her daughter, her eyes expressed the churning turmoil taking place inside her.

Emma and Vinny were involuntary spectators. With Connolly, Helena and two uniformed officers, they faced this grim tableau from the opposite end of the room. The air seemed charged with enough static electricity to power a small town. 'I don't need this,' Helena snapped, moving towards Grace McCormick.

'Stay exactly where you are,' Grace ordered. 'Tell me again why you've brought a whole entourage with you?'

'Fuck this for a game of soldiers,' Helena replied, still moving forward. A shot rang out before she'd managed to take a second step. A bullet whistled past the side of her head, close enough to disturb a few loose strands of hair. A pain-filled howl came from the officer standing next to Connolly. The bullet had ploughed into his shoulder. He staggered for a moment then stumbled heavily to the floor. His face distorted in agony, his hand clutching the wound, his eyes appearing to pop out of his head. Blood leaked from between his fingers. Connolly made a move to go to his aid but stopped when another bullet ripped through the air. This time the bullet lodged in the plaster on the wall to one side of his head.

'For God's sake man,' Connolly shouted, holding his hands in the air, 'can't you see that a man's been — '

'Shut it,' the man named Gerard yelled back, 'next person to move gets it in the head.'

The officer on the floor moaned as his

body writhed in a spasm of agony. Grace McCormick looked at him dispassionately then turned to Helena. 'This wouldn't have happened if you'd done as you were told.'

Helena stared back at Grace, anger and bewilderment in her eyes, 'What the hell's the matter with you, Grace? This is *my* house . . . we are partners in this . . . what's got into you?'

'You need to ask? You arrive with a police escort and you ask what's the matter? You turn up with the reporter you were supposed to take care of — '

'Well, you were supposed to take care of her husband and he's here too. Looks like you fucked up as well.'

'I'm not sure which side you're on any more,' Grace said.

'Don't be daft. We're in this together . . . that's what we agreed. It's what we planned. It's — '

'You've been compromised, forced to work with the enemy.'

'You're wrong! I was — '

'If I'm wrong I'll apologize later. Meanwhile, I have to finish what I came here to do.'

'I'm *with you* in this, damn it,' Helena shouted. 'I'm the one — '

Grace cut across her. 'You can help . . . but

you must keep your distance. I don't want any tricks.'

Helena glared at her. 'What do you want me to do?' she asked sullenly.

'Strip the cops. Remove their clothes. Make sure they've no weapons.' Grace turned her attention to Emma and Vinny. 'Move back against the wall.'

Emma and Vinny took a step backwards. They watched in stunned silence as Helena removed the officer's uniform. With nothing more than vest, boxer shorts, socks and shoes, the officer was ordered to sit on the floor. Helena confronted Connolly. 'Strip,' she ordered. Connolly took off his jacket, waistcoat, shirt and tie before removing his shoes and trousers. He handed them to Helena, the expression on his face grimmer than Emma had ever seen. Emma held her breath, waiting to see what would happen when Helena discovered the pistol. She remembered seeing Keenahan hand Connolly the gun that Prof had used in her apartment. Helena felt the pockets before folding the clothes and placing them on the floor. 'All clear,' she said to Grace.

Grace nodded. 'Now cuff the two cops to each other . . . back to back.'

Helena's body language was openly rebellious but she carried out the task without complaint. After clicking the cuffs in position she moved to the wounded officer. 'What about this one?' she asked.

'Leave him,' Grace replied, 'he's not going anywhere.'

Emma wondered about the gun. Had Helena lied about her search or had Connolly somehow managed to get rid of the weapon?

Grace McCormick cleared her throat. 'Ten years ago,' she began, her arms held aloft, her hands opened in an imploring gesture, 'Susan Furlong met with an untimely death.' She paused for effect before continuing. 'The poor demented soul was driven to take the action she did . . . hounded by people in this room. Her death went unpunished. No one bothered to seek justice, no one that is, until the Spirit of the Lord interceded and spoke to me.'

'What about me?' Helena said through clenched teeth. 'I too have sought justice. Without me, you would never have — '

'This is not about you, Helena,' Grace replied, 'it's never been about you.' She stopped, bowed her head reverentially before continuing. 'A far greater power than either of us is responsible for the deliverance visited upon us today. Granted, my mission would have been more difficult without your assistance. For that I'm grateful. I know you've suffered . . . haven't we all? . . . but your suffering is as nothing when compared to what Susan Furlong endured. Besides, Helena, it was your rejection of your mother that made her finally snap. You pounded your fists against her, told her she was a bad person.'

'That's not fair,' Helena cried, 'I was a child then, didn't know the facts. How could I — ?'

'You're right, Helena. It's not fair. I have, through my intercession with the Lord, forgiven you your act of cruelty and absolved you of sin. But I could never allow the others to go unpunished. I swore an oath to Susan and to my Saviour, a sacred vow that I've never once deviated from over this past decade. For His glory I have travelled this path of retribution.'

Grace stopped talking for a moment, a wild fervent sheen in her eyes. She looked directly towards Emma. 'I hadn't planned for you and Vinny to be present today, but it is surely fitting . . . part of the great design; you were present to bear witness when Susan died; it is right and fitting that you should be here to commemorate that sad event.'

There was something lurking in Grace's eyes that Emma should have picked up on before: the woman was totally insane. Emma opened her mouth to speak but was silenced by a flick of the wrist from Grace.

'Don't you dare speak,' Grace said, 'or I'll have Gerard drop you where you stand. You have forfeited all rights in the matter.'

Emma reined in her fury, hoping a better opportunity would present itself to reason with Grace. She watched the psychiatrist remove the gag from Joan Quinn's mouth. With the cloth removed, Joan looked to her mother's chair but she seemed incapable of speaking. All the while, Gerard stood guard, gun in hand, alert to everything as Grace removed the gag from Niamh O'Flynn's mouth. True to her political credentials, O'Flynn had no hesitation in speaking.

'This is madness,' she said defiantly, 'I insist that you stop this — '

Grace slapped her across the face with enough force to knock her head sideways. 'Speak again and the child gets hurt,' Grace said, as she untied the cords that secured O'Flynn's right arm to the chair's armrest.

What happened next only took seconds to complete but would live in Emma's memory forever. Gerard placed his gun in Niamh O'Flynn's hand and forced her fingers around the grip. Without a word being said, he positioned her index finger in front of the trigger, clasped her hand in his and forced the barrel towards the side of her head. She had barely time to register what was happening when pressure was applied to her trigger finger.

An explosive sound boomed around the room. O'Flynn's head jerked violently. A hole appeared in the side of her head; wisps of smoke issued from her mouth and nostrils. A terrible, reverberating silence followed. Gerard unclasped her fingers from the gun, one by one, and wiped the barrel clean against the sleeve of his jacket. A smile lingered on his craggy features as he watched O'Flynn's head slump to her shoulder.

Joan's shrill scream shattered the momentary silence. The child stared at her dead mother, opened her mouth and continued to scream.

'She's in shock,' Grace shouted to Gerard, her words barely audible above the din. 'Slap her face, snap her out of it.'

Gerard moved in front of Joan, looked to Grace before lifting his hand to slap the child. Grace nodded for him to proceed. As Gerard hit Joan for the first time, Emma could see that Helena had now got a gun in her hand. Emma had somehow missed seeing her extract the Beretta from Connolly's pocket. Helena was crying. 'No, no, Mum, don't . . . don't . . . don't.' Her voice had taken on the cadence of a child. Before Gerard or Grace knew what was happening Helena fired the gun. The first bullet caught Gerard in the small of his back before he had time to react.

'Don't beat me . . . don't beat me,' Helena wailed in her child-like voice. As Gerard swung around, a second bullet ploughed into his neck. A third bullet slammed into his chest. Helena continued to pull the trigger as the big man fell heavily to the floor. The gun was now making clicking sounds. All the bullets had been used up but Helena continued to pull the trigger again and again and again.

Emma's ears were ringing from the repeated gunshots. She could see Helena holding on to the gun, shaking from head to toe.

Joan Quinn stopped screaming.

Grace McCormick stared into the middle distance. She tugged at the beads and crucifix round her neck, involuntarily snapping the chain. Beads cascaded on to the floor, some landing in the freshly spilt blood. Grace didn't seem to notice; she held on to the crucifix and began mouthing the *Hail Mary*.

The Beretta fell from Helena's hand and clattered off the side of a chair and on to the floor. Moving as though sleep-walking, she clasped her arms around the static figure of Grace McCormick. Through sobs she spoke in her eerie child's voice, repeating the same phrase, 'Don't leave me, Mum, please don't leave me again.'

Neither Helena nor Grace noticed the two police officers entering the room by the side door. Both moved cautiously, their weapons drawn. Emma recognized them as part of Connolly's team, detectives McFadden and Dorsett. They walked slowly over to where Gerard's body lay, circling the bulk, making sure he was not a threat. Taking no chances, they kicked his gun across the floor, out of reach from the splayed fingers of his lifeless hands.

Emma hunkered down next to Joan Quinn and put her arms around the child's shoulders. There was no response. It was as though Joan was in a comatose state. Emma continued to hold the child, telling her that everything was going to be all right. But Emma knew that things would never be right for Joan Quinn again.

McFadden and Dorsett cuffed Helena and Grace and ushered them out of the room. Vinny made himself useful by removing the handcuffs from Connolly and his colleague. Both policemen were badly shaken. The sound of ambulance sirens filled the air as they struggled to get into their clothes. Seconds later, several paramedics hurried into the room. Their immediate concern was for the dead and wounded. They quickly established that Niamh O'Flynn and Gerard Dean were beyond medical aid and placed sheets over their bodies. Until the technical experts arrived to examine the scene, the bodies would remain where they lay.

The wounded officer was eased on to a stretcher and despatched to a waiting ambulance. At first, no one seemed quite sure what to do about Joan Quinn. While hushed discussions took place between the various personnel in regard to the child, Mary-Jo Graham made an appearance. She embraced Emma, saying, 'Oh, thank God you're all right. I was so worried.'

'How did you get here?' Emma asked. 'Why are you here?'

'I called for help, got on to Detective Connolly's office and got through to Chief Superintendent Smith. I told him what was happening.'

Their discussion was interrupted when a nurse brushed past Mary-Jo and attempted to take care of Joan Quinn. The little girl clung to Emma, unwilling to let go. Emma hunkered down once more so that she was face-to-face with Joan. 'You're going to be safe now,' she told the child, 'this nice lady is a nurse; she's going to look after you.'

After a little hesitation, Joan allowed the nurse to take her by the hand. 'I think I should accompany Joan in the ambulance,' Emma said to the nurse. 'The poor little mite needs all the support she can get right now.'

Connolly glanced at the caked blood on Emma's knee. 'Might be a good idea to have someone see to that knee of yours.'

'I'd almost forgotten about it. Stings a bit, now that you mention it. I suppose I'd better get it dressed.'

Mary-Jo and Vinny both offered to accompany her.

'No, it's OK,' Emma replied, 'too many of us might frighten Joan.'

'You're sure?' Vinny asked, disappointment in his voice.

'Yeah, sure, I'll be fine. You'd better bring the car back to the apartment. I'll call you as soon as they get through with me in the hospital.'

Vinny placed an awkward kiss on her cheek and squeezed her hands.

As the doors of the ambulance were about to close, Emma looked to Mary-Jo. 'How'd you know what was going on here?'

'I followed you all the way from your apartment.'

'What? But why? I mean, *why* were you following me?'

'It's a long story, Emma. I'll tell you when you get back to the newsroom. In the meantime I've a front page story to write for the *Post*.'

39

Bob Crosby sat across from Emma taking up most of the space available at the coffee shop's small corner table. Mary-Jo Graham looked as though she'd been inserted between them with a tweezer. Their waitress had promised to find them a better table as soon as one became available. That had been twenty minutes earlier. It was coming up to six o'clock, a busy time in and around the Temple Bar district. Carol singers stood in the street outside the coffee shop trying their best to sound joyous even though the biting cold was making itself felt. Strains of *Deck the Halls* struggled to find harmonious expression above the Yuletide hustle and bustle and clamour. Emma ignored the singers. Her interest focused on what Bob and Mary-Jo were saying. The promised change to a better table had not materialized.

A week had elapsed since Emma and Joan Quinn had shared an ambulance ride to hospital. A more eventful week would be hard to imagine. The death of politician Niamh O'Flynn had been the biggest story of the year. People from all walks of life had joined in a groundswell of revulsion. The murder had galvanized the nation into demanding action: *Something must be done* became the common cry. Guns must be outlawed; bigger jails built to house the criminals. Television reports and tabloid headlines fanned the fire of outrage. That it should follow so fast on the heels of the 'unexplained' death of Niamh O'Flynn's husband in Brussels added poignancy to the terrible event. Tributes had come from all sides of the political divide. Even O'Flynn's greatest detractors managed to find a few kind words.

Emma's role in the events leading up to O'Flynn's death had been well documented. Even rival newspapers gave her the full treatment. Both broadsheet and tabloids featured her picture almost as prominently as that of Niamh O'Flynn. The *Post,* proudly claiming proprietary rights, had given her iconic coverage. The gunshot wound to her knee had taken on a life of its own. She was the heroine of the hour. With just a small white bandage on her knee to indicate the part she played, Emma had left the hospital's A&E department. Her departure was marked by the accompaniment of flashbulbs, television cameras and microphones. Since then shc'd been sought as a guest on all the current events programmes on radio and television.

The late Gerard Dean, on the other hand, was cast as the villain, vilified by all and sundry. His history of mental illness and criminal record was exposed and raked over in the full glare of publicity. Like the man calling himself Prof, Dean had been a former patient of Grace McCormick. The two men were alike in many respects: in the past they'd both stood trial for murder. Both had escaped prison terms by virtue of being declared insane. And both had come under the influence and care of their psychiatrist, Grace McCormick.

Pictures of Dr Brian Whelehan, sitting up in his hospital bed featured on most papers and even made the evening television news. He was being hailed as a 'brave survivor', his role in the recent events benefiting from a most benign interpretation. One tabloid went so far as to suggest that Whelehan should come out of retirement and run for the country's presidential office.

Overshadowed by these dramatic events and consigned to the inside pages of the press, the death of Bernadette Maxwell, *aka* Joan of Arc, got scant attention. According to reports, she'd passed away peacefully in her sleep after earlier meeting for a birthday celebration with some of her old comrades-in-arms. Her death contrasted greatly with those lives of innocent men, women and children she'd wasted during her notorious bombing campaign in Britain back in the seventies. Much to the disgust of the relatives of those she killed and maimed, her burial had all the usual paramilitary trappings that one associates with such so-called freedom fighters.

Because of *sub judice* restrictions, coverage given to Grace McCormick and Helena Andrews remained low-key. Helena was in the Dochas Centre, the female unit of Mountjoy, the largest committal prison in the State. Grace was placed in St Patrick's Institution undergoing psychiatric evaluation. The institution's findings would determine whether or not she was mentally fit to stand trial. A report would then go to the office of the Director of Public Prosecutions. Until the DPP's decision was announced, the media had to exercise caution in what they reported. However, in the background, feverish activity was ongoing in relation to the two women, everyone gearing up for the onslaught that would inevitably follow the DPP's decision.

Detective Inspector Jim Connolly had come in for something of a lashing from the media, his contribution to the events in Helena Andrews's house being linked to headlines that contained the words *Botched Operation*.

Young Joan Quinn was protected from the glare of publicity. She was being treated for shock. More than anyone else, she represented the real victim in all that had occurred. Her ordeal at the hands of Grace McCormick and the loss of her father and mother were bound to have long lasting effects. Emma had made discreet enquiries about the prospects for Joan's future and welfare. Apparently, Niamh O'Flynn had a brother and two sisters, all of whom were willing to look after the 9-year-old. Only time would tell what kind of psychological damage had been inflicted on her.

Less serious were the effects being experienced by Vinny. Nevertheless, the whole episode in Cobh had unsettled him, the upheaval leaving him with an uneasy feeling. Since his arrival back in Dublin he'd felt both mentally and physically divorced from his wife's world. Discovering that she was smack-bang in the thick of things, exposing herself to all kinds of danger did not sit well with him. On their first evening together in the apartment, after she'd returned from the hospital, the atmosphere had been strained. When things were going really well they tended to slag each other off and play little practical jokes. But when things weren't so hot they became overly polite and civil to each other.

Using this barometer it was pretty obvious that something was amiss. Emma had a fair idea what was going through Vinny's head; he was working up to telling her, once again, to give up her job and take on something less hazardous. The row that seemed inevitable would invariably turn to the question of starting a family. That old chestnut again. Rather than go home after work this evening she had agreed to meet Bob Crosby and Mary-Jo Graham for coffee in Temple Bar. They had already told her about some duplicitous actions they had indulged in over the past number of weeks.

Bob Crosby ordered another round of coffees and stared intently into Emma's eyes. 'I'm sorry about the deception,' he was saying as he reached across the small table to squeeze her hand.

'Ditto,' Mary-Jo said.

'Not good enough,' Emma replied, giving them both a stern look.

Crosby's eyebrows shot up, concern on his face. He was about to say something when he saw her smile.

'The two of you are right shits,' she said, trying to remain serious. 'Have to admit though, you had me going there for a while.'

A big smile lit up Mary-Jo's face. 'Well, at

least you won't have to put up with me in your work space any longer,' she said.

Emma pulled a phoney frown. 'I see. So, the truth is I was just a piece of research for you, that it?'

''Fraid so.' Mary-Jo admitted. 'I need an investigative journalist in my next book and you fitted the bill perfectly.'

Bob Crosby had been the one to tell Emma the truth. Mary-Jo Graham was his niece. She'd come to him with her idea of using an investigative journalist as a central character in her next book. Initially, she hoped he'd be able to give her enough information but he had come up with a better idea; he'd offered to let her work alongside a real journalist for a few weeks — Emma being the person he had in mind. For the idea to work, he explained, it was essential that Emma remain unaware of the real intent.

'As it turned out,' Mary-Jo said, 'I got more than I bargained for.'

'Serves you right,' Emma said.

'Yeah, I know, but I wouldn't have missed it for the world . . . and to show my appreciation I've decided to dedicate my next book to you, Emma.'

Before Emma could react, Mary-Jo launched into a colourful description of how she planned to develop her 'Emma Boylan' character. The proposed scenarios as outlined by Mary-Jo caused Emma to wince. She couldn't relate to the fictional character as envisaged by Mary-Jo but she was reluctant to dampen the writer's enthusiasm. She was glad when the sound of her mobile halted the conversation. The number displayed on the small screen let her know who was calling. Her face lit up. 'Hello,' she said, turning away from Bob and Mary-Jo.

'Hello, Emma, Connolly here, can you talk?'

'Yeah sure, sure. How are you?'

'I'm fine, just fine. I was wondering . . . wondering if . . . '

'What, Jim? You were wondering what?'

'Later this evening, a meal, a drink? Would you join me . . . ?

Emma had a thousand excuses ready, all of them sound arguments for not meeting him. 'Yes, Jim, why not?' she said. 'I'd love to.'

We do hope that you have enjoyed reading this large print book.

Did you know that all of our titles are available for purchase?

We publish a wide range of high quality large print books including:
Romances, Mysteries, Classics
General Fiction
Non Fiction and Westerns

Special interest titles available in large print are:
The Little Oxford Dictionary
Music Book
Song Book
Hymn Book
Service Book

Also available from us courtesy of Oxford University Press:
Young Readers' Dictionary
(large print edition)
Young Readers' Thesaurus
(large print edition)

For further information or a free brochure, please contact us at:
Ulverscroft Large Print Books Ltd.,
The Green, Bradgate Road, Anstey,
Leicester, LE7 7FU, England.
Tel: (00 44) **0116 236 4325**
Fax: (00 44) **0116 234 0205**

THE CORPORAL WORKS OF MURDER

Sister Carol Anne O'Marie

Sister Mary Helen is once more in the middle of a murder case. She holds a dying young woman, shot in the street outside the Refuge for homeless women. Grieving over the loss of life, Mary Helen spots something strange about the victim. Her ragged clothing is at odds with her healthy looking unblemished skin; her perfect teeth are white and unstained. Her appearance belies that of a woman living in poverty on the streets. With the weapons of her logical mind, will Sister Mary Helen solve the case and prove once again to be the bane of Inspector Gallagher's life?